THE ISLAND GIRLS

RACHEL SWEASEY

B
Boldwood

First published in Great Britain in 2024 by Boldwood Books Ltd.

Copyright © Rachel Sweasey, 2024

Cover Design by Becky Glibbery

Cover Images: Shutterstock and iStock

The moral right of Rachel Sweasey to be identified as the author of this work has been asserted in accordance with the Copyright, Designs and Patents Act 1988.

A CIP catalogue record for this book is available from the British Library.

Paperback ISBN 978-1-83533-106-4

Large Print ISBN 978-1-83533-107-1

Hardback ISBN 978-1-83533-108-8

Ebook ISBN 978-1-83533-105-7

Kindle ISBN 978-1-83533-104-0

Audio CD ISBN 978-1-83533-113-2

MP3 CD ISBN 978-1-83533-112-5

Digital audio download ISBN 978-1-83533-109-5

This book is printed on certified sustainable paper. Boldwood Books is dedicated to putting sustainability at the heart of our business. For more information please visit https://www.boldwoodbooks.com/about-us/sustainability/

Boldwood Books Ltd, 23 Bowerdean Street, London, SW6 3TN

www.boldwoodbooks.com

For Ben, Henry, Georgie, Naomi & Matt: my team, my best mates, my loves.

PROLOGUE

POOLE, DORSET, ENGLAND – MARCH 1941

My dearest Darrell,

If you are reading this letter, then I am so terribly sorry for your loss. But I promise you it is my loss too. As I write this, you might think nothing more of me than I'm just a girl you met in a pub: a girl you went out on a day trip with. But, for me, I want you to know that I want this to be more. I barely know you, Darrell, and so this is so strange to put into words, but at this moment, I hope to spend the rest of my life in your arms. I hope that this terrible time of war will end, and that Hitler can be stopped and driven back. I hope that peace, and sense, will prevail. I hope for a time of plenty: of food, and homes, and work for all. For a time when we can sit in the sun and enjoy life together. But, if I have my way, you will only be given this letter to read if I have lost my life before you in these dark days.

I will not have told you why I am behaving so differently at this time; why I am spending less time with you and more time with others – with one other in particular. You may even believe that I don't love you with the same passion you do me…

...but I need you to know this, Darrell – I will love you, and only you, for all eternity, and I will see you when you get here. I will be waiting for you.

With all my love, forever,

Peggy

1

ROTTERDAM, HOLLAND – MAY 1940

The eerie calm that had settled over the Nieuwe Maas river in the last few hours was now a deathly silence. Supressing the chill that prickled his spine, Hans looked up and down the quayside for anyone who might catch hold of his mooring line. He was alone – more alone than he'd ever been in his life before – too far from the action to find a Dutch soldier and too far from the families gathering nearer the mouth of the river and preparing to flee. The dock workers had all disappeared like rats running from a sinking ship.

He brought the launch into the dockside and, holding the rope, jumped to the ancient and worn stone steps. Normally, this part of the dock would have been heaving with industry and at different times in the preceding days, there'd been activity enough, but not now. With nobody to take his line for him, Hans swiftly tied the rope to the old worn cleat himself, with the figure eight and locking half-hitch knot he could create in his sleep. The rope worked through his fingers along the pronounced calluses that a decade of boatmanship had worn into his hands. A hasty glance around the quayside showed no more signs of life. There wasn't a dockhand or boatman to be seen or heard. And he wondered now, in the strange silence like the midnight hour on this mild, sunny, spring morning, if he was dreaming. Was it over already? Had Holland surrendered, and Germany taken control?

Three nights had passed since the onslaught had started – since his world had crumbled to this other thing, this existence that was no more than dust on the air. Distant gunshots, then the low hum of dozens of tanks rumbling towards Rotterdam had heralded the arrival of the *Wehrmacht*. He'd heard on the wireless the news of the German Army invading Holland, and had gone out looking for them, filled with an inexplicable kind of dreadful thrill for the spectacle of disaster.

He had left Katrijn in bed, nursing baby Anika close to her chest.

'Do you have to go, Hans? Isn't it dangerous out there? Stay in here with us, where it's safe,' she'd said.

'I'll be fine, my love. I'm fast, and young,' he'd said to his wife with a wink, kissing the sweet, soft head of his baby girl and breathing in the milky scent of her. Katrijn had pulled him back and kissed him, firmly, fully, and lusciously on the lips like she had when they'd first found each other.

At the foot of the stairs to their attic apartment, as he'd shut the door behind him, Hans had been surprised to meet Klaus, who seemed to have been waiting for him. They'd met with a firm shake of the hand and together, they'd gone in search of the soldiers and the fighting and the horrible excitement of it all on that first day of the invasion. They'd been met by a crowd of panic-stricken families coming in the opposite direction, fleeing the soldiers, evacuating their homes and clutching everything they could carry in their arms: a few items of food, a baby, a cat in a basket, a bundle of blankets. Once the two young men had pushed through the tide of humanity and into the open square, they'd been greeted with the sobering sight of the source of all the distant noise they'd been hearing.

A grey Panzer tank, formidable in size alone, even without the firepower it was wielding, had stood in the middle of the square firing at the buildings on all sides in turn. Two soldiers had walked behind the tank carrying some kind of gun that was attached to a pack they each wore on their backs. When the deafening din from the tank's fire had ceased, the men walked forward and unleashed the dreadful power of the flamethrowers they held. The flames had roared like dragon fire and reached the full height of the buildings, setting each one alight with such incredible power and speed that the young men had ducked back around the corner for cover. They'd realised then that the exodus they'd witnessed a few moments earlier must have been the residents of these homes, warned to evacuate and then shown exactly what would happen if they remained inside.

Hans emptied his stomach into the gutter before he even realised he felt sick. His legs buckled and his head thumped as the panic released adrenaline that raced through his bloodstream. *Escape*, his body told him. *Run away. Save yourself*. In that moment, understanding the terror of the German power, Hans knew they would win. He hadn't a shred of doubt that Europe was going to become a very large German empire. No question. Holland could never withstand this level of attack. Where the hell were any Dutch soldiers now, anyway? And what did they have to fight back with? They were too busy holding the north bank and there just weren't enough of them to go around. If this nightmare was the way Germany invaded and took over a country, the rest of Europe didn't stand a chance. And neither did he and his fledgling family. At this point in his life, Hans still consid-ered himself very much a *Nederlander*, because of his Dutch mother. But he would remember to his dying gasp this moment when he had the idea to cast off his ties to the country he thought of as home and decided he would become fully German instead, taking on the heritage of his proud German father.

In the nightmare of that moment, Hans saw an image of his sweet Dutch mother, happy at home, pouring coffee for guests, feeding them sweet treats she'd baked and serving it all on the pretty blue Delft pottery she treasured. If she'd still been alive now, his choice might have been different. Perhaps he would have decided to take Katrijn and Anika, run back to Utrecht to join Mother, gather her up and take her somewhere inland – anywhere – that might offer them all safety, at least out of the city, even though he knew full well there was nowhere left to run. But she'd died some months before Anika was born and now his two girls were all he had.

In the face of this dreadful power and brute force, he now saw the German father he remembered from his childhood. Strong, intimidating, content when he was getting his own way, and not afraid to show Hans and his mother exactly who was in charge.

The image of those crowds he'd seen just minutes before reminded him of how he and his mother must have looked as they'd fled Düsseldorf by night, walking for two days until they reached the safety of the little Dutch village where they had hidden from Father. Hans and his mother had fled in terror and that's when he became a *Nederlander*. And now, Hans – the fully grown, strong boatman – decided he must join the force instead of running from it. He would never allow himself to be the weak prey of a tyrant again. He must become German to survive.

Klaus was no more than an acquaintance from the docks, but Hans knew him to have even stronger ties with Germany than he had himself, and as he'd talked through his plans with Klaus, he had been emboldened by the encouragement of the other man.

'You're right, Hans,' he'd said with an eager nod. 'The Germans are going to win, and they need men like us on their side. I've already made contact with a man I know, and there's work for us to do. You should come with me to meet him,' Klaus had encouraged him.

For the next two days, while Hans worked through this solution for protecting his wife and child, becoming formally German and joining the winning side, he had heard the onrushing destructive forces of the German advance, and every hour, it seemed there were fewer people around than the hour before. There was a constant haze of smoke over the city and a background noise of firearms, with the occasional Luftwaffe plane overhead dropping a bomb.

That first night back at home, when Katrijn had greeted him with relief as if he was back from the dead, he'd collected his prized identity documents, both those that showed he was Dutch and the others, indicating his right to German citizenship, and tucked the folded papers neatly into a buttoned pocket on his shirt. He'd drunk in the sight of his beautiful family, and watched Katrijn, totally lost in this love affair with their new baby daughter. He'd sat beside her on the bed and tried to phrase the thoughts in his jumbled head; the plans he thought might save them all. But he hadn't been able to bring himself to trouble her with this nightmare from out there, instead choosing to leave her unaware and resting in the beauty of this time, treasuring every moment with her newborn.

The next morning, the second day of the invasion, he'd discovered, quite by accident, the few families at the fishing port who were planning on running away to England. In the madness and chaos of the invasion, he had taken his boat to the mouth of the river to see what was happening in other parts of the city. There were a dozen or more boats that had been stripped of their fishing gear and were being loaded with some basic supplies: drums of water, piles of blankets. On the quayside, beside the boats, families had gathered, with a few small bags. Their faces had been strangely marked by a mix of desperation and eager hope.

'What's going on?' he'd called to the man on one of the boats, who seemed to be giving out instructions.

'We're out of here, friend. I'm taking my family to England. So is Dirk, and Pieter you see along the way. This is hopeless,' he'd said with a nod in the direction of the clouds of smoke beginning to form over the city of Rotterdam.

'What do you think you'll do in England? This is your home. And don't you realise the Germans will be there soon as well?' Hans had asked, unable to see the sense in their flight.

'Look, son, I'm a man of the sea. England is surrounded by it. I'm sure I'll find work there, and even if we get a little head start on the Hun, I have more chance of saving my wife and children than I do if I stay here. Want to come with us?' he'd added with a look of real fatherly concern that irritated the independent young Hans.

'I'll stay, I think. Take my chances. It can't be that bad,' he'd replied as he held up a hand to signal farewell, turning his boat back upstream again. But as he'd chugged slowly back towards the dock he knew so well, Hans had begun to wonder if his plans to become German might be simply scoffed at by the advancing *Wehrmacht*. Who was he, anyway? Why would they want to take him? And what about Katrijn? She was Dutch through and through, with no hint of German blood. Would they accept her as well, simply because she was his wife? And when he'd seen her again that night, he still hadn't been able to bear telling her of the things he'd learnt – that the city around them was virtually deserted, and people were fleeing the country any way they could.

Now, on this third day, with his boat safely tied up, Hans walked the deserted streets and alleys towards the attic room they called home, with the thought of at least gathering a few important belongings and keeping them safe in the small, enclosed cuddy cabin of his boat, just in case they should need to flee. He still hoped to meet Klaus's German contact and explain that he himself was German, and save his family that way.

The battle noise still echoed around the city, much quieter today for some reason he'd yet to discover, but he made sure to keep it at a muffled distance from his path. As he walked through one dark alley and out into a slightly wider street, he was brought to a halt in shock as he saw the sky turn blood red above him. The grey, brown smoky clouds were mingling with red shot. In places, it almost looked like a floral display, but in others, all Hans could see was blood. Somewhere to the south, red flares were being set off into the skies over Rotterdam. Was this the surrender? Did it signal the end? In his gut, Hans knew – whatever he'd seen of the German wrath so far, it was about to get worse. Much worse. And he was still on the wrong side.

The planes seemed to come from every direction possible, bringing with them a crescendo of the dreadful noise of war. Through the smoke from the previous onslaught, they came in their dozens, from the north and the south, and when overhead, they rained bombs on the ancient city as indiscriminately as if they were farmhands scattering grain for the hens. Had the city been hens and had the bombs been grain, the feed would have been so plentiful that day as to smother the creatures to death.

He ran back to their apartment, crashing into people who seemed to have been shaken outdoors in their hundreds just like cockroaches fleeing the light. For the last three days, Hans had been in a state of high alert, but the start of the bombing that would be the destruction of Rotterdam had him quivering with fear like he'd never known. He raced up the street and flung open the front door, hurling his way up the stairs three at a time until, without warning, the world exploded around him.

Hans was flung down one flight of stairs and lay there aching in every limb. The world had gone strangely quiet, as if he'd been thrown into the bottom of a deep pool and his eyes were blinded as if they were filled with salt water. The world stopped turning and slipped from a freeze frame into slow motion. When his sight returned, and he could hear again a little more clearly, the air around him roared and the staircase he was lying on was open to a gaping hole where the top three floors of the apartment building had been. Flames crackled at the foot of the stairs and dust and smoke and debris of varying sizes flew all about him.

He pulled himself up and kept going up the stairs and, though the part of his brain that wanted to survive screamed at him to go back down, he reached forward and opened the door to their room.

The wardrobe still stood on the edge of the room and the curtain flapped in the wind that howled through the broken glass where the front-facing window had been. But there in the middle of the room where the big bed had stood, and where he'd last seen Katrijn and Anika, there was nothing: a hole that dropped into an abyss of smoke, and flame, and rubble.

Hans lunged forward to the splintered edges of the wooden floor and peered down through the gloom, screaming their names into the black hole that was the grave of his wife and daughter. As the dust began to settle, he could see nothing below but an enormous pile of rubble and flames. He ran down the three flights of stairs again and ploughed into the midst of the debris, hoarse now from screaming for Katrijn and Anika, yet also knowing, somewhere deep inside, that they would never hear him. He pulled blocks of concrete and broken pieces of furniture and bricks and lumps of timber frame from the pile in the middle of what had once been the ground floor of his small apartment building. His hands were torn raw and bloody, and the smoke and dust filled his eyes and lungs, but nothing would stop him from trying to find his family beneath the rubble.

He saw the baby's fist first. Just a chubby little hand, clenched as always, on the end of an arm and sticking up from the rubble. He gently released Anika, pulled her clear and held her to his chest as if the nearness of him might revive her. She didn't seem broken, even, except for a channel of dust-encrusted blood that had run down the side of her head from her ear.

He howled like a dying bear and sobbed as he clutched the tiny body close. Then, he found a torn fragment of curtain in the rubble and made a soft bed on the edge of the room and placed the body of his daughter safely there, as if to put her down to sleep. And his search continued until he found Katrijn. But her legs were firmly trapped underneath a steel girder, and her face had been smashed by bricks that had rendered her almost unrecognisable. Her hands were growing cold already, and her skin was paler than he'd ever seen it. He couldn't pull her body out and hid his face in her chest and cried like a baby as the bombs still fell all around in the streets outside.

He did not know what to do with Anika's body, and he couldn't move Katrijn. She was already buried. So he brought the baby back to Katrijn and rested Anika in her mother's arms, then covered them both with the curtain and hoisted a piece of tin over the top of them both, as if to protect them further. Then he climbed the precariously dangerous staircase back up to what was left of their little apartment.

For hours, he stayed curled in the corner of the room, crying their names, and roaring his anger at the air around him, while outside, Rotterdam was bombed to shreds. Then it was as if he woke up, knowing with clarity what he must do next. Hans reached into the wardrobe, now teetering on the edge of the cliff that his room had become, grabbed his small canvas bag from the cupboard and threw in the few spare clothes he could reach. He owned little of any value, but grabbed the two pictures that lay smashed under the windowsill: one of his mother and the other of he and Katrijn, taken last spring when they'd taken his boat down the river for a picnic in the meadows. That day was the first time they'd made love, gently, tenderly, in the open air of the cockpit because there wasn't a soul around to see, or hear, or care.

As he turned to leave, clinging to the edge of the room around the huge hole in the floor, the deafening sound of the Luftwaffe planes overhead was smothered by the almighty noise of another bomb dropping just feet away from him, in the house that stood the other side of his staircase. Despite the terror he felt – or perhaps because of it – he flung himself down the stairs, three at a time, pulling the canvas bag behind him, missed his footing mid-flight and tumbled head first down a run of six stairs at once. A black shroud like night enveloped him and the deafening sounds ceased. But his reprieve only lasted a minute or two until he regained consciousness and the searing pain in his left leg brought him back from restful sleep into his nightmare again. He sobbed and coughed alternately until the buzzing in his ears stopped again and the noise of terror came back.

He got up to run but found the best he could manage was a painful limp. His whole leg felt as though it was on fire. When he stumbled out into the street, he saw that the staircase and the walls either side of it were all that was left intact of the two adjoining apartment buildings, which had now disappeared completely. There was just a fragile-looking stairwell left with rubble either side of it. The smoke and dust were beginning to clear from the base of his building and his heart stopped as he peered into the space to see if they were still there. But the two girls he loved were both now buried underneath several feet more of bricks and timber and rubble that had fallen deep into the basement. And still the planes roared overhead, spreading fire and death like dragons from a horrible fantasy tale of tragedy.

Hans looked down at the bag he held, which signified everything he had left in the world. And though his heart whimpered, *Lie down and die with them too*, his head showed him the memory of the families preparing to flee at the mouth of the river. His boat. He still had his boat. He reached a hand wearily to the pocket holding his identify documents and, as another bomb fell across the street, he set off, dragging his injured leg and zigzagging his way back to his boat, dodging the bombardment falling from the skies. The Nazi plan for Rotterdam must be nothing less than complete annihilation, he realised.

As Hans staggered around the last bend at the docks, he groaned in relief that his boat was where he'd left it earlier and he leant on the corner, doubled over to catch his breath. Moments later, he struggled down the steps and threw his bag forward into the cabin then painfully climbed back up to the stores where he kept spare supplies for his daily runs. He had two cans of fuel so, with a huge effort, he stowed those in the boat then went back for an empty water can. As he watched it filling from the tap – which miraculously still ran amidst the destruction – he counted the bombs as he heard them fall. One, three, nine by the time the container was full and he was screwing the lid on. He hauled it to the quayside and down the steps, placing it safely forward.

He felt sick to his core and didn't know which was worse: his wretched broken heart, the excruciating pain in his leg, or the fear that the next bomb would kill him too. He stood on the deck of his launch and ran his hands through his hair, wincing as he found some small pieces of glass still lodged in his thick curls. The pain spread from his fingers to his heart and the aching emptiness in his soul which, without his girls, threatened to end him. He collapsed onto his knees in the cockpit and howled like a wounded animal until the anguish subsided to quiet sobs again. Sniffing, he wiped his face on his sleeves then raised his head to think about what he should do next. The way his mind took him from despair to rational thought and back again was like rolling on the roughest of seas in the smallest of boats.

Hans remembered he had a couple of blankets he always kept in the boat, together with several tins of food, and that would have to do. There was no more time for thinking or planning – and nowhere else to get anything from, anyway.

From the moment that they'd killed his family, the idea of handing himself over to the Germans to fight on their side had become enough to make him vomit. The Germans – everything that his father represented – had killed his wife and child and he would hate them forever for this. He could never join them. All Hans could do now was respond to his body's insistence that he escape, survive, run away, and live.

He undid the line that signified his last permanent attachment to Holland and threw it into the cockpit, started the motor, and was turning away from the dock when he heard a shout behind him. Hans looked back along the smoky dockside to see Klaus running towards him, arms flailing, calling his name.

'Stop Hans, Stop! Wait for me!'

For a moment that might have changed the whole course of his life, Hans hesitated, while he decided whether to 'hear' Klaus or not. He knew Klaus as a workmate but little else, and over these few days he'd learnt that Klaus intended to work for Germany. But they weren't really friends, and Hans wasn't sure he wanted this man's company in a small boat for the next few days, especially now he'd completely changed his mind about his plans. But if he left Klaus here in the dockside, he would surely die.

The better side of Hans's conscience took over and he turned the boat back. He used the docking technique that had been his daily bread and held the launch almost motionless a few metres away from the wall. He looked at Klaus and lifted his chin a little in greeting.

'Take me with you?' shouted Klaus over the din.

'You don't even know where I'm going,' called Hans.

'Are you staying in Rotterdam, then?' Klaus's expression told Hans that he knew the answer already.

'Of course not. But I'm going a long way – to England. And I only have enough food for one. Are you ready for a trip that far?'

'England is my top choice of destination, Meyers. Take me with you, please?' he said, holding up his bag and showing Hans the stash of food he'd brought with him. Hans realised now that if he'd not come for his boat when he did, Klaus would likely have stolen it anyway. But Klaus had brought with him more than twice the food Hans already had, and he was someone to share the night watches with, at least, whatever else happened when they reached England.

Hans breathed out his frustration and took the boat in close enough for Klaus to make the jump. Klaus greeted Hans with a warm handshake and, with a sincere smile of thanks, coiled the docking line that lay in the floor of the boat and took a seat. And as Hans piloted his launch towards the mouth of the river and the place where he'd found the fleeing families earlier that morning – a lifetime ago, back when he had a wife and child and a future, and when Rotterdam was still recognisable – Klaus told him his plans, and how his industriousness was going to give them both a ticket to freedom once Germany conquered England as well.

Hans gritted his teeth, horrified now at the very idea of helping Germany, and tried to drown out the sound of Klaus and his plans.

2

BROWNSEA ISLAND, POOLE – SUMMER 1998

Rebekah waved to the tired and happy visitors as the last ferry of the day left the island and made its way back across the harbour to Poole Quay. The other guides and volunteers had left as well, taking the shorter ferry ride for staff to Sandbanks, and, as always, she felt her heart swell with joy for the evening's solitude ahead of her.

Ben had seemed to want to hang around a bit more than usual today, and just as he'd been about to get on the boat, he'd turned back as if to say something to her, but then changed his mind. He was several years her junior and a great worker as a volunteer, but just lately, it had seemed he was angling to spend more time with her – time that Rebekah was not interested in sharing with anyone.

Rebekah took a moment to take a deep sniff of the sea air and turned towards the harbour entrance to watch the chain ferry as it glided across from the Haven Hotel to the Studland side. When it reached the shore, the front end of the car ferry lowered slowly like a giant jaw dropping open. It issued a groan of rusted metal, as if its old joints ached and complained, and then the cars began to roll off the deck and up onto the road beyond, headed for the little toll hut, and then along the road, where perhaps the visitors would take an evening swim on the beach or travel to Studland village and the seaside town of Swanage beyond.

She walked back along the little quay, pausing to look down into the clear, shallow waters for fish or crabs, then headed through the National Trust reception, locking the quayside door behind her. Rebekah checked that the cash tills were all switched off for the night, and the day's takings locked in the safe. She closed the windows, then she locked the island-side door to reception as she walked through it and left 'work' for the evening. Rebekah then took her last stroll of the day around the eastern end of Brownsea Island on her way to Rose Cottage for the night.

She ran her fingertips gently along the ancient brick wall to her left, as if to say goodnight to the tiny Italian snails she seemed to have spent hours searching for earlier in the day. She loved telling visitors to the island about this rare little snail – so small you could barely see it – that was thought to have travelled here on the slabs of Italian marble brought to be used in the building of the castle, in its more extravagant era of refurbishing, over two hundred years earlier.

Rebekah smiled at the cheeky red squirrel who crossed her path and seemed to be saying, *Catch me if you can*, as it scampered up the oak tree beside the path.

At St Mary's Church, Rebekah walked up the ancient stone steps and along the gravel path to check that the church door was shut and locked, and then looked around the Church Field and the open-air theatre site to make sure none of the campers, or more likely their children, were up to any mischief among the half-built stage and seating gallery.

Every year, the island became home to an open-air theatre that had staged a different Shakespeare play ever since 1964. For several months, the activity of building the stage, the set, and the seating gallery created excitement. And then hundreds of play-goers would come over on a special evening boat to watch the play over a fortnight in summer.

More than once, she'd found some cheeky kids acting out a few lines of *Romeo and Juliet* on the set, and though she was bound to chastise them, she loved their adventurous spirits, though she scoffed at the naturally romantic heart that all young teens seemed to have. She supposed she'd felt that way, briefly, too, despite knowing from her mother that romance only led to anguish, and she learnt it for herself the hard way eventually. Shakespeare was probably making the same point in *Romeo and Juliet* though, she thought to herself as she regarded the stage set for the next display of the bard's works.

Only a few more weeks now until the next play would be showing – *As You Like It* – for the thirty-fifth consecutive year of the Brownsea Open Air Theatre plays. Soon her evenings wouldn't be so quiet when hundreds of people would make their annual pilgrimage over on the late-afternoon ferry, bringing their picnics and chilled wine and blankets, and settling in for an evening of outdoor Shakespeare. Every Monday, Wednesday, and Friday for a couple of weeks, the atmosphere on the island would throng with the excitement of the theatre. She loved it, really, though the influx of people was always a strange change to her peaceful island life.

Rebekah climbed the hill up to the lookout and paused to take in the view she knew would never grow old for her: the sweeping vista of Studland, beyond it to Old Harry Rocks, and around towards the west across the heath and the Purbeck Hills. This was the view that had helped her fall in love with this island in the middle of the harbour. The tales she'd grown up with, told passionately by Aunty Peggy, had sparked her curiosity, and the disaster that had been her first love-come-hate affair had cemented the idea of running to the other side of the world. But when she had first arrived here in the flesh, she'd been left speechless by the beauty of the place. And, for Rebekah, Brownsea Island was the gem, the pearl in the oyster, of everything Poole and this beautiful stretch of Dorset coastline had to offer.

Rebekah always marvelled that though destiny had set her birthplace on the other side of the world, in Australia, she'd been allowed to come here to Poole, where her neighbour Peggy had grown up, and she realised now that she'd never found out exactly why Peggy had left Poole, or what could have been a powerful enough inducement to take anyone away from this paradise.

Despite Rebekah's attachment to Brisbane, Poole was now home too, and her love for the limestone hills and cliffs of the Isle of Purbeck and Poole Harbour, and especially the most wonderful place of all – Brownsea Island – was all the proof she'd ever need that she was right where she belonged.

Her first winter had been a trial of perseverance and new experiences: the bitter chill of wind that felt sharp enough to cut her throat; the feeling that her feet might never be properly warm again and the pain as they tingled back to life in front of the fireplace; the dark of night that began at four in the afternoon and went on until eight the next morning, and even then the thick blanket of grey cloud seemed to hang over all of England and didn't let the sun shine through. But within a couple of months, spring had sprung with bright daffodils, bluebells, warmer weather and longer days. Now that her third summer was here, Rebekah could understand why so many poets of old had saved their best words for their adulation of the English summertime.

The distant sounds of happy campers floated up from the

campsite down near the shore and mingled in the evening air with the aroma of sausages and bacon cooking on campfires. Rebekah saw children playing on the beach below, throwing little pieces of driftwood into the water and collecting shells, while their parents were preparing their dinners. All was well.

Rebekah turned towards home. She passed one of the remaining stands of rhododendrons that still needed to be dug out and burned. There were remnants of them everywhere, even thirty years after the National Trust had taken over and started eliminating the invasive weed, clearing the way for native trees like the oaks, hawthorn, and yew. The heathland was beginning to return to its natural glory, with purple flowering heathers and the buttercup-hued gorse thriving once more. Even now, late in the afternoon, Rebekah could see the benefits of the clearing work that had been done in the pine stand as dappled sunlight fell around her feet on the woodland floor.

As she unlatched the squeaky gate to Rose Cottage, her island home, and walked through the garden and up the path to the front door, she was grateful that she had finished all the human interaction needed for the day, and thanked the fates, or destiny, or the stars, or whatever spirit it was who was responsible for her life winding up this way. At her age, most of Rebekah's friends both here and home in Brisbane were married, and many already had a few children, but life as a ranger on Brownsea Island suited this introverted young woman perfectly. Wildlife, peace, no traffic, no crowds – absolutely no men trying to tease her into that thing they called love, but which only led to pain and hate – and hours and hours of spare time for reading.

Inside the comfort of the little cottage, Rebekah took off her walking shoes and headed to the kitchen. She opened the fridge door and pulled out the newspaper-wrapped parcel that she'd placed there earlier. When Ben had arrived on the staff ferry that morning, he'd greeting her with a grin and held out the parcel.

'Something from the seafood kiosk on the quay for you, Rebekah.' He'd winked as he handed over the gift. She had thanked him and reached out to give him a little pat on the arm, and then regretted it as he turned and gave her a full and tight hug – exactly the kind of physical contact with a man that she hated. He was a nice enough chap, but Rebekah was not in the slightest bit interested in anyone that way.

She'd called her thanks again over her shoulder as she pulled away and went to stash the parcel in the staff fridge until she had a moment at lunchtime to run it up to her own kitchen in Rose Cottage. Ben had been a constant in her life ever since her arrival on Brownsea Island and was one of those people she knew would always be there for her. She had never had much time or interest in socialising once she'd made Brownsea her home, and so as Ben came to the island twice a week, they had fallen into what had become one of her most constant relationships. He seemed to bring her gifts like this more often than not on Fridays when he came to the island to volunteer.

Rebekah wondered now whether she ought to give him something in return, but there wasn't any produce grown on the island to share and she felt bad that the gift giving was so one-sided. Perhaps she should offer to pay him. But perhaps what he really wanted was the one thing she was not prepared to give.

She opened the parcel on the aged wooden table to reveal a pile of shiny black mussels. Rebekah tucked her loose, cinnamon-brown hair behind an ear before bending to sniff the smell of the sea that had come into the room as she opened the parcel. She tapped each shell, checking to make sure none of them were open and ensuring they were fresh enough to eat still, then rinsed them in a colander in the old stone sink of the cottage kitchen.

After taking a saucepan and a frying pan out of the cupboard, she set water to boil, then reached for the spaghetti from her larder.

Rebekah stepped outside into the garden and picked a bowl of warm, shiny, red, cherry tomatoes from the vine growing against the south-facing wall, popping one straight into her mouth and feeling the warm burst of sunshine tingle on her tongue as she exploded it with her bite. Back in the kitchen, she crushed some garlic and fried it in olive oil, then added some chilli and the tomatoes before dropping the spaghetti into the bubbling pot of water. She added capers and olives to the frying pan and then the mussels, covering them with the glass lid and watching the slow process of each mussel shell opening as they steamed. Then she popped the cork on a bottle of chilled Chablis and enjoyed the welcome chuckle of wine poured into a glass.

The aroma of the Mediterranean filled her little Dorset kitchen as she drained the pasta, then scraped the mussel mix, and all its delicious garlicky juices, into the spaghetti. She served herself one portion and set aside the remains for tomorrow's dinner.

With a deep sigh of satisfaction, Rebekah gathered her pasta bowl and wine glass and sat down in her favourite window seat to eat until she'd licked the bowl clean. She rested, enjoying the warmth in her belly and the sensation of the wine reaching her fingertips while she watched the tops of the trees move gently in the light evening breeze and the summer sunlight outside. She drained her wine glass as she set the dirty dishes in the sink, and then poured another as she settled in for a night with Thomas Hardy.

Rebekah was part way through *Far from the Madding Crowd*, for about the fourth time, and though she knew full well that Sergeant Troy was a cad, she couldn't help but feel for poor, romantic Bathsheba, who wanted more out of life than stability and sense, and a husband who promised little more than determined constancy. What woman wouldn't fall for a tall, handsome romantic who promised her excitement with every twinkle in his eye? Actually, Rebekah thought to herself, she knew she wouldn't. Not any more.

Rebekah's life had been perfectly adequate without a man around, ever since the last time. She had learnt by watching her mum and her neighbour, Aunty Peggy, that a woman didn't need a man in her life to make her happy. Still, she seemed to have always known that singledom wasn't the first choice for either woman, and though love and marriage had never been modelled for her at home, something inside her had sometimes longed for it, all the same.

The thing with Andy had started out so well. A bond over their joint love of bushwalking had seen them spending more weekends together than not, and the nights they'd shared together in a two-man tent had soon turned into weeknight study sessions that led to sleepovers at his flat in the city. And she'd been happy with the fun and the company, and loved being around someone who made her laugh and treated her well on their occasional splurges for dinner in the city.

The trouble had started at a party with all their friends, when she'd found herself deep in conversation with someone from school that Andy didn't know. When Lloyd had got up to get her another drink from the bar, Andy had appeared from nowhere, grabbed her by the arm and frogmarched her out of the bar. She was too shocked by his outburst to understand that his jealousy was the tip of a controlling nature she'd never seen before. Within a few weeks, he'd begun to ask her details of everywhere she'd been, and who she had been with, insisting on driving her to and from every social engagement she had. And when Lloyd turned up at a friend's dinner party and she'd greeted him with a friendly hug, Andy's true nature was fully revealed.

Afterwards, when he had crossed the line that she knew she would never let another man cross again, she'd packed up everything that she kept at his flat immediately, and taken a taxi straight to her mum's place. There, in the sanctuary of home, her black eye, cut lip, and traumatised soul were mended with love, encouragement and a protective shield that could have kept off an army of demons. She'd tried to report him to the police, because both Mum and Aunty Peggy persuaded her that rape was rape and should be punished as such. Peggy had driven her to the police station, making no attempt to conceal the burning rage she felt for the man who had so hurt the girl she loved like her own granddaughter.

'Rebekah, my love, men have been treating women with this kind of disgusting disrespect for hundreds, thousands, of years. But it is so wrong. And they must be made to stop. The last thing any woman needs in her life is a man who treats her worse than an animal. We just won't stand for it,' she'd seethed. But the off-hand way the middle-aged police officer dealt with her in the suburban station told Rebekah that if she had a boyfriend, she should expect a bit of rough now and then. So from that moment on, supported by Mum and Peggy, she'd stayed well away from all men. The threat of tying herself to one and being stuck with him for life had brought her up sharp and she'd chosen singledom instead.

The only thing she could remember about living with a man in the house as a child was loud arguments, shrieks of fear, and the occasional crash of breaking furniture. The experience with Andy had only solidified her understanding. And perhaps, quite apart from that and the childhood trauma she barely knew she harboured deep in her heart, she'd also learnt from Bathsheba

Everdene, or Tess Durbeyfield, or all the fictional women she'd read about who'd learnt their lessons the hard way. Men were either trouble in disguise, or boredom personified. She would stick with squirrels and trees. Birds and books. Her island home in paradise.

'God bless Thomas Hardy,' she said out loud and laughed at the sound of passion in her voice. She took another sip of wine, put her feet up and opened her book with a satisfied sigh. This, she agreed with herself for the billionth time, was a life of utter perfection.

3

POOLE – JANUARY 1941

Peggy Symonds took one last look at herself in the mirror – crisp, white-collared shirt, navy-blue woollen slacks, and a navy-blue jumper with the British Overseas Airways Corporation 'Speedbird' insignia on the front. She picked up her flat, peaked cap and trotted down the stairs.

'Put the kettle on for me would you, Peggy love?' Peggy's sister Molly had called from her bed as Peggy was getting dressed for work. Peggy popped her head into her sister's room to see Molly curled on her side, hiding her face with her arm.

'Not feeling too good today, my love?' asked Peggy, coming in and perching on the edge of the bed.

'I'm exhausted all the time. I feel sick all day and all night, and having to spend hours outside in that freezing shelter just about did for me last night. I don't know how I can survive any more of this,' Molly groaned, and Peggy could see her sister was a very pale shade of olive green. Like hundreds of other young brides, Molly had moved back into her parents' home once her husband was called up and went off to war, unable to manage the rent on her own and with her husband only sending back a minimal army pay.

'You poor love,' Peggy said as she softly stroked her sister's hair back from her eyes. 'Have you been sick this morning?'

Molly shook her head and grimaced in response. 'It doesn't make any difference anyway – it's more like seasickness than a tummy bug. It just never stops.'

'Nurse Wallace said it should get better after the first three months. You must be about there by now, surely?' Peggy asked, counting the months out on her fingers, back to the time this baby must have been conceived last year, when Molly's husband was home on leave. 'I'll go and make you that cup of tea. Anything to eat?'

The muffled noise of disgust that Molly made into her pillow was enough to tell Peggy that her sister couldn't face food. But Peggy knew she needed the strength.

'I'll make you a bit of dry toast and bring that up too – just for a nibble, Molly,' she said, giving her a gentle pat as she went downstairs to the kitchen.

It had been a rough night, even for Peggy, who was fit, healthy, and not expecting a child. The air-raid siren had sounded early, at nine o'clock, and the whole family had rushed out to the Anderson shelter still dressed from the day. But nothing seemed to come of it, though they heard a few planes go overhead, and only an hour later, the all-clear had sounded. Once back inside, they all got themselves undressed and tucked up in their warm beds, only to be woken again at midnight by another siren. Molly was all for giving up and staying in bed, but Peggy and their mother wouldn't hear of it and had dragged her up, taking extra blankets into the shelter. And there they'd stayed until four o'clock in the morning, with the sound of bombs dropping, the ack-ack guns blaring, and fire engine bells ringing the whole time.

By six in the morning, with only a few hours' sleep in her own bed, Molly was exhausted, but at least she could stay there all day if she wanted. Peggy was up and dressed and ready to put a brave smile on her tired face as she worked her launch in the harbour all day. Father was already up and had been out on a fishing run since before dawn, and Mother had gone to check on the neighbours after the air raid.

As Peggy went past the door to the front room, she ducked in to open the curtains, take down the blackout lining, and light the coal fire in the grate, stopping to look at the pictures of their brother, Samuel, and Molly's husband, Bill, both dressed in their new uniforms, one in the navy and the other the army. Peggy said a quiet prayer for their safety today then headed into the kitchen at the back of the house. She filled the kettle with water then lit the gas stove, placing the kettle on top to boil before setting out two cups and saucers. While the kettle was boiling, Peggy opened the back door and braved the chilly air to use the outside lavatory.

Their home in Ballard Road backed on to the little bit of shore in Poole Harbour where most of the fishermen kept their upturned dinghies, ready to row out to their boats in Fisherman's Dock. Peggy looked past the rabbit hutch and saw her dad's tender was out, as she had expected it would be, and there were a few other fishermen sat about, balanced on their dinghies, mending nets, or ropes. Gulls squawked overhead, somehow able to smell the fish on the nets even when there were no fish to be had yet today.

She bent down to open the rabbit-hutch door and poured a portion of food pellets into their bowl and broke the sheet of ice that had formed on their water bowl, making kissing noises to them all the while. It was difficult to see them as anything but cute and fluffy, even though they were all destined for the stew pot sooner or later.

When she was back inside the warm kitchen again, the kettle boiled and Peggy completed the tea routine, pouring a little water into the teapot, then swirling it around to warm it before tipping the water down the sink. Then she dropped in two heaped spoons of tea leaves and poured the boiling water on top. She gave it a stir, popped the lid on and stuck the knitted tea cosy on to keep the pot warm.

She cut two slices from yesterday's loaf of bread and stuck the first with the toasting fork, holding it near the gas flame to toast it before turning it over, then doing the same with the other. She went to the front door, wondering if the milkman had managed to deliver anything this morning after the air-raid disturbance overnight. There on the doorstep was their bottle of creamy-topped milk and Peggy smiled at the reassuring sign. All was well this morning – the world still turned as it should. Fish were being fished, rabbits were growing plump, milk was being delivered, and babies were growing strong and healthy inside their mothers' bellies. The world had not ended last night, after all.

'There you go, Molly love: hot tea and dry toast. Try and get a bit of that into you. I've got the fire going in the front room for you, and I've hung the big kettle on it for later,' soothed Peggy.

Molly grunted her thanks and grimaced as she lifted herself up to sit and drink the tea.

'The ration books are on the kitchen table,' Peggy continued, 'so if you could help Mother and pop out later to see if you can get us a bit of meat for dinner, that would be...' Peggy didn't get chance to finish before Molly leant over the side of the bed to the bucket she kept there, retching up the few mouthfuls of tea she'd just drunk.

'Sorry, Peg,' Molly mumbled, wiping her mouth on a hanky. 'It was the thought of raw meat. I can't go near the butcher's shop, let alone inside it.'

'Never mind, Molly – Mother will go if you can't,' said Peggy, patting her sister's hand. 'And failing that, Dad will have some fish for us again. But I would like a change.' She sighed. 'I'll be off then. See you at dinnertime,' she added as she headed down the stairs and started the process of rugging up into her coat, scarf, and gloves, for the freezing though brief walk to work this morning. Just as she was opening the door, the telegram boy arrived with something addressed to her parents. She thanked him with a tight smile, but backed into the hall shakily, shutting the door again and putting the telegram down on the hall table.

Would this be a notice of leave for Samuel? Or something much more sinister? She was desperate to open it but knew she shouldn't. She picked it up again and turned it over, then opened the door a crack to look up and down the street for her mother. There she was, across the road with Mrs Skinner, laughing away, probably both rejoicing in their good fortune at not being hit overnight. Peggy didn't want to be there to see her mother's life destroyed if this was the dreaded news that Samuel was hurt, or worse. But she couldn't go all day without knowing. She shut the door again and made her choice, peeling open the envelope and scanning it quickly, her heart beating as loud as a drum roll all the while.

Samuel's ship was coming in and he would be home on leave in a couple of weeks' time, the telegram read. Peggy dropped the message onto the hall stand and buried her face in her hands, sobbing with relief and joy and gratitude for a few precious moments. She still had a brother. Life would go on today.

She dried her face and picked up the telegram, rushing out

the door and running across the road to her mother to bring her the good news.

'Mum! It's Samuel!' she called, careful to plaster a big grin in her face so that Mum would know the news was good. 'He's coming home to see us, Mum, in two weeks' time,' Peggy said as she held out the telegram for her mother to read.

'Oh, bless my soul, that is wonderful news! Did you hear that, Mrs Skinner? Our Samuel coming back to see us, safe and sound,' Mrs Symonds cried gleefully. 'Oh, Peg love, we shall have to save up some rations so we can give him a feast: a cake, at the very least, don't you think?'

'We'll do what we can, Mum, but I'm sure he'll be happy to just come home and sit by our fire and sleep in his own bed a while,' said Peggy. 'Anyway, I'm off to work now, so I'll see you tonight.' She gave her mother a peck on the cheek.

Peggy ducked back into the house, put on her gloves, picked up her gas mask and walked out the front door and towards Poole Quay and the Flying Boat offices, happy from the morning's surprise and bemused at the way things could change. The telegram might just as easily have brought news that her family was about to start falling apart. And now there was cause for celebration. These were the moments that made up their lives, like morsels that were part of a bigger meal. Each bite was to be savoured for what it was.

The bitter wind howled down Ballard Road as Peggy braced herself against its chill, and she pushed her chin down into the folds of her scarf, creating a haven of warm air inside the cavern there with her breath. But she was grateful that she had a scarf, and gloves, and shoes, and work, and a home to go back to this evening where the fire would be roaring. And her brother was still safe and coming home to visit. This was the way to find joy.

To feel the gratitude for every small and wonderful blessing, despite the hell of war.

Her cheeks stung and her eyes watered and the cold was so biting, she suspected there might even be ice on the launch boat this morning. But it was early yet, not even seven in the morning. The air was cold, but the sky was clear, and the sun would soon be bright, so at least she wouldn't have to deal with rain or sleet today.

As Peggy passed around the back of the lifeboat house and looked to her right, up Stanley Road, she saw the rubble where a house had been hit in the night. She heard the fire bell ringing and saw the truck coming down South Road. Peggy paused for a moment, wondering if she should go and help, but then thought of her incoming C-class this morning. She had a flying boat to meet, passengers to fetch and an important duty of her own to carry out.

Peggy walked briskly on, passing the Poole Pottery buildings, and along the quay to the Harbour Office, which now housed the newly installed BOAC offices. She paused to look out over the harbour on the way, pleased to see the stiff breeze was one-directional at least, and not squally. She would know how to handle her launch just fine this morning.

Peggy's father, Brian, had been taking his children out to fish and row and handle anything necessary on a boat in Poole Harbour ever since they could stand up and hold a rope between their chubby little fingers. She could row herself to Brownsea and back by the time she was twelve and, between them, the three siblings could handle the fishing boat without their dad before they were old enough to legally drink a pint of beer with him in the Jolly Sailor. So, when the call had gone out for workers to operate the launches for BOAC, with all the young men and many of the harbour's older boatmen away at war, the daughters of Poole fishermen and lifeboat crew were the pick of the crop. Young women like Peggy had lived and breathed the harbour, knew every sandbar, every channel, and could almost find their way from Poole Quay to Pottery Pier on Brownsea Island with their eyes shut – which was sometimes quite necessary in a dense fog.

'Good morning, Miss Symonds,' called the bright voice of the harbour master as she pushed open the door into the warmth put out by the little coal fire.

'Morning, Mr Hewitt. Chilly one today,' she replied as she went through to the BOAC room and collected the key to her launch and her orders for the day.

'You've got the *Clare* coming in from Lisbon this morning, Peggy. Twelve passengers aboard and some cargo to unload,' said Patricia, the traffic manager, as she greeted Peggy. 'Nora and Eileen are crewing for you today.'

'Rightio, Pat, see you later,' called Peggy brightly as she went back out into the cold, across the quay to the ancient Custom House steps on the quayside, and down into her waiting launch. She was pleased to see no ice on the craft, and started the motor to get it warmed up, checking the fuel supplies, when she heard the familiar distant drone of the flying boat coming in over the harbour to land on the trots in the main channel.

Peggy stood upright and turned towards the sound, shielding her eyes against the morning sun, to watch the beautiful sight of the big-bellied flying boat coming in to land. The plane dropped down to what looked from this angle like one end of Brownsea Island and, as she hit the harbour waters, sea spray splashed past the windows, soaking the hull of the vessel up to the wings. Peggy had not yet had the chance to fly in one of these beauties – her job was simply to meet them and help them moor up, take the passengers and crew to and from either the quay or Salterns

Marina, and carry any cargo backwards and forwards – but she hankered for the thrill of flying.

'You'll get a go one day, for sure, Peggy,' said Nora as she stepped into the launch and patted Peggy on the shoulder as she passed.

'Eileen's going to marry a toff from America and get herself flown over to Hollywood to be in the movies like Maureen O'Hara. Isn't that right, Eileen?' and the three girls laughed as they readied the launch to head out to the flying boat as it taxied towards its mooring spot.

Peggy checked that the dock lines were cleared away from the quayside, turned the launch out towards the middle of the harbour and set off at a speed that froze their faces in the chill.

When they reached the *Clare* as she came to the end of the water runway and into her mooring spot, Peggy skilfully manoeuvred the launch in under the wing, close enough for Nora to climb aboard up the rope ladder on the bow, to help the stewardess who waited on board with the mooring line, while Eileen secured the launch to the flying boat at the stern. The stewardess opened the main passenger door and greeted the seawomen with a hearty 'Good morning, ladies!' before turning back to help her passengers out.

Eileen slipped on board to start collecting luggage and crates of cargo while Peggy helped all the passengers aboard the launch, and into the covered cabin where they'd be warmer than out on deck. Among the men in smart suits who stepped off the vessel carrying briefcases, which must be full of important documents, there were just two women.

They wore lusciously thick fur coats, had their wavy hair perfectly curled and pinned into place, and their flawless, pale skin was made up with bright-red lipstick and smoky, dark eye makeup. As Peggy held her hand out to help each of them on board, she felt the softness of their delicate leather gloves in her calloused, seawoman's hands and caught a whiff of what must be an expensive scent – Chanel No.5, Peggy assumed, though she'd only ever read of it in a magazine and never had the chance to smell it. But it smelled like class, and these women reeked of everything Peggy admired that was fabulous and classy and elegant.

She set her shoulders back and turned her head to show the best of her cheekbones in the morning sunlight, conscious that she wanted these women to see her as one of them, and not just some nameless fisherman's daughter.

Next came the six crew members, each carrying a box or a suitcase, one at a time until everything was unloaded, and the stewardess carried out a case of empty thermos flasks, used to make the serving of hot tea and coffee on demand easier than lighting the galley gas stove on the flying boat every time a passenger fancied a brew.

Peggy caught another scent on the air now, something tropical – oranges and bananas – and there was even a small box of pineapples with their spiky tops and strangely tessellated, prickly skins. She was lost in thought for a moment, wondering exactly which ration coupons would cover such rare and exotic delights, as the captain went through his last few security checks, then with everyone on board, he gave Peggy the nod to head back into the quay.

'Thank you, Captain, we're ready when you are,' he said with a tiny wink that drew Peggy's warmest smile. She loved the way the pilots treated her with such respect – one captain to another – with no distinction made about class or gender or the size of the vessel in their command. In times not so long ago, it would have seemed impossible that a job as important as ferrying passengers around the harbour to flying boats could have been undertaken by women. This was clearly a man's role, just like all the other jobs that required the operation of machinery or handling of maritime equipment. But with all the men away at war, and important jobs like this still to be done, the call had gone out to women to do anything they could. This, Peggy felt, was one of the only good things to come of the war. And it was always worth looking for those little highlights to be grateful for.

With practised ease, Peggy turned the launch back towards the quay and brought it in to the Fish Shambles steps, nearest to Poole Pottery. It was unusual for passengers to be brought direct to the quay, as the launches usually took them to Lake Pier in Hamworthy or into Salterns Marina, but the radio call had been clear: VIP passengers alighting at Poole Quay to be transferred to Poole Railway Station ASAP by BOAC security staff. Waiting for their arrival on the quay stood Major Carter and Rose Stevens from the BOAC security, customs, and immigration control office that was now housed in what had been the Poole Pottery showrooms.

Rose, not nearly so used to the outdoor work that Peggy did, stood cocooned in her long, double-breasted coat, buttoned up to the neck, with her scarf wrapped around her ears. She wore knitted mittens and clapped them together in muffled applause to keep them warm as she stamped her feet on the icy cobblestones. Peggy had known Rose, and her twin sister Daisy, ever since they were schoolgirls together, but among all the women now working in this men's world there was a shared private agreement that they kept their friendly relationships at bay in front of the men.

Like Peggy, Rose now wore a little cap that bore the 'Speedbird' insignia of the British Overseas Airways Corporation. The uniform made them all aware that they were working in a terribly important men's world now.

Peggy helped her passengers step off the launch and watched as Major Carter checked through everyone's passports and tickets, aided by Rose. This was an unusual transfer today. There were three cars waiting on the quayside to take most of the passengers directly to Poole train station. With all the passengers off the launch, the flying boat crew helped Peggy, Eileen and Nora unload the luggage and crates of fruit, every one of them secretly hoping an orange or two might 'fall' out of the crates and into their pockets.

When the last box was heaved up onto the quayside, and the passengers were all safely installed into the cars, Major Carter and Rose prepared to drive them off to the station. Just as he was about to get into the car, Major Carter stepped back to have a quiet word with Peggy. He cleared his throat gently and lowered his voice as he caught her eye and called her name.

'You're a fine seawoman, Miss Symonds. Your supervisors tell me you're doing an excellent job,' he began.

'Thank you, sir. It's as easy for me to handle this launch as it is for one of your potters to cast a china plate. I've been in and out of boats all my life,' she said with a wave towards the harbour she knew and loved.

'And how well do you handle other means of transport? Have you learnt to drive a car?' he asked with a frown of concentration on his face.

Peggy was surprised by the question, but not thrown by the idea.

'I've had a bit of a go in the grocer's van – my friend Isabel is the grocer's daughter and she showed me the ins and outs of it. But I've not much experience,' she said, wondering where this might be leading.

'That is good news,' he added with a nod. 'And so, do you think if you were asked to occasionally help out with driving passengers or goods to and from the quay by car, as well as by launch, you'd be up to the task? We would ensure you felt confident first, of course. Rose would teach you all that you'd need to know.'

'I'd be happy to help if it was required. All part of the BOAC service, I suppose,' said Peggy with a happy shrug.

'Absolutely, that's the ticket,' said the major. 'Well, I'd best get these chaps off to the train station, but I'll have Rose get in touch with you about some training and then some trips when they come up. In fact,' he said with a glance at the crates of fruit, 'we may even need these delivered up to the Harbour Heights Hotel later today. Perhaps you could go up for a run with Rose then, and she can give you the drill?'

'I have some passengers to take from Salterns Marina out to meet their plane after lunch, but until then it should be all quiet. I'll come in and check with Rose when I'm done here, shall I?'

He nodded and thanked her as he stepped into the car and set off with his passengers. The flight crew had loaded the crates onto a handcart and one of the dockhands was pulling it over to the harbour master's office, where the crew were following.

'Driving a car now too?' teased Nora as the three women closed down the launch and secured it before walking back into the offices. 'You'll be meeting more of the rich and famous than our Eileen here. You'll have to watch she doesn't get too jealous.' She winked, and the three young women linked arms and laughed their way back to the office.

4

POOLE, DORSET – MAY 1940

Hans Meyers peered at the white cliffs on the horizon and watched England drawing closer with every passing minute. The ache inside his chest was spreading like a cancer to his sore gut and up into his throat, which was as dry as the dust he'd breathed as he'd fled Rotterdam. He'd spent much of the journey with his teeth clenched shut to stop the anger and tears and fear from erupting.

Klaus had talked non-stop from when he'd jumped onto the boat until Hans had finally taken him by the shoulder and told him to shut up and listen to what had just happened to him. What he'd just lost. Why his life was over. Klaus had stayed silent then, until they'd joined the other refugees at the river's mouth and headed out to sea and he had others to talk to – shout to – across the water. The launch was meant for rivers and harbours, not the open sea, but thankfully the weather had been calm, and they had been kept safe by the sheer number of other vessels travelling with them. Hans had thought their small boat was not much use to anyone else, but when they saw the mass of humanity trying to get onto boats, he felt he had to offer space to any who wanted to brave the trip in his little open launch. Instead of just the two men as he'd imagined, his boat took twelve men, women, and children safely away from Holland's shores.

And in the end, Hans was glad that Klaus was there. He became the go-between with the other refugees. Hans held firm at the helm for most of the trip, and Klaus did all the communicating about where they were headed, how much water was left, and if there was room aboard for any others as some of the boats were far too crowded. Hans was able to stay locked inside the dark cavern of his grief, his eyes set on the prize of escaping the hell that Rotterdam now represented to him.

Every now and then, he heard the call of a woman's voice or the cry of a baby and he pictured them, his own wife and child, there with him, where they should have been. Katrijn and Anika: his life, his world. Why he hadn't thought to take them away with him earlier, he would never know, and he knew now he'd never stop regretting his foolish mistake.

But now he and Klaus were simply single men travelling together. None of the others knew his history, his family, the trajectory his life had been on until just days ago. The two young men were understood to be friends, or brothers even. And regardless how the others saw them, they were all Dutch refugees – simple fishermen and their families – fleeing the Nazi onslaught. Hans gripped the wheel and bile rose in his throat as he remembered his plan to simply give up on Holland and become German. The idea of siding with the monster that had killed his girls was now so disgusting that he hated himself for ever thinking of claiming his German heritage. He harboured a niggling worry about Klaus and what he intended to do, with his German nationality and the contact he claimed to have made with the German Army. But Hans had neither the heart nor the headspace to deal with that problem.

And it was all such a mashed-together mess anyway, he mused as the blur of the English coastline gradually morphed to reveal the detail in the limestone cliffs, the trees, the beach. When a man is born in Düsseldorf, with a Dutch mother and a German father, the lines between Germany and Holland become blurred, and it is only the tragedy of war that makes the borders real.

Klaus, it seemed, was determined to offer the victors something useful to keep himself safe, and certain that German invasion would become a reality for England within days or weeks.

But the idea of claiming his German heritage now repulsed Hans to his core. And all he could see in his mind's eye when he thought of Germany was blood: the blood-red flare smoke that had hung over Rotterdam on the day Germany had destroyed the beautiful city and everything he loved with it; the dried trickle of blood that stained the head of his precious baby girl; the blood that had drained away from Katrijn's face; the red of the Nazi flags that had hung from the Panzer tanks.

* * *

The fleet of a hundred or so little boats, overcrowded with terrified Dutch families, had taken two days to journey here to the south coast of England from Holland, and others were now on their way from Belgium too. The horrors of Nazi attack and the swiftly gained occupation, and the threat of Hitler's plan of total control over Europe, had become clear to every man, woman, and child swept up in the debris. Those desperate enough to escape by sea who had the means, and the contacts, had taken to the little boats with only the scantest of belongings. Yet although these folks were headed for England, what they'd seen of the speed of Hitler's attacking armies and the lack of mercy shown to any who stood in their way told them this was no place to hide. America was their only hope and plans on how to get there occupied most of the men along the journey. England would soon be occupied by Germany as well; that was a certainty.

There was nothing but this tiny strip of water between the English coastline and the most powerful and determined army the world had ever seen, and these humble Dutch fisherfolk intended to get far, far away. Hitler was surely coming soon.

* * *

'Do you have all the papers ready?' asked a red-faced and exhausted-looking woman, holding a toddler on her hip as she stood on the starboard side of Hans's launch. As she turned around to face the shore again, her heavily pregnant belly loomed before her. Her husband tapped his coat pocket and spoke soothingly to her. Her features relaxed a little and she took deep breaths as she lightly swayed along with the motion of the boat, slowly chugging towards the harbour entrance.

There was a small boat belonging to the British Royal Navy ahead of them, and another not far behind the fleet of refugees, who'd been guiding them along the coast towards Poole Harbour ever since they were first intercepted in the east, off the coast of Kent.

The sound of the water splashing the side of the boat had been the constant companion to the noise from the motors for the whole journey, and although the passengers had often scanned the skies for enemy planes, they had – so far – heard none. So, when the distant deep drone of a plane now hit the airwaves around them, a quickening, animal-like sense of mild panic stirred them all at once. Hans's heartbeat skipped one or two beats faster as he frowned into the skies, looking for the planes. He crouched, as did the others, ready to duck and hide, though that would have been utterly fruitless in the event of an attack. But there was just one plane, and it didn't look to be any kind of fighter.

Hans relaxed a little as the plane flew overhead on its descent towards the vast, shallow harbour beyond. The plane was an unusual shape, with a much larger belly than any he'd seen before, and the wings seemed to be attached too high, rather than central to the main body of the plane as they were more used to seeing.

At the harbour entrance, a small gap between two long, sandy beaches, Hans took in the sight of an imposing white hotel building, three storeys high with a red-tiled roof, and dozens of windows looking straight out to sea. Between the two sides of the harbour entrance a long, low barge ran on chains that made a rhythmic chug, chug, chug sound as the ferry pulled itself on the chains across the stretch of water. Steam chuffed from the chimney stacks on either side of the ferry and it was packed with cars, army trucks, and even a bus being taken from one side of the harbour entrance to the other.

A navy guide boat signalled to the flotilla to slow their speed and they were led into a calm, expansive natural harbour, so vast it was more like an inland lake that followed the curve of a varying and mostly unseen landscape. There were several islands in the harbour, the main and most central one appearing to be over a mile long, and almost as wide, with a number of ancient buildings and even a castle at its eastern point.

Almost every direction the refugees looked, they saw the vessels with wings like the strange plane they had seen earlier, moored in channels near the islands, or taxiing across the calm waters. Hans followed the instructions to take his boat alongside the largest island, towards a mooring in a channel further along.

As they passed the island with the castle, he saw there were tents and huts being erected, and a small army of people in various uniforms – both men and women – milling about, unloading crates onto the short jetty, setting up small tents and tables, carrying baskets of food. Klaus caught the mooring line that was offered to him and tied the boat securely to it.

And now they waited. They were safely nestled within a calm British harbour, unoccupied by the Germans and yet, they were not allowed to land. Alarm ran through the body of refugees who feared being sent away, back into the English Channel.

Patiently, the thousands of refugees stayed on their moored boats while the naval officers moved, one boat to another, with painfully slow, meticulous attention to detail, checking the identity documents and credentials of all the boat owners and pilots. And although it was plain for all to see the Dutch were relieved to be there, their terror of what they believed to be coming close behind them was palpable to all the navy and army staff who greeted them.

After hours of waiting, and a full day since all their food had gone, the turn came for Hans's boat to be checked. As the small navy launch pulled up beside them, Hans helped tie the two boats together.

'Good afternoon,' the naval officer greeted them with a stiff smile. 'Who's in charge here?'

Hans stepped forward and doffed his cap, reaching instinctively to his pocket for the identity papers. His hand froze midway to his chest as he remembered that both the German and the Dutch papers were still there together. In his stupor of grief, he had forgotten to separate them on the journey. He would never be able to sort through them now, unseen. His palms began to sweat, and he licked his lips nervously at the thought of being considered German. He would not make it on to British soil before they shot him, surely? Hans dropped his hand to his trouser leg, wiping it there and waiting for their next instruction.

'Papers?' the naval officer asked curtly, looking to both Hans and Klaus, who had come to stand beside him.

'Good day to you,' Klaus offered. 'I am Klaus Schmidt, and I work with my friend, Hans Meyers,' he said in remarkably good English, and holding out his papers as he did so. 'Hans, you should get your papers from the cabin,' he said with a look in his eye that only Hans could read.

Of course. Hans recalled how, one quiet hour on their journey, between his grieving and his worry, Klaus had talked more of his plan once he reached England, and had asked to see Hans's two sets of papers. He knew now that Klaus was giving him a way to step down into the cabin and separate the papers, hiding the German ones there. Hans nodded to Klaus and ducked down into the clammy darkness of his small cuddy cabin. His hands shook as he unbuttoned the pocket, keeping his back to the hatch. He took the German papers and spread them open, then unbuttoned the cover on the cushion he kept in there as a pillow. This was the pillow that Katrijn had used to rest her head, that day of their picnic.

He paused to lift it to his face, hoping to sense some aroma of her still lingering there. But now it just smelled of salty sea water and engine oil. He sighed deeply and slipped the German papers inside, smoothed them flat, and rebuttoned the cover, throwing the cushion into the very front of the cabin. He held his Dutch papers in his hand and, taking three deep breaths to calm himself, climbed back up into the warm May sunshine.

The naval officer stared at his papers for an age while time stood still. He compared them to Klaus's, and then handed both sets to another officer to study while he began his questioning. Where had they come from? Why were they here? Who were the others in the boat with them? What work did they do? Where were their families?

At this last question, Hans's patience and resolve to remain calm exploded. His tolerance for the 'normalness' of this standard processing had reached its end.

'My family is dead,' he spat with bitterness. 'The German bombs have killed my wife – she was beautiful, and kind, and talented – and my baby girl with her. Anika was just three weeks old. Three weeks! She had barely breathed a lungful of fresh air, only seen the sun a few times, and the Germans have killed her in the bed where I left her safely in her mother's arms!' he shrieked at them now, tears pouring down their well-worn rivulets in his face.

The naval officers looked at one another, quietly clearing their throats and wiping their brows. The first one held out a hand to quiet Hans, and spoke a few words to placate him, and offer his brief and polite condolences.

An hour later, they were delivered to the shores of the large island, weary past the point of being able to think any more.

'Welcome to Brownsea Island,' called a cheery young woman in a uniform that wasn't quite military. She gave them water and hot tea to drink and then beckoned them to cold-water troughs and showed them the basic washing set-up that had been made ready for them. The mothers washed their children and then themselves, and the men poured the fresh water over their heads, faces and hands, and the life began to return to their bones.

* * *

A chubby-legged little boy with a round face and dark, curly locks tugged at his mother's hand, demanding that she look to the imposing castle they'd seen as they first arrived in the harbour.

Hans had wondered himself about this ancient-looking castle, but realised it was in prime position to protect the harbour entrance from advancing foes. He wondered if it would be used soon as a defence against the Germans. But now he was too exhausted to think any more, and the pain in his injured leg was immense. They had walked, and he had hobbled, for what seemed far too long to such weary people, up a hill and over to the southern side of the island, to a clearing not far from the beach, where the welcome aroma of hot soup wafted on the warm summer afternoon air. The tents were all erected here, and Hans recognised the site that they'd passed on the way to their moorings.

'One bowl of soup and a bread roll each,' called out a stern, stout woman overseeing the distribution of a thick, hot vegetable broth from a camp kitchen. She wore a long, dark coat, and a woollen hat, even though the summer weather was mild and sunny. 'There will be more later,' she enunciated slowly and loudly, as if the Dutch might be a little bit deaf and stupid as well as foreign. 'This will have to do for tonight, but more supplies will be here by morning.'

The expectant mother took her place in the queue for soup, and when the broth was ladled into the dish she'd been given to hold, she made a point of searching out the eyes of the bossy lady serving her.

'*Ontzettend bedankt*,' she said earnestly. 'Thank you, thank you so much.'

In response, the English lady nodded curtly but gave no hint of a smile.

'My name is Lotte,' the Dutch woman tried again. 'And you?'

The ladle hung still for a moment as the older woman seemed to battle with herself about how to respond. She sighed and, glancing down at the little boy beside the woman, she answered, 'Mary. My name is Mary. This is my island. I'm not used to people. I don't allow anyone to visit, you see. The island is just for the animals and the birds. For me, and the trees.'

'But it is a very beautiful place,' said Lotte with the warmth of hot Dutch chocolate in her voice. 'Thank you.'

Tents were being set up by soldiers and others sat at temporary desks rechecking papers and handing out basic supplies. The queue of refugees snaked forever and as they stood in line, waiting to be processed through the next stage of bureaucracy, all were amazed at the activity in the harbour around them. The sound of a thousand bumble bees thrumming around a massive hive signalled to the refugees that another of the strange planes was coming into the harbour and they turned as one to watch in awe as it came down so low, they thought it might crash-land, but it splashed onto the water beside the island, sea spray shooting into the air behind it, apparently quite deliberately.

The more watchful of the refugees could see that others like this were being towed about all over the harbour, closer to the town beyond. These weren't just strangely shaped planes. They were planes that were built to float on the water. Flying boats.

* * *

After almost a week of tense waiting, Hans had successfully passed the processing station, and been accepted by the British security forces who were manning this camp. He was granted refuge in the United Kingdom until such time as it was safe for him to return to Holland. He walked away from the first processing desk and on to the next where he was handed a small bag of food supplies to take with him to the mainland. The soldier then pointed in the direction of the large tent that had been home since his arrival.

'Go and get your things, son,' said the soldier. Hans under-stood him perfectly, but simply shook his head.

'Bags? Clothes?' asked the soldier. Hans held up his small bag, the one containing everything he needed for his new life: a change of clothes and the photos of his beloved wife and mother. He'd kept it close to him the entire trip and hadn't let it out of his hands once since he landed on this island.

'This is my bag,' said Hans in his thick Dutch accent. 'I have other things on the boat. My boat,' he said, pointing in the direc-tion he knew the channel lay where his boat was moored.

'The boats will remain where they are for now. There is a possibility the Royal Navy might require the use of them for a military operation in the next few weeks. Check in with officials on Poole Quay in the next week, and there might be more infor-mation,' the officer told him.

Hans had no power to do anything but nod and accept what he'd been told. He glanced around him, wondering where in the system Klaus was. In the blur of his vision to one side, he noticed a small group of men stood around another desk, and then he saw Klaus, following not far behind. But he chose not to see him. He'd never asked for Klaus's company, and didn't welcome his strange allegiance to Germany. The sooner he could get away from him, the better.

'Take the walk across the island and down to the quay please, young man, and a ferry will be along soon to take you into Poole. The nice ladies from the Wrens are along the way to guide you, so as you don't get lost,' said a kindly Englishman wearing a uniform that wasn't quite the same as the English soldier. Perhaps this was the costume of a member of the reserves.

The German identity papers grew so large in his mind, he imagined them swelling up and spilling over the side of the boat. How he would ever get to them, he couldn't imagine, but he could not raise the issue now. Getting off this island was the most important thing for now. Hans nodded and smiled his response, muttering a 'thank you'. He limped away from the clearing where they'd been camped, leaving the hubbub of the processing station behind him, trying not to look back to Klaus.

A peacock called in the distance and Hans stopped to rest his aching leg and looked up to see him stretching his tail feathers, chasing a hen across the open field. He rubbed his knee and studied his leg again, as he'd been doing these last few days. There was no sign of an injury, no cut or bruise, but something seemed to have happened inside his leg, to his knee, that continued to cause him pain. It simply wasn't healing. He gritted his teeth and walked on, passing the church that had become familiar in these last few days and took in a deep breath of the pine-fresh air of the island. A cheeky little red squirrel ran across his path, then paused at the base of a tree, looking back at Hans as if to say, *Catch me if you can.*

When Hans reached the island quayside, he found a place to sit down along with the others being released today, in the warmth of the evening sun, and he hoped that Klaus was far behind and would not get onto the same ferry as him. The ferry arrived and Hans, along with around thirty others, was guided aboard for the short trip to the town quay. He sighed with relief. His connection with Klaus Schmidt was over forever.

Eager to take in all he could see of the harbour and the flying boats, he took a seat on the top deck of the ferry. There might be good work here for a boatman, he realised. There were dozens of those flying boats moored in different places around the harbour and, hearing the roar of its engines before he saw the plane, he turned his head back towards the harbour entrance and watched one taking off as his ferry boat approached Poole Quay. The big-bellied plane lifted itself off the water as gracefully as any seabird

Hans had seen, despite the fact it was built like a pregnant whale. It flew off into the setting sun over the top of Brownsea Island and into the hills on the far side of the harbour. West, then.

He heard the familiar sound of a motor launch not unlike his own and watched to see it leaving from where the flying boat had taken off. He peered closely to see the pilot and felt sure it was a woman, with curly, blonde hair tucked underneath her cap, strange as it seemed.

Hans saw that the ferry's deckhand was eyeing him with a smile as he watched the activity. His face warmed as their eyes connected.

'I like these seaplanes,' Hans offered pointing to the flying boat.

'Not a seaplane, matey – that there's a flying boat. See this one over this way?' the deckhand asked, pointing towards the inside of the peninsula where several smaller planes were moored on the water, seeming to stand up on stilts. 'The bigguns are called a flying boat because they're technically a boat that flies, rather than a plane that can land on the water like these tiddlers, which is called a seaplane, by rights,' he added in his thick Dorset accent. Hans nodded and thanked the man for his help.

The journey from the island to the surprisingly industrial quayside took almost half an hour. At the quay, a man in uniform was waiting to greet them. Standing beside this gentleman who wore a major's stripes on his shoulders was a striking young woman, with dark, wavy hair and a smile that lit up her face like the sun when she laughed at whatever it was the major was saying to her. But the sense of delight in this young woman's carefree laugh soon turned to bitter guilt in his throat as he compared it with that of Katrijn. He knew then that he would never stop missing her. This hole in his heart could not heal.

'Up you come then, miss,' Hans heard the local ferryman say

to a young girl as he helped her off the boat. Hans and the other refugees on this ferry were guided a little way along the quay towards another officer who, they were told, would help them with travel arrangements or accommodation here in the town.

The welcoming committee here appeared calm, and genial even, compared to the intensity of the arrival on the island, and in the midst of his pain and grief, something warm sparked in him, a little like the feeling of coming home on a cold night.

5

BRISBANE – SUMMER 1971

The slow-flowing, warm water trickled over Rebekah's toes as she sat perched on the edge of the narrow creek bank, wearing no more than her underwear and her floppy, yellow, terry-towelling sun hat. Birds chattered in the tall trees overhead and the high-pitched ticking of cicadas filled the humid afternoon air as the distant sound of a growling lawnmower hushed abruptly after what seemed like hours. Rebekah leant forward and picked up another handful of gritty mud and dribbled it onto her feet and legs, then rubbed it all over her knees, the grit lightly scrubbing her skin. She peered back over her shoulder, up the little hill from the creek and into the backyard.

No one was watching. Mum must have finished taking the washing off the line and gone back inside to fold and iron it. Even Scat the cat was sound asleep with her head on her paws in the shade and relative cool of the back verandah. The sun was at its highest and Rebekah knew that if she made any sound and reminded Mum that she was out here frying her shoulders and back in the mid-afternoon heat, she'd be called inside.

Rebekah firmly pushed her palms into the warm, prickly

brown grass on the creek bank and lowered herself carefully down to sit in the trickle of water that she called her creek. It was only just wide enough for her tiny form to sit inside and there was never more than a trickle of water except in the middle of a rainstorm, when it ran like a torrent from the big overflowing water tank at the top of the hill all the way down until it disappeared into the stormwater drain at the low end of the street.

The backyards of all the houses in Barrawondi Street had no fences to the rear so each one opened out onto this stretch of bushland that seemed to be owned by nobody, though if the residents had tried to build anything there, the Brisbane City Council would surely have had something to say about it. Rebekah's creek was no more than the downhill route that the stormwater run-off took through the empty land, but to her four-year-old mind, it was a wild waterway full of fascinating creatures, rocks, and her favourite part – the mud.

She scooped up more water and washed the mud off her skin until she was meticulously clean, and then started the process again. A handful of mud, dropped onto her feet, shins, knees, and thighs, then rubbed in all over. She scooped the next handful of mud and, looking out from underneath her long, dark eyelashes, chin low to her chest, she did one more check for anyone who might be watching. Then she slowly lifted her hand to her mouth and did the one thing she was not allowed to do with the mud. But she couldn't resist the sandy feel as it crunched between her teeth and Rebekah closed her eyes against the sun to better hear the crunch and grind inside her head as she bit down on the grit. And while she was crushing it, feeling the textures on her tongue, she scooped up more soft, warm water and washed her legs clean again.

The cicadas sang their endless chirpy background music and she looked, trying to see them, to find where their chirruping came from, but they were like the hot air she breathed – always there but impossible to see. A kookaburra laughed overhead, and Rebekah looked up to the top of the gum tree, through the blue-green haze of eucalypt leaves that hung like rain from the branches, to find the bird. Was he laughing at her? Afternoon thunder rumbled from miles away and within a few minutes, a flock of rainbow lorikeets had filled the branches of the giant tree, chattering to each other about the coming storm.

Rebekah knew what was coming next in her summer afternoon play ritual. Soon Mum would come and call her out of the creek, hose her down and get her inside, safe from the storm that would soon come to fill the creek with fresh, cool rain.

But the sound when she heard it was not her mum's sweet call, or the sound of a loud and close thunderclap. It was that sound she had begun to dread. The angry yell of her dad, home from the pub after his long lunchtime session. He was perennially angry now. Either he was angry after he came in smelling of beer, or he was angry in the morning when his head hurt. Sometimes, he was angry with Mum for not cooking his steak the way he liked it, and other times he was angry with Rebekah for leaving her toys on the floor. Whatever the reason for his erupting temper, Rebekah had learnt to hold her chin on her chest and put her hands over her ears when she heard him shouting, so she could hide and wait for the storm to pass. She stayed that way, in the creek, until her hands hurt and her ears burned from squeezing them so tight.

She let go cautiously and, fearing what she might hear next, the unexpected voice, when it came from behind, though known and loved by Rebekah, was a surprise.

'What are you doing in there, muddy miss? Doesn't your mother have a proper bath indoors?' Aunty Pig's chuckle was warm and soft, and she held out her hand to Rebekah to help her climb out of the creek. 'Come on indoors with me, my lovely, and you can have a bath and a pikelet or three.'

Rebekah obeyed without question, knowing and trusting her neighbour as if she were her own mother, but still she looked back to her own back verandah with a frown.

'Where's my mum, then?' she asked as she grabbed a few treasured rocks in her chubby hand to bring indoors for later.

'She's very tired today, love, and I think she and your dad have got some business to attend to. You come in with me for a while. Is that all right with you?'

Rebekah nodded as they walked into the backyard of Pig's house next door, past the timber hut that housed the outdoor dunny, the big, rotary washing line, and up the little concrete path to the base of the timber steps that led to the back verandah of Rebekah's next-door neighbour's home.

'Let's have a look at you then, Becky. Do we need a hose-off first?'

Rebekah held her arms up and turned around to show off her muddiness, giggling at the prospect of the jet of warm hose water on her skin.

'I reckon you could do with a once-over. Don't want too much of that creek in our bathtub, do we?' Pig laughed. The rubber hose had been lying in the full heat of the Queensland sun for hours, so Pig held it away from Rebekah's delicate skin until all the burning hot water had passed through the pipe, and it ran lukewarm, safe for a little girl's shower.

'Got any in your hair today?' teased Pig as Rebekah laughed under the shower of water, then stood still as Pig dried her off, wrapped her in the old towel that always hung on the peg near the hose, then carried her inside.

'Have you got bubbles, Piggy?' Rebekah asked as the bath water was run and she dropped various plastic cups and jugs into the tub to play with. Pig dribbled in some bubble bath and dropped the lavender soap for Rebekah to chase around the tub.

'In you get then, missy. I'll be back in a minute. Then when you've had enough, you can help me mix up the pikelet batter.'

Rebekah lay down in the warm water and floated on her back, dropping the bubbles onto her tummy and blowing them away again until the water was almost the same temperature as the creek.

Pig came in and dried her properly when she climbed out of the tub, and dropped a clean sundress over Rebekah's head, then she helped the little girl step into her clean undies, as Rebekah leant on Pig's shoulders.

'You're all set, gorgeous. You smell pretty good now, chicken. Have you had a nice bath?'

'Yeah, I was a bit muddy in the creek, but now I'm nice. Are we gonna make pikeliks now, Piggy?'

* * *

Half an hour later lightning lit up the kitchen and thunder rumbled around the suburb while the rain pounded on the tin roof, sounding like the fat from a giant's frying pan sizzling his sausages for tea. Rebekah sat with her elbows on the Formica kitchen table, kneeling up on the vinyl-covered chair as she licked butter and strawberry jam from her fingers and told Pig all her discoveries of the day.

'And there was a kookaburra, and lots of lorikeets, and I think they were all talking 'bout the rain—'

'Are you sure they were lorikeets and not budgies, Bek?' interrupted Piggy.

'Yep, lorikeets – too big and noisy for budgies,' she answered with a firm nod of the head and another mouthful of pikelet. 'And in the creek, there were rocks with shiny bits, see?' she said, pointing to her now clean and lavender-smelling creek treasures lined up on the table beside her plate.

'Did you have to dig them out of the mud, or were they in the dry grass?'

'These were in the mud. I like how it feels on my fingers when I find them all hard in the squishy mud.'

'I like that feeling too,' said Piggy. 'When I was a young girl, I used to row my dad's boat across the harbour to the beach on the island—'

'To Brownsea Island?' asked Rebekah.

'That's the one, love, to Brownsea Island in the middle of the harbour. I would land my boat on the shore and paddle in the water in my bare feet and feel in the mud with my toes for the cockles. Then, when I found one, I would reach my hand down and pull it out of the mud, give it a little wash, and put it into my bucket. And then, when I had collected enough, I would take them home and we'd boil them up and eat them for our tea, with vinegar and some lovely bread and butter,' Piggy told her, with that faraway look in her eyes that made Rebekah's heart feel full and happy.

'What did they taste like?' Rebekah asked, as fascinated as ever by Pig's tales of the magical harbour with its beautiful island where she used to live, in the 'olden days' of the war.

'They tasted salty and vinegary, and they're a little bit chewy and a little bit soft,' replied Piggy thoughtfully.

'*Pikeliks* are a bit chewy and a bit soft,' said Rebekah, making Piggy laugh. 'What colour are cockles?'

'The shells are white and brown, a little bit stripy. You have to make sure the shells are shut tight before you cook them else they might be no good. You soak them in salted water for a few hours, which cleans the grit out of them, then pop them in a pan of water and boil them. When they're cooked, the shell opens and you can see that they are white with a bright-orange beak. Very tasty, they are, too.'

'I'm goin' there to eat some cockles, too,' said Rebekah in the matter-of-fact way that Pig seemed to love about her surrogate granddaughter.

'Are you, Becky? When's that then?'

'When I'm big and I know all about the animals and birds and trees in Australia. Then I'm going to England to learn all about the animals and birds and trees there too.'

6

POOLE – JANUARY 1941

Peggy loaded all ten passengers into the launch from the pontoon at Salterns Marina and, with Nora's help, got them settled into the cabin, safe from the cold wind and rain that was beginning to fall. They'd mostly been brought there directly from the train, but there was one couple who'd had an extended stay at the Harbour Heights Hotel. She glanced up in the direction of the beautiful and very classy hotel building on the hill as she navigated her way out of the marina and into the main channel, headed for the C-class. The plump seabird waited patiently for them to arrive, bobbing on its moorings looking just like any other boat in the harbour, except for its wide wingspan with two propellers on each wing.

She drew the launch in to nestle under the protection of the flying boat's outstretched wing, just like a duckling diving for cover under the safety of mother duck. As the last of the passengers were settled aboard, she turned the launch carefully away and heard the engines start up behind her and build to a powerful roar. The cabin crew took in the mooring line and the flying boat began its slow taxi to the start of the runway trots.

Peggy picked up speed and, with one eye on the flying boat, she took the launch as fast as she dared, sea water spraying out beside and behind her just as it did on the flying boats as they took off and landed. She felt the freezing wind in her face and, closing her eyes, imagined she was flying the plane and could take off, rising clear of the harbour at any moment. But she knew the launch and the harbour so well, with all its busy activity and deadly sandbars that she only gave herself a second or two before she dropped the speed, opened her eyes, and hoped nobody had noticed her speedy little escapade.

The tone of the engines on the flying boat stepped up a few notes and she turned back to watch it begin its take-off, speeding down runway number one, directly parallel to Brownsea Island, then it lifted off and left the harbour below as it climbed fast and disappeared over the other side of the island, heading westward.

Peggy turned her face towards the quay where she was headed and was soon gliding in past Fisherman's Dock and expertly bringing the launch alongside the quay. She noticed the two cars and a small truck parked outside the pottery and knew that Rose Stevens would be waiting for her. The plan had been for Peggy to go and see about the driving instruction before lunch, but some other jobs had cropped up so all she'd had time for was a quick visit to tell Rose she'd be back after her last run of the day in the early afternoon.

Peggy's hands were cold and stiff from the freezing salty sea spray, so she first went inside to warm them by the fire and swallowed a quick cup of hot tea to warm her insides. Then she took the brisk walk down the quay to the front of the pottery and went in to find Rose, who looked up from her desk with a warm smile.

'Ready for the off, Peggy?' Rose asked, as she picked up some keys and led the boatwoman back downstairs to the cars waiting outside. Peggy simply nodded with anticipation. She had revelled in the chance to captain her own boat, and now the idea of taking charge of a car was just as thrilling.

'The fruit and other supplies that came in from Lisbon this morning are due up at the Harbour Heights Hotel, so we've had them loaded into the back of the truck. It drives just like a car, so there's nothing difficult there – especially as you've already driven a grocer's van. But it is just a bit less comfortable and ornate on the inside than the major's car,' Rose said and laughed as she unlocked the doors. 'How confident do you think you are to get right into the driver's seat Peggy? Would you prefer to watch me first?' Rose asked.

'It's been a little while since I first had a go at driving, so perhaps I should watch you first, just to be safe,' said Peggy.

'Rightio, then. You jump in the passenger side, and I'll take the driving seat. I'll explain everything as I go, then we'll stop halfway so you can have a turn,' said Rose, as she started the engine and began to run through the motions, explaining everything to Peggy with practised patience.

'The clutch pedal is the hardest thing to master, as I'm sure you'll remember, but it just takes practice,' said Rose as her own foot slipped off the clutch and she crunched the gearbox, wincing as she did.

'Yes, I remember that was a bit tricky, but at least I remember the order of things. Clutch down, into first gear, clutch up slowly and press on the accelerator,' said Peggy.

'You've got it. And you use the same foot for the brake as you do the accelerator,' Rose said to remind Peggy. They had driven away from the quay and up the High Street, and were just pulling into the gates of Poole Park.

'Shall I pull over here in the park, Peggy? There are hardly any other cars around, so this would be a good quiet place to start, I think,' said Rose, more to herself than as a question to

Peggy. She pulled into the side of the road near the big boating lake then opened the door and got out. Peggy did the same and felt her heartbeat quicken as she sat in the driver's seat and took hold of the big steering wheel firmly. Rose had left the engine running, and reminded Peggy what to do first.

Both girls laughed at Peggy's first attempt to raise the clutch slowly, which meant they bunny-hopped a few yards while she was getting used to things, but by the time they made it through to the other side of the park, she was in third gear and the knack had all come flooding back.

'You're a natural, Peggy Symonds. It took me a week to become as confident as you are already!' cooed Rose.

'I have done it before, of course. But I'm also used to listening to the hum of an engine and hearing what she wants from me,' said Peggy, feeling almost as though she should apologise for being able to pick up the new skill so readily.

'You'll be a great help to us if you can manage some driving from time to time. Things are getting more and more busy, and I'm flat-strapped just seeing to all the security paperwork that is coming through the BOAC office these days. We could really do with an extra pair of hands, but it is so hard to find anyone. I don't suppose your sister is interested in working?' asked Rose.

'She might get back to it at some point, I suppose, but I don't think that's likely. She's simply too unwell at the moment, and before too long, the baby will be here. She can't get through a day without being sick and feels absolutely rotten all the time,' Peggy offered with a grimace.

'My sister's been the same too, though thankfully she's past the worst of the sickness now. But she's too tired for any work. She's managing the house for the pair of us while I'm working. It will be lovely having little babies around to play with, won't it?' Rose beamed. 'Something to brighten the days a little.'

Peggy nodded and smiled but remembered last night's raid and the way the morning had begun. This afternoon, she was smiling and chatting and learning a new skill but her brother and brother-in-law were away in the war, and just this morning, the telegram that had arrived might have changed her life forever and brought news that Samuel was one more statistic. It was the same for Rose and her sister, Peggy thought solemnly, as both their husbands were also away defending England from Hitler.

Just last year when the Germans had taken Paris and invaded Holland and Belgium too, it had seemed certain that England would be invaded within weeks. Peggy had woken up in a cold sweat on several nights, fearing she could hear German soldiers landing on the little shaley beach at the back of her parents' home and coming to knock the door down. And all of England had lived in the same fear. The Dunkirk evacuation had been an amazing feat, but it was still just a retreat away from the winning side, and all those refugees who'd arrived on Brownsea Island seemed shell-shocked from what they'd seen in Holland.

But the months had gone on and no invasion had happened. With every passing day, there was hope that England might have time to bolster their defences and be able to ward Hitler off when he came. But they knew he would come. The air raids that were destroying half the country were a clear sign of his intentions. Peggy was just beginning to realise how long both she and Rose had remained quiet when they passed the site of a recently bombed home, still smoking and surrounded by people who were searching through the debris.

'I hope there's nobody trapped inside there,' said Rose quietly. If there was, there'd be no hope for them now. Suddenly, the thought of bringing new babies into this world didn't seem quite such a jolly idea, after all.

They reached the peak of Evening Hill and both glanced out

across the harbour to Brownsea Island and the Purbecks beyond, each one taking in the more cheerful sight than the bombed house they'd passed.

'Always such a lovely view,' said Peggy, noticing the strength of the tide as it pulled all the moored flying boats so they pointed the same direction. A small seaplane flew in and landed on the waters, heading towards the Royal Motor Yacht Club where the Royal Navy base was stationed.

'That reminds me,' said Rose with a jollier tone in her voice once more, 'did you hear about the Australians moving in at Hamworthy?'

'Australians? No, I hadn't heard. Why Hamworthy?' asked Peggy.

'They're a squadron of the Royal Australian Air Force, come to fly Short Sunderlands with the RAF and Royal Navy. They're taking over the base at HMS Turtle in Hamworthy, just by Lake Pier, as an RAF base. There've been trainloads of equipment coming in and the airmen are starting to arrive now too. We're sure to meet them before long. They're moving here from RAF Mountbatten in Plymouth, so I heard,' explained Rose.

'Well, that's all right with me,' Peggy said, 'a whole squadron of Australian airmen visiting town! That will make things interesting at the dance on Saturday night.'

The two girls laughed, and Peggy pulled into the driveway of the Harbour Heights Hotel.

'Shall I just go up the main driveway to the hotel front doors?' asked Peggy, wondering if there was a deliveries entry she should aim for instead.

'Yes, that'll do. Stop here and I'll nip inside to see where they want these crates.'

Peggy pulled on the handbrake and sat at the wheel, still enjoying being in control of the vehicle and more than a little pleased with how well she had handled her first driving job for BOAC. Within a few minutes, Rose returned and a man in cook's clothing came out from a side door to meet her, then they walked over to the truck and Peggy got out to help with the unloading.

'What will you be doing with these pineapples, do you think?' Peggy asked in wonder as the aroma of the tropical fruit hit her senses for the second time that day.

'Fruit salads, cocktails, and some fresh juices I imagine,' replied the cook as he heaved the last crate inside, then he winked and beckoned Peggy and Rose to the kitchen door with him. He looked around the kitchen furtively, then picked up a couple of oranges and handed them one each.

'Don't tell anyone, or you won't be seeing me here again, if you get my meaning,' he said quietly, then beamed and winked as he waved them goodbye and shut the door. Rose and Peggy quickly stashed the oranges into their coat pockets and once back inside the truck, they let their laughter rip.

'Fresh oranges! Who'd have thought we'd be so blessed today, hey?' asked Rose. 'My sister will love this. We'll share it after tea.'

Peggy agreed it would be too delicious to keep to herself and knew she'd be eating only a quarter of hers once she'd shared it with Mum, Dad, and Molly, but she was already enjoying the look of delight she anticipated she'd see on their faces.

'There have to be some bright spots in these dark days, and this is one of them, don't you think?' Peggy asked Rose, who agreed heartily.

As Peggy drove them back to Poole Quay, it was nearly four o'clock and the deep mid-winter dusk was settling in for a dark night ahead. They made it back before lights were necessary, which was just as well seeing as they were not allowed in the blackout. Peggy parked the car up outside the pottery, and Rose shook her hand as they parted.

'Consider yourself inducted as a driver for BOAC, Peggy Symonds. You're as fabulous behind the wheel of a car as you are at the helm of a boat,' said Rose with a bright smile. 'I'll let Mr Carter know – Major Carter, I should say – in the morning when I see him, and whenever you aren't needed on the launches, we will get in touch if we need a driver.'

* * *

By Saturday night, it was widely known that there were some very friendly Australians in town, and all the single girls – and a few of the not-so-single girls – were looking forward to the chance of a dance with their first ever Australian airman. But Peggy already had her dance partner fixed and, as she dressed, pulling on a precious pair of stockings and painting on her lipstick on Saturday night, she smiled and hummed to herself as she remembered meeting Flight Lieutenant Taylor earlier in the week.

After she'd heard about the arrival of the Australian squadron from Rose Stevens on Monday afternoon, she'd quickly put the thought aside as she had walked home in the cold and the dark, clutching the sunshine-infused orange in her pocket. She had found Molly in the kitchen helping her mother to prepare dinner, and her father was just coming in from the back garden having finished with his nets and jobs for the day.

'I've got a wonderful surprise for you all,' she said with glee and waited until all eyes were on her before she theatrically pulled the orange from her pocket and put it in the middle of the kitchen table, to the delighted sounds telling of her family's joy. They'd all wanted to know at once where she'd got it from and when they'd finished their meal, mother had carefully cut it into quarters so they could all enjoy the treat.

'Well, this is one bonus to you meeting flying boats that are coming in from the warmer climes, my love,' crooned her father as he licked the orange juice from his lips.

'Mmm, I can't remember when I last had an orange, Peg; it must be well over a year ago now. Certainly not since rationing began, that's for sure. I feel so much better tonight, after that dinner, and now this lovely fruit is just the icing on the cake,' said Molly.

'That will be good for you, Molly love – bound to help you feel a little better,' said Mother, clearly thinking of the vitamins she knew her expectant daughter needed.

'It's put me in a mood to celebrate,' said her father. 'How about we all go down to the Antelope for a quick pint, hey? A bit of stout would do our Molly good, and we could all do with a pick-me-up after last night.'

So far there had been no warning signs of another air raid, and the whole family – the whole nation – hoped for a peaceful night's sleep ahead. But the Symonds family readily agreed to an outing to celebrate the 'night of the orange', and wrapped themselves up in scarves, hats, gloves, and coats and headed off towards their favourite inn at the bottom end of the High Street. They had only intended to stay for one drink, but once they opened the doors and went inside, they discovered the bar was alive with a party atmosphere, and the uniforms were a mix of English Royal Navy and Royal Australian Air Force. The Australian airmen were being treated to their first Poole pint by some of the local Royal Navy boys.

'Let me give you a hand, Dad,' said Peggy. 'You'll never get to the bar in this crush.'

She found that heads turned and a path was made between the men when she waded through the crowd towards the bar, with her father following in her wake. Peggy ordered a half a pint of stout for her sister, a pint of best bitter for her dad and two glasses of port and lemonade for herself and her mother. Her father paid and turned back to the corner table with the beers in his hand, and just as Peggy was about to pick up the glasses for herself and her mother a manly hand reached out and collected them first. Indignant, Peggy looked up into the cheeriest face she'd ever seen on a man. He had a wavy, blonde fringe and tanned skin that spoke of summer in just the same way that the orange had done.

'Let me help you with these, can I? This mob will knock you and spill them in no time. You make a path and I'll follow behind,' the rather forthright Australian said.

Unable to think of any reason not to accept, and yet feeling a little put out that he'd taken charge so easily, Peggy did as he suggested. But she couldn't help noticing the looks of envy in the eyes of the other men in the bar between whom she made a path, and she held her head a little higher. When they reached the corner table where her family was sitting, all eyes were on the Australian. Mr Symonds put down the two beers and stood to greet him, shaking the man's hand and introducing his wife and daughters.

'Darrell Taylor's my name – Flight Lieutenant Darrell Taylor, of course, but Darrell will do just fine.' He beamed, and soon he was regaling them with tales of kangaroos in the streets, which delighted them, and of snakes in the roof, which horrified the women.

'Yeah, but it's a ripper place, though. And I've never in my life been so cold as I am here this winter. How do you all survive it year after year? And how long until summer starts?' he asked them, astounded to hear that it might not be what he would call properly warm until late May or June even.

'And what are your squadron doing here, Mr Taylor?' Peggy asked him politely.

'Darrell, love, just Darrell. We fly Short Sunderlands back at home, and we've been running them down at Plymouth – and they've moved us here. Getting a bit crowded in Plymouth it was, and you've got a real beaut big harbour here. Plenty of room for us to share it with the civilian flying boats, and lovely shallow water too, perfect for landings and take-off.'

'Our daughter here, Peggy, works with the flying boats, you know – the civilian ones that is. Tell 'im all about it, Peggy,' encouraged Mrs Symonds.

'We're a fishing family, so I know how to handle a boat, thanks to Dad, and I run one of the launches that take the passengers and crew in and out to the BOAC flying boats,' said Peggy, a little embarrassed about putting herself forwards.

'Well, I never – a working woman with a real skill. That's impressive, I'll say,' said Darrell, taking a big swill of the beer his mate had brought over to him, but he made a sour face as he swallowed.

'Can't say as I'll ever get used to this grog though,' he said, nodding towards his beer glass. 'This is not what we would call beer at home.'

'That's a good pint of proper bitter, that is,' said Mr Symonds proudly. 'It'll put hairs on your chest, son.' The women squealed with delight as Darrell made as if to peer into his uniform shirt to see if it was working yet, and by the end of the evening, the Symonds family had named Flight Lieutenant Darrell Taylor as a close family friend who was welcome at their table, any time.

They'd seen him a couple of nights later as well, and that's when Molly had told him about the dance on Saturday night.

'How many of you will be going along, do you think?' she asked him. 'I'll not be there, being a married woman and needing to put this baby to bed early,' she giggled, patting her now obvious baby bump. 'But Peggy will go, won't you Peg?' said Molly, giving her little sister a big nudge in the ribs.

'Will you, Peggy? Well, if you'll be there, I will be as well – provided we aren't called out on a run, that is. But I should be getting Saturday off, all being well,' Darrell said with a smile that was meant just for Peggy. And by the end of that night, it was fixed that she'd be dancing with him, at least the first three.

And now the night of the dance had come, and Peggy realised how much she was counting on Darrell being there. As she walked up the street, arm in arm with her friends whom she had gathered along the way, she checked herself, remembering that it was never a certainty that a serviceman had the power to be where he had said he hoped to be, but all the same, she was so looking forward to seeing that smiling face.

Peggy hadn't even reached the dance hall when she saw a half dozen or so of the RAAF men whose faces had become familiar through the week. They had been waiting at the doors to the dance hall and, as Peggy approached, Darrell stepped out of the crowd and came to take her arm.

'Miss Symonds, I believe you've promised to dance with me?' he teased her, and before she even stepped into the dance hall, Peggy was certain she could predict exactly how the next year of her life was about to develop. And nothing would have convinced her on this happy night of dancing and flirting to imagine anything like the strange reality that was about to unfold.

7

POOLE – FEBRUARY 1941

Charlie Edwards checked the clock at Waterloo Station and saw he had time for a bite of lunch before his train was due to leave. He stepped across the road from the train station and pushed open the door to the tea shop where delicious aromas hit his senses like a melody from the past – a past filled with warmth, and home-cooked meals.

'What can I get you, love?' asked the waitress, with a tenderness in her voice that he'd not heard in so long now that it prickled the back of his throat. He wasn't from these parts, and had never been accepted as a local, yet now, just as he was giving up and leaving, this woman reached out to him with the kindness of family. Even though half of London was missing some or all of their family after the Blitz, he sensed there was a stigma to being the only one left. For months now, he'd had nothing but hard stares and cold shoulders. So, he had decided to move on, and reinvent himself as someone who might fit in better where he was going next.

His practised accent now was southern, but not quite London. West Country, but not deep Somerset. Local, but not too local to anywhere in particular. He could have come from Oxford, or Basingstoke. Reading or Andover. Rochester or Hastings. Bath or Bournemouth. He'd already decided the answer to the question about where he was from: 'All over, really – you name it, I've lived there.'

'I'll have a nice cup of tea and your soup and toast, please, love.' He smiled, winningly.

'The soup is leek and potato, today. Is that all right for you?'

'Sounds just the job to warm me up,' he said, rubbing his hands together with glee, much more thrilled that she'd not even flinched at his accent than he was about the bland-sounding soup.

'Right away then, sir – I'll bring it back in just a moment.'

Charlie enjoyed the soup surprisingly more than he had expected to. A meal without meat or cheese or fish didn't sound like a meal at all, but the texture was thick and soothing on his tongue, and the hot toast was dripping with margarine and was delicious dipped into the soup bowl. The meal warmed him and filled his belly. He made his way to the counter to pay his bill, handling the coins in his pocket carefully, picking out the pennies from the shillings between his fingers to help him speed up the process once he pulled them out into his palm.

'That'll be threepence please, sir.' She beamed, and he handed over the three big, round, bronze coins.

'How do you manage to charge so little? You can't get a meal like that for less than a shilling anywhere else,' he answered as she rang up the till.

'We're subsidised now, as a part of the Ministry of Food scheme. Simple meals like the soup are only tuppence, so as everyone can afford a feed. A nasty German did that to you, did he?' she asked, nodding in the direction of his leg. She'd noticed the limp he tried to hide. The sudden change of subject took him back to the battleground and made him flinch, and he saw by her response that she knew she'd troubled him by bringing up thoughts of war.

'No, I've had this since I was a kid,' he replied, more curtly than he had meant to.

'Sorry, I didn't mean to upset you. Glad you're home safe now though,' she said. 'My John is in the navy, you know. He's out there doing his bit to protect our merchant ships so we've a hope of getting some more food in.'

'He's a good man, then,' said Charlie. 'And you make a lovely soup, too, miss.'

'We're all doing our bit. My grandad grew the veg himself, you know,' she added with pride.

Charlie nodded his thanks, then left the tea shop, closing the door carefully behind him and bracing himself against the sharp winter winds that howled down the street. He slung his bag over his shoulder, pulled his coat collar up and gripped it with one hand, then headed back into the train station. Once on the platform again, he found a quiet corner and settled in to await his southbound train.

When the whistle blew to sound that the train was ready to board, he made his way towards the central carriage. He wanted to be not the first, not the last, just one of the crowd going about his business in a way that nobody would notice. A fresh start in a new town meant blending in as soon as he could. He shut the door behind him and walked down the carriage looking for just the right spot. He was relieved to see there were some passengers, but not too many. Plenty of people to get lost amongst, but not so many that the crowd would be pushing up close to him.

Women seemed the safest bet. So far, he'd had the most generous treatment from ladies. He chose a compartment with a mother and her two little children and another lone man in uniform. Charlie sat beside the window so he could watch the scene go by, field by field, town by town, until the fields became more than the towns and he could almost smell the sea air of the south.

When the journey was over and the train pulled into Poole, Charlie was pleased to see almost all the passengers spill out onto the platform – a perfect crowd to get lost amongst. He picked up his bag, put his head down, and went with the flow of the crowd out from the station and into the High Street.

He knew that anyone who had a spare room would have a little notice in their front window. All he needed was to find the best spot. He walked down the High Street towards the quay, as far as Castle Street, and turned in to the left. Here were the lanes and alleys that ran back and forth behind the quay, and here would be the ideal place to settle – close to the water and the action of work that went on there.

The houses were all terraced together with doors that opened directly onto the pavement at the front. Each one had a small, bricked courtyard at the back. Every few houses, the terrace was broken by a ground-level alley that ran through to the lane at the back. These lanes separated the back courtyards and each had a wooden gate in the high brick wall, giving access into the courtyard. He could see that, in this part of the town, there was only one shared toilet between four houses, and through a gate that was left hanging open, he saw a communal water pump. The many chimneys atop each house all piped thick smoke into the air from the fireplaces and wood-fired kitchen ranges inside.

The dank air smelled faintly of fish and smoke, and of the coming winter night. It was only three in the afternoon, but dusk was hanging around the chimney tops, ready to settle the town under its dark blanket for night-time. Charlie wondered if he'd find a place to stay today, or if he'd be better off paying for a room in a pub for the night.

As he turned a corner, he came across a pair of young boys, playing with marbles and sticks on the edge of an alleyway. They looked up to him, then gave him a second look, obviously realising he wasn't someone they knew.

'Evening, lads,' Charlie started. 'Know of any rooms to let around here? I'm looking for lodgings.'

'My mum's got no rooms, what wiv me and me brothers and the *vacees*. But Mother Rogers has got a notice up in her window.' He pointed to the end of the lane. 'Down Strand Street, then down Blue Boar Lane. Just a few places back in from the quay,' he added.

'Sounds perfect to me.' Charlie smiled and fished a farthing out of his pocket, flipping it up in the air for the lad to catch.

'Cor, thanks! C'mon, Frank, let's get some sweets at Setch-fields,' he cried as they ran off towards the High Street. Charlie smiled as he watched them run, remembering the rows of glass jars full of all kinds of different-coloured sweets that he'd seen that the little shop sold as he'd passed.

The boy's directions were good, and he easily found Mrs Rogers' home in Blue Boar Lane. He could hear the industry of the quayside going on at the far end of the narrow, dark lane and he followed the sound. At the end of the lane, where it opened onto the quay that he recognised, he saw that on one side was the Lord Nelson, and on the other the Jolly Sailor. Across the water, between the quays, a ship was being unloaded of its cargo and he could hear the noise of the gasworks coming up from the east. There was plenty of work here, and Blue Boar Lane would be a very handy spot to base himself.

Just as he turned to go back into the lane, he heard the hubbub from inside the Jolly Sailor as someone opened the door.

Perhaps there was time for a quick half pint before knocking on Mrs Rogers' door.

The pub was warm and welcoming, and he found himself in easy conversation with the barman while he drank his beer, and might have been tempted to stay for longer. But it would never do to have too much beer inside him as he met a new landlady. He said a cheery farewell to the men at the bar, and stepped back outside. The night was dark now.

Turning back into the lane, the reek of old fish and the filthy state of the drains hit his senses. Overhead hung a line of laundry, strung across from one side of the lane to the other. These must be the poorest of the poor, he thought, looking at the tiny houses in the dank, darkening light, though he had seen there were alms houses just a stone's throw away too. At least this woman could afford her own home. There was the notice in the window, as promised:

Room to let: 8s per week
Full board (coupons required)
1s extra for weekly laundry

That she was charging less than she could get for an evacuee spoke volumes to Charlie. This woman's home must not be considered suitable for the children sent down from London, and she must have found it difficult to get boarders. He was pleased to solve one of her financial worries today, and smiled as he knocked on the door and readied himself to impress Mrs Rogers with his best manners.

8

Rebekah lay in bed with the curtains wide open, watching the steady progress of small puffs of dark clouds as they sailed across the moon. The sounds of the sleeping island soothed her through the open window and she smiled to hear the occasional pipping of the little pipistrelle bats as they flew between the trees. The sound always reminded her of a little clay bird whistle she'd been given as a child, which she would fill with water and then blow into the pipe, making a tiny, warbling sound just like the call of the bats she now knew so well.

An owl called softly in the distance and Rebekah drifted to sleep, nestled luxuriously in the softness of her down pillows and quilt, overcome by tiredness as only can be felt after a day spent walking and working in the fresh pine-scented woodlands of her island.

The knock, when it first sounded, went unheard, as if it was simply the breeze getting up a little and rapping a branch against a window on the other side of the cottage. But with its second report, it became strong enough to rouse her and she lifted her eyelids a touch. The third knock created the moment of her waking fully. She thought through the possibilities as she slipped her feet from under the soft covers and pulled on her robe. There were only the staff of John Lewis who were staying as guests within the castle walls overnight, or else the campers on the island with her tonight. One of the former could have wandered off for a midnight walk and lost their way back to the castle. The latter could be more worrying – there was nothing any of the campers could need from her unless there was a real problem; perhaps a child had gone missing, or a camp fire was out of control?

She turned the landing light on as she passed the top of the stairs, not that she needed to see where she was going, but rather to let the knocker know she was on her way.

Rebekah unlatched the door, flicking on the porch light to better see who was responsible for disturbing her sleep. She put in a substantial effort to change her facial expression from a somewhat grumpy *you woke me up* into the perfectly composed customer service provider's *how may I help you?* But as the light shone onto the warm and lovely face that greeted her when she opened the door, Rebekah knew that she gaped with a look that read quite obviously: *I wasn't expecting anyone like you.*

He stood taller than Rebekah so that even though he was beneath her on the step of the porch, his eyes looked down a little into hers. He was large without being bulky, and probably muscly beneath his waxed raincoat. He had an aura of strength mingled with gentleness, a face that exuded meekness. In the dusky gloom of the yellow porch light, the shadow of dark, bristly stubble lengthened, making him look more haggard than he probably was. There were delicate laughter lines around his eyes but deep creases in his forehead that reminded her to breathe and ask him what was wrong.

'Firstly, I am so very sorry to wake you at this awfully late hour,' he said, glancing at his watch and covering his face with one hand. 'But I saw the cottage and at first thought I might just sleep here until I realised someone probably lived here, and after I'd opened the gate – which has such a loud squeak to its hinges, don't you think? – then I was worried that you – or whoever lived here – might hear me and be worried about intruders, so I decided to go ahead and knock. I'm so sorry. I'm rambling. Actually, that's probably where I should have started,' he said and seemed about to continue but Rebekah took this opportunity of a minor break in the flow of his very long account to interrupt him.

'Is anyone in danger?' she asked, pointing down towards the campsite.

'No, no, not at all. Sorry. It's just me – and I'm fine, but—'

'Then why don't you come inside. We'll have a cup of tea, and I can see how I can help you,' Rebekah offered. Tea. She'd been awake now for several minutes and if she was expected to stay awake any longer, she was going to need a cup of tea. Strangely, it wasn't until later that it had even occurred to her that this might have been dangerous – the business of welcoming a completely strange man into the cottage at night, while she was half undressed and all alone. But something about his meekness had spoken safety to her, even in those first few seconds of meeting him.

He followed her inside, pattering out apologies and politely taking his boots off at the door before slipping off his wax raincoat (quite unnecessary on this balmy summer night, Rebekah thought) and hanging it over the back of a kitchen chair.

'How do you like it?' she asked him over her shoulder and saw in his face something of a frightened rabbit. 'Tea,' she explained. 'How do you like your tea?'

'Oh, right. White and no sugar, thanks. This is so good of you. I'm Paul, by the way.'

'Paul.' She nodded. 'Nice to meet you. I'm Rebekah Martin – the ranger in residence – but I imagine you knew that?' she said as she filled the kettle and set teabags into two matching mugs. She turned and leant against the kitchen sink, waiting for the kettle to boil, and watched him as he seemed to notice for the first time that she was wearing a light silk robe with barely anything underneath it. Colour blushed his already tanned face and she felt his anguish and so, as he was about to open his mouth to apologise again, she stopped him.

'Take a seat, Paul. Would you be more comfortable here at the table or on the settee?'

'Here's fine, thanks,' he said, pulling the heavy wooden chair back and scraping it on the slate tile floor. The kettle boiled and Rebekah poured the water over the teabags, gave them a squish with a spoon after letting them steep, and fetched the milk from the fridge. She carried the two mugs over to the table, sat down opposite Paul and watched him cup his hands around the mug. He'd been wearing just a T-shirt and shorts underneath the raincoat and now she saw why he'd put it on. He had the tell-tale red marks of many mosquito bites on his arms and legs.

'So, what's up then, Paul? How come you're wandering about the island at this time of the night, getting eaten alive by our vicious wildlife?' she said with a cheeky smile and a nod to the bites.

He snorted in response, nearly choking on his tea.

'It's a short and incredibly stupid story, I'm afraid. I'm embarrassed to tell you, really, and feel so awful for waking you now – but once the mozzies started having a real go at me, I didn't think I could cope with another six hours of this torture.'

'So, where are you supposed to be right now? At the castle?' asked Rebekah, blowing on her tea and taking a delicious sip of her favourite drink of all.

'No, I'm supposed to be in a comfortable king-sized bed at the Harbour Heights Hotel.'

'And yet, you chose to walk around Brownsea Island at midnight and become mozzie fodder?' she asked with one eyebrow cocked higher than the other.

And then he laughed. Perhaps it was the tea warming him, or maybe he was just relieved to be indoors, or possibly her dry sense of humour really tickled him, but his laugh was a deep chuckle that shook his broad shoulders and lit up his eyes.

'Naturally, yes,' he said, flashing a wide smile. 'Why sleep in a bed when there's heather to lie on? I blame it all on Enid Blyton, myself,' he added. 'No, that's not fair. It's not her fault at all. She only tempted me here. I was the fool who succumbed to the heather.'

'So, you have actually lain down on a bed of heather tonight then?' asked Rebekah.

'Not tonight, as such, no. That happened around five o'clock. I came over on the ferry this morning, and I had a wonderful time looking all over the island. I spent quite a while at the lagoon, trying out all the hides. I'm not much of a bird spotter usually, but it was addictive once I learnt to sit there in silence and just watch – like viewing a nature documentary. I could almost hear David Attenborough's voice telling me all the bird names and describing what they were up to. Then I went up to the daffodil fields to eat my lunch and watch the peacocks and went on down to the ruins of the village at Maryland and Pottery Pier – fascinating, isn't it?'

Rebekah nodded enthusiastically and went to get out a few biscuits and boil the kettle again for another cup, as Paul carried on.

'Then I did a tour of the other side of the island, the scout camp site, and all the views of the Purbeck hills from up there. I just wandered until I found some heather and the kid in me wondered if all the *Famous Five* stories could really be believed. Was the heather such a wonderfully soft bed to sleep on? Turns out, when the prickles are kept off your skin by a good, strong, wax jacket with a padded lining, it's a perfect mattress. So perfect, in fact, that I didn't wake up until hours later when the sun was beginning to set and the mozzies came out. I raced down to the jetty but I knew I'd missed the last ferry. I did think about going to the castle but the signs were pretty clear about it being private property, and entry being only for staff and their pre-booked guests. So, I realised I was a bit stuck.'

'I'm sure if you'd gone to the kitchen door at the castle and explained your situation, they'd never have turned you away, but you're right. They are pretty fierce about their private castle,' groaned Rebekah. 'Still, I mustn't grumble. The private lease of the castle is a huge bonus to the National Trust work here, as they pay so much for the privilege. So how did you end up here at Rose Cottage?'

'My next thought was to head to the campsite to see if some kind campers might have a spot in a tent for me. But when I drew near, it was all in silence and total darkness by then – being nearly midnight by this time – and I realised I'd be a terrifying prospect to them all, if I woke them from their sleeping bags. And then I remembered seeing this cottage and wondered if it might be empty, and unlocked even. I saw the curtains in the window, and wellington boots outside the front door and realised my mistake. But by then I was worried about being caught tres-passing and thought it best to just come right up and knock. And wake you up. I'm so sorry for that, Rebekah,' he said as he sighed and reached a hand across the table as a gesture of repentance.

She studied his face again and saw the warmth and honesty in his eyes. Rebekah had read of enough Troys, d'Urbervilles, Willoughbys and Wickhams to be sure of her own judgement.

This one was a Jude, a Gabriel Oak, a Colonel Brandon – it wasn't his fault that everything had been against him, and she knew he would never harm her.

'Are you hungry, Paul? It sounds as though you didn't get any dinner?' she asked.

'I've been trying not to think about it, but yes, I'm famished.' He laughed again.

'Do you like seafood? Mussels? I've some tasty leftovers in the fridge if you'd like some.'

He groaned with delightful expectation. 'That sounds amazing, if you're sure I'm not too much of a bother? I feel so bad...'

She shushed him and went to warm the pasta bowl in the microwave, momentarily sparing a thought for poor Ben who had meant the mussels as a gift entirely for her pleasure. Then she fetched a spare blanket and pillow from the cupboard under the stairs.

'I'm sorry, there's no spare bed here – only mine – but you're welcome to kip on the settee for the rest of the night. I'll even give you breakfast if you make me a cup of tea in the morning,' she joked.

'You're an angel, Rebekah. An absolute angel, and this,' he said with a mouthful of mussel and tomato pasta, 'is the food of the gods. Did you cook this?'

'I did. The mussels were brought over from Poole this morning. Good, isn't it?'

'Good? It's heavenly. Oh, sorry, I'm being so selfish – here, share it with me,' he said, pushing the bowl into the middle of the table and handing her the unused spoon, while he held the fork. She paused for a moment before realising that sharing a bowl of pasta with Paul, this man she'd never known before she'd gone to sleep just a few hours ago, seemed the most natural thing in the world.

9

POOLE – FEBRUARY 1941

Peggy, Nora and Eileen worked together like a well-oiled machine to get the launch ready for their first trip of the day. The morning was bright and the sky blue, but the choppy water of the harbour showed the reason for the bite in the air. They'd be fighting a cold wind today. Peggy became aware of steps drawing closer and looked up to the quay to see a young man had arrived and was watching them work. He wore the uniform of the Home Guard, which was unusual in one so young, Peggy thought.

'Good morning,' Peggy called, cheerily.

'Good morning, ladies,' the man offered, tipping his cap. 'Can I help you with your line?' he asked, laying his hand on the large cleat on the quayside as Peggy made a move towards the steps to cast them off.

'The girls and I can manage quite well, but if you'd like to help, you're welcome,' she said. 'Do you know your way around a mooring cleat, then?' she asked with a hint of tease in her glance towards him.

'I most certainly do. I'm a dockworker and I've been running a launch like this on the Thames. Just moved to Poole to find lodgings. So many places getting bombed out in London, a room is hard to find now,' he offered.

The captain of the launch cocked her head and looked him over appraisingly, in a way she would never have done for fear of causing offence to a man before the war. Before everything had changed.

'I've seen you making your way up and down the quay. That limp doesn't hold you up much, does it?' she asked him, and he stood more upright, as if aware that he might be seriously considered for work here.

'No, it doesn't hold me up at all. I've had it all my life, and I can do most things, except run, of course. But they didn't want me in the army with it, so I'm Home Guard. I'm working as a dockhand over on the other quayside,' he said pointing to the Hamworthy side. 'But I'm really looking for work on a boat if I can get it.'

'What's your name? I'll put a word in for you with the boss. Goodness knows we are short-handed, and there's more work all the time. I've just started doing some driving as well as running the launch so we could use a spare pair of hands, I'm sure.'

'My name's Charlie. Charlie Edwards.'

'Pleased to meet you, Charlie. I'm Peggy Symonds. Where can I reach you?'

He gave Peggy the address of his boarding house with Mrs Rogers, then bid them farewell as he threw down the neatly coiled dock line into the front of the launch and Peggy got set to race off out to the middle of the harbour with her two crewmates.

* * *

'He's nice, Peggy,' cooed Nora with a wink and nudge to Eileen as they pulled away from the quay and out of earshot from the handsome young man Peggy had struck up a conversation with. 'You've already got Australian Darrell at the dance hall as your man, and now you'll have chirpy Charlie, too.' She giggled, and all three girls laughed.

'Darrell is not *my man*, and Charlie is simply a willing pair of hands who seems to know his way around a boat. Settle down, ladies, I'm thinking of the business here,' she said with a mock-stern tone, though Peggy did really want to discourage their ideas that she was becoming something of a flirt. She changed the subject as quickly as she could.

'You seemed to be getting pretty pally with our Samuel in the pub last night, anyway, Nora. I'll have you know we have very high standards for our little brother.' She laughed, poking Nora in the ribs.

Samuel had come home on leave as promised, and though it had only been for the standard seventy-two hours, he had made the most of it, and thrilled his family with his happy smile and light-hearted disposition. He'd made a fuss of his mum's wonderful cooking, enjoying a Sunday roast with the family – though it was mostly vegetables from the garden and only a little bit of chicken – and he had been out for a couple of nights on the quay, where he'd taken notice of Nora for the first time.

'He's grown ever so much more handsome since he started wearing that sailor's uniform, Peggy,' Nora replied. 'Perhaps you and me, with Darrell and Samuel, will be making up a foursome sometime, hey? But what about Charlie?' pushed Nora again, annoying Peggy.

'No, seriously, I'll simply let Pat know when we get back in later, and she can get in touch with him if she would like to talk to him about some work. That's all,' she said with a shrug of her shoulder, then turned back towards the C-class they were headed for that had just come in to land.

Peggy was keen to keep the girls quiet on the subject, but she did secretly like the sound of the way they called Darrell 'her man', and she tried to hide a tiny smile as she thought of him now. He was lovely to look at, and gentlemanly in the way he treated her, and yet also relaxed and laid-back in a way she'd never known any English young man to be. He was confident without being cocky: sure of himself without being in any way stuck-up or proud. Darrell had told her as much as he was allowed to about the life of a pilot in the RAAF and the different types of missions he flew on from the RAF base in Poole Harbour.

Mostly they went on reconnaissance trips across the channel, out into the Atlantic and down into the Bay of Biscay, looking for enemy ships and submarines so they could report their positions back to the British control. But, from time to time, they were caught up in real action and though a Short Sunderland was not built as a fighter, it had guns installed and would shoot an enemy ship or plane if necessary. Once, he had told her, they had come across a merchant navy ship that had been hit by a torpedo. They had flown down to sink the submarine that had issued its deadly weapon, and then circled back and landed near the flailing British ship, taking on board the sailors who had bailed out and would have been lost on the edge of the Atlantic Ocean had Darrell and his crew not been there.

The idea that Darrell's role was to protect England's ships and shores, and even to rescue the English sailors, filled Peggy's heart with warmth and soothed her soul like a balm of honey. Her brother, Samuel, seemed safer than he had done before, now she knew there were airmen like Darrell looking out for him. And so, without even really trying, Darrell had become a source of strength and hope for her.

And the way he made her laugh was like a bright shaft of sunlight on a dim and gloomy day. He didn't even have to be trying to tell a joke, but there was something in the positive way he saw the funny side in the silliest of situations that made Peggy laugh, filling her soul with food like sweetmeats from heaven, in these dry and restricted times of rationing. He had spent a few evenings with her at the Antelope and had danced most of the night last Saturday with her, and then walked her home. But this week, he must have been out on a series of missions as she hadn't seen him for days. There hadn't been as many of the Australian airmen around town, generally. Still, today was Friday, and she hoped she might see him again tonight. There were a few questions about his home and his future that she'd begun to wonder about.

Later that morning, when she had delivered her passengers to Salterns Marina and put the launch away, she nipped in to see Pat about Charlie.

'He seems genuine enough, Pat, and it would be good to have a strong man around for some of the heavier lifting jobs,' Peggy said, as she put the launch key back on its hook and warmed her hands by the little coal fire.

'But what about that limp of his, Peggy? Surely he isn't that able-bodied, else they'd have him in the army,' asked Pat with concern.

'He says he's had it since he was a kid, and it doesn't bother him at all. Polio, I suppose. But the recruiting officers thought it would slow him down, so he's on Home Guard. It really is only a slight limp and doesn't seem to cause him pain. He doesn't have any trouble at all walking, or with balance, and his upper body looks strong enough to me,' Peggy said thoughtfully.

'Had a good look at his muscles, did you?' teased Pat.

'Not you as well, Pat. I've already had this from Eileen and Nora.' She laughed. 'No, honestly, I just think he'd be a great worker. He must be – hauling sacks and crates in and out of ships' holds on the main dock over there.'

'You're right, Peggy, I'm only teasing you. I think he'll be a great help. I'll send a note to ask him to come in for a proper chat. What's up for you next?'

'Just popping in to see Rose Stevens at the pottery, to get the run-down on some driving jobs, then I'll be back in after lunch to go and meet the *Clyde* when she flies in. See you later,' Peggy called cheerily as she shut the door behind her.

As Peggy made the short walk from the harbour master's office to Poole Pottery where Rose Stevens and Major Carter were based, she heard the familiar sound of a Sunderland taking off and looked over to see the plane decked out in its red, white, and blue roundels, rising from the Hamworthy RAF runway. She stopped to raise a hand to her eyes and peer up at the cockpit, wondering if Darrell was flying this one. She smiled to herself and she remembered the way he had tenderly held her arm as if to protect her on their walk home from the dance last Saturday night. She wondered if he might be there again tomorrow.

'Thanks for popping in, Peggy. There's lots going on at the moment so let's have a cup of tea and a sit-down so I can run through it all,' said Rose as she greeted Peggy and led her through to the passengers' tea lounge. Rose took out her dark-red, leather-bound ledger in which she recorded all the flights and the passenger lists, as well as the names of the seawomen who ran the launch to and from each flying boat and the crews that flew them in and out of Poole Harbour. She made a pot of tea and set it on a tray with two cups and saucers and a plate of biscuits, then carried the tray to Peggy, who was more than a little bit surprised – and delighted – to be given such special treatment.

'You'll be driving some passengers from the train station up to the Harbour Heights Hotel early this evening, and then in the morning, they fly out on their way to Sydney, so you'll pick them up in the launch from Salterns Marina after they've had their breakfast at the hotel and someone from there has dropped them down to the marina for you,' Rose said as she put her cup back in the saucer and ran her finger down the ledger, looking at the plans for Friday.

'And tomorrow afternoon, there will be a large delivery of cargo coming in, some for the hotel and some supplies going to RAF Sandbanks and RAF Hamworthy. So I've been sent some paperwork from London that I need to give you so they can grant you a special pass for access. The RAF business is quite separate from us here at BOAC of course, but it seems more and more that we are to be involved in the RAF's war effort here in Poole. I hear you might be on your way to getting your own special access to some parts of the RAAF though, Peggy,' teased Rose.

'Not you as well, Rose.' Peggy giggled. 'We've only had a dance and a few evenings together in the pub.'

'But he does seem like a very lovely young man, don't you think?' asked Rose with a more motherly tone than before. 'In times like these, I'd advise you to grab at any opportunity for happiness, Peggy. We don't know what tomorrow will bring.'

Both women sipped their tea silently for a few moments, remembering all those friends of theirs who had already lost husbands, brothers, and lovers. Peggy knew that Rose's own husband and brother-in-law were away in the war and the twin sisters lived together waiting for news of their safety, while Rose's twin Daisy was growing a baby at about the same rate as Peggy's sister Molly.

'You're right, Rose. Today really might be all we have. And I agree, he does seem lovely. He's fun and caring. And solid – dependable too,' she mused.

'And strong, I should think – looks like he'd be a great help around here with those muscles of his.' Rose laughed.

'Actually, that reminds me. There's a man working on the docks – Charlie Edwards – arrived fairly recently in Poole from London, and he's got experience with boats. He's in the Home Guard – has a limp, which I think must be from polio from what he's said, and so he can't serve, which is good for us. We can train him up and know he would have a chance of staying, unlike all the other fellows around here. Patricia is going to see if she can get him some work on the launches and I wonder if he could help with the driving, or at least with the loading and unloading for us,' offered Peggy.

'Which leg is it that has the limp? He would need a strong left leg to handle the clutch so that might stop him from driving. But extra muscles with those crates would be an enormous help,' said Rose. 'I'll ask Pat to send him up to me if she takes him on, then I can check him out and give him a pass for the RAF bases too. You might have some company on the run tomorrow.'

Rose turned over the page in her book and tapped it with her pen.

'Now, I'm not certain who they are, because I've not been given any names, but next week, there's a VIP coming in to the hotel, spending a day visiting places I've not been told the where-abouts of, and then flying off somewhere as yet to be discovered,' said Rose with an arch brow, which told Peggy this was the way of things these days. Major Carter, with his history of serving in the Great War, might be in charge of field security in the harbour now, but Rose was just his secretary at the pottery, not military personnel, and so was never privy to the details. So much was on a need-to-know basis, and apparently, neither Rose nor Peggy needed to know these details.

'But Major Carter has asked for you, personally, to be the taxi driver and the launch pilot – on the day that I cannot yet name. I just wanted you to be aware that when you hear from Pat that you've been called for, you're not to swap your shift with any of the other girls,' said Rose.

'Fair enough. Intriguing, but I shall not ask or probe. Loose lips and all that,' said Peggy, tapping a two-fingered salute to her temple as Rose shut the ledger with a thwump and stood to show Peggy out.

'Absolutely. Both Major Carter and I know we can trust you on this. England is counting on us all to do our part.'

10

BROWNSEA ISLAND, POOLE – JULY 1998

Rebekah began to stir, and in the space between sleep and waking, she heard the sounds of gentle summer rain splashing on the roof and gurgling from the gutter down the drainpipes. The rain brought the scent of the woodlands into her bedroom and for a few moments, she enjoyed the luxury of having woken naturally before her alarm, knowing it was Saturday morning, so she relaxed and enjoyed the softness of her pillow a while longer.

The tap on her door was brief and hesitant, and barely loud enough to wake her from the doze she had fallen into. The second knock was a little more insistent but accompanied by a shy cough, which brought back all her memories of Paul from the night before. When she came to her senses and realised it was Paul knocking, she jumped up and opened the door. But he wasn't there. She looked around and found a cup of tea waiting for her on the landing table.

Perhaps it would be a bit too much to greet him this early in the morning, and at her bedroom door. She took the cup of tea back to bed and sat up, nestled amongst her pillows, to enjoy it. For the first time now, she wondered at the wisdom of letting him into her home last night, this man about whom she'd known nothing. She had known Andy for over a year before they had meandered from friendship into a relationship, and she thought she knew him completely until his controlling side had come out. What if Paul was someone with a dark and crazy side too? Strange how she felt she could trust him, despite what her head told her now. And he'd made her a perfect cup of tea. He'd certainly had chance to learn how she liked her tea after they'd had three cups together last night, in the end. It had been after two in the morning before she had finally said goodnight and climbed the stairs to bed while Paul settled down on the settee.

And when, as they had said goodnight, he had leant in to kiss her warmly on the cheek, and touched his hand to her shoulder as he did so, there'd been nothing even strange about it. They seemed to know each other so well by then. Nothing strange at all, except the way her cheek and shoulder had tingled all the way up the stairs, and she had lain awake in bed with her hand to her cheek, while she pictured him downstairs, slipping off his T-shirt and lying down, bare-chested, on her settee for the night.

The idea of Paul now filled her with warmth and an excitement that she couldn't explain, so when she heard the front door open and click shut again shortly afterwards, the sense of panic that he might be leaving without saying goodbye, and that she might never see him again, filled her with an unexpected rush of dread that frightened her. Why should she even care whether he was here or not? Rebekah knew that she had never needed a man in her life, just like her strong mother and Aunty Peggy had been perfectly happy alone. A woman should be strong enough to cope on her own and not need the fluff of romance in her life to make her happy – especially when a man could bring the kind of horror that Andy had, and that she remembered her mum had suffered at the hands of her father. But what if, even though she knew she didn't need to know Paul, she wanted to anyway?

She leapt out of bed and ran down the stairs two at a time, pulling on her robe as she went, and reached the front door in a matter of seconds, flinging it open and rushing out into the light rain, down the cottage garden path. He was nowhere to be seen and she could see a good hundred metres in every direction. How could he have gone so far, so fast? Had he run? Had he developed an urge to get as far away from her as possible?

'Are you okay, Rebekah?' asked the voice that had become so familiar to her in the middle of the night. She spun around and there in her open doorway stood Paul, a look of deep concern on his face. 'What's wrong?'

'Oh, Paul, you're still here! I...' she began, then ran her hands through her hair and tied her silky bathrobe around the middle, catching her breath and taking the moment to calm her thoughts. 'I thought I heard you leaving. I heard the door,' she added, waving vaguely in Paul's direction.

'Oh, sorry. I opened it to have a look outside and see what the weather was doing. Quite a heavy rain shower – and I'm so glad I didn't wake up drenched on that heather this morning.' He grinned, looking to the rumpled blanket on the sofa where he'd slept. 'I've been waiting for you to wake up.' He smiled, his eyes crinkling at the corners. 'Did you find your tea?' He held the door open for her as she slowly walked back inside.

'Yes, thank you, I did. And I believe I promised you breakfast in return,' Rebekah said, going to the kitchen and taking out eggs and a pan, and trying to look a little less ruffled. 'Would you like an omelette?' she asked.

'That sounds perfect, but I don't want to keep you. It's already eight o'clock. When do you have to start work?' he asked with concern.

'It's Saturday. I don't have to start at all. There are staff to run the island reception, and plenty of volunteers to help, and a weekend ranger will arrive on the first ferry this morning,' she explained.

'Where does she stay?' asked Paul, looking up the stairs with a frown to where Rebekah had told him there was only one bedroom.

'*He* – his name is Michael – chooses to camp out instead of enjoying the luxury of my humble abode. It's only one night, and he brings everything he needs in a pack on his back. His choice, of course – I should really vacate the cottage for him at the weekends, but as I don't have another base in Poole and he would rather camp anyway, it works perfectly for both of us,' she said as she cracked eggs and beat them into a basin. 'I like coffee with my breakfast. Can I interest you in one or are you strictly a tea man?' she asked as she put a filter paper into her coffee machine.

'I'd love a coffee, thank you. This really is first-class accommodation, Rebekah. You're something of a threat to the hotel, you know,' he said with a wink.

'Talking of the mainland,' she said, grating cheese into the eggs as they bubbled in the pan, 'what do you do when you aren't spending unexpected nights on islands in the middle of Poole Harbour?' she asked, surprised to realise she hadn't asked him that last night. They'd talked about Brownsea, and Poole, and the ferries, and her job as ranger, and where they'd both been born, and how much he'd always wanted to visit Australia, but somehow, they'd not gone into the details of his life or his job.

'I'm a professional historian,' he said, taking a big breath, and Rebekah realised her face must be telling him she needed much more information than that. 'I work freelance, sometimes for museums or government agencies on particular projects as they come up, but often in the corporate world. I'm in Poole to work on some artefacts at Poole Pottery. It's moving away from its original site on the quay, and I'm working through the archives. The ultimate aim is to create a written history of the pottery, but for now, I'm employed to ensure we save everything with important information that might be helpful in future.'

'You know, I don't think I had any idea what kind of job you might have, but if I'd had a million guesses, I bet I would never have come up with that,' she said as she poured them both coffee and went back to the stove to finish the omelettes.

'Well, I did have a bit of an advantage on you – finding you here doing your job as I did. If you'd first met me while I was doing mine, you would have had a much better chance of success. If, for example, I'd met you while you were looking around the showrooms at Poole Pottery, what chance would I have had of guessing you were an Australian trained conservationist working as a ranger for the National Trust on Brownsea Island?' he asked with a chuckle, and she laughed.

'I think I would have guessed you were an accountant. Or a banker,' she said, thoughtfully.

'And what is it about me that says I would be remotely interested in adding up profit and loss sheets?' He laughed, and she joined in.

'I can't say. I suppose you just seem very professional, and that's what came to mind.'

'I am – I hope – very professional. But as a historian, I'm much more interested in people than facts and figures, though of course there are plenty of those to account for as well.'

'And I'm sure there are plenty of interesting characters buried in the history of Poole Pottery,' said Rebekah as she plated up their omelettes and carried them over to the kitchen table. Paul poured the coffee and sat down opposite her.

'There are some incredibly interesting characters. Did you

know that the pottery more or less closed down during the war and became the security and customs offices for the flying boat port here in Poole?' he asked as he took a forkful of fluffy omelette and made appreciative sounds.

'I did not know that – but I'm not exactly a Poole local so there are all kinds of details that others would probably know.'

'The owner of the pottery, a Mr Carter, was given a military position and became Major Carter – head of Field Security in the harbour, possibly owing to his previous army service during World War One. But still, that was probably quite a shift from managing staff and clay purchases, don't you think?' asked Paul.

'I'm sure it was. Did you know about the old pottery here on the island? The whole beach down there at the western end is still littered with bits of clay pots and pipes, and some ruins of the pottery building are still there if you look for them, though much of it was destroyed in the war apparently.'

'Yes, that's one of the reasons I came over here actually: to have a good look at the pottery. But I've read that there was no connection at all.'

'That's right. One of the owners of the island found that there was clay here and set up the pottery intending to make a real go of the business. They invested everything they had, and employed dozens of people, but it turned out the clay wasn't good enough quality for fine china. In the end, the business failed but there was such a thriving community on the island that farming took over – and daffodils became the centre of business for a while,' said Rebekah, watching Paul clear his plate and dab his mouth with a napkin.

'Mmm, that was delicious, thank you,' he said.

'And what does a professional historian do on a Saturday when they've woken up in the wrong place?' she teased him.

'I'm supposed to be going into the pottery offices to do some more work for a few hours. It's easier to get at things when the office staff aren't all there. But I don't need long. There are a few more files for me to go through before I head back to London tomorrow,' he said, and he seemed to have caught the brief look of sadness that Rebekah had tried to hide. She paused and looked into her coffee for a moment before taking a breath and voicing the suggestion that could go one of two ways.

'I have to go into Poole today myself, to pick up some groceries and get a few jobs done. Perhaps we could catch the same ferry across?' She couldn't explain why she felt like holding her breath, or why she cared if she never saw this stranger again. *Come on, Rebekah, remember who you are. You don't do relationships. Not any more. This isn't going anywhere.* But then he smiled at her so broadly and with a sigh that she was sure meant relief. And hope.

'I'd love that, Rebekah. Let's spend the day together.'

11

POOLE HARBOUR – FEBRUARY 1941

When Peggy arrived at the harbour master's office the next morning, she was surprised to find Charlie there waiting for her by the fire.

'Morning, Miss Symonds.' He smiled brightly, and Peggy thought she heard a quaver of nerves in his voice. 'Miss Foster asked me to wait here for you this morning,' he said, nodding in the direction of Pat's office.

Peggy raised an enquiring eyebrow to Pat as she went in to collect the launch key.

'I met him yesterday afternoon, Peggy. I sent a note round to his lodgings and he got it when he went home for dinner, then he came in to see me late in the afternoon. He seems to know the ropes pretty well, so I thought the best thing was for him to spend a day with you and you can work out what he's capable of,' Pat explained.

'No problem, Pat, I'll take him with me now. Later today, I have to do some driving deliveries so he might come with me then too. Will you organise that with Rose Stevens, or shall I leave him behind?'

'I'll telephone through to Rose with all the details, and when you come back in with him after this run, send him up to meet her so she can cover anything she needs to,' she said with a nod as Peggy took the key and gathered Charlie up with her as she left.

'We've got one of our usual runs to Salterns Marina and out to a waiting C-class, and then we can take you for a little run of the harbour if you like. And perhaps you can take the controls for a while – show me what you can do,' Peggy told Charlie as they stepped into the launch with Eileen and Nora, then cast off to start the day's work.

Within an hour, the crew, passengers, and luggage were all loaded onto the C-class and Peggy had overseen the take-off from the main runway, then she turned to Charlie who had been more than helpful with the work so far.

'We're at high tide right now, so there aren't many places we can't go as the launch doesn't draw very much, but at low tide, we have to stick to the main channels. You've seen the marker buoys, of course,' she said as she saw him taking in the familiar signs that he obviously recognised.

'There's a chart below that stays on board, and others back at the office we can lend you to learn your way around. Right then, take over, Charlie, and we'll go on a little trip around the island,' said Peggy as she handed the helm over.

* * *

They were facing west and so they passed the Pottery Pier on their left as they rounded the western end of Brownsea Island first, and Peggy noticed that Charlie was taking a keen interest in the island, and the channel markers around it.

'Just up around that way, on the southern side of Brownsea

Island, is the Upper Wych channel. There're quite a few flying boats moored up here, though some of the moorings are still taken up by some Dutch boats that came over with the refugees last year,' she said, and Charlie seemed surprised at the news.

'How many boats were there?' he asked.

'Oh, around a hundred originally, I believe. Some of them went off to Dunkirk and never came back, and some of them have left with their owners for other parts of the south coast. A few have remained in the harbour, but they anchor elsewhere now. There are just a handful left here,' Peggy said as she pointed out the few *schuyts* and one barge, which were left moored up now.

'Can we go and take a look?' asked Charlie, and when she nodded, he slowed the launch and drew into the channel.

Charlie seemed to use the opportunity to demonstrate his skills, coming up close by one of the boats with expertise as if they had been about to board her, then took off again to continue on their jaunt. Peggy was impressed, and was happy to tell him as much.

'You certainly do know how to handle a boat, Charlie. You'd have no problem at all doing what I do,' she said, a comment that she knew must sound strange to his ears when he'd probably been handling boats his whole life. But so, she realised, had she. Times had changed. This was no longer a man's world.

'Thank you, Peggy,' he said with a smile and the acknowledge- ment that they'd agreed on first-name terms earlier in the day. 'I must admit I've missed this.' He sighed and indicated the boat and harbour before him. 'I'd be very glad to have some work with you if there's any going.'

Peggy nodded in response but was determined not to make any commitments to him now.

'You mentioned the Dutch boats are in other parts of the harbour. Where else have they ended up?' he asked.

'There are one or two up the Frome River – on the way to Wareham – and I think I saw one at anchor over by Arne a few weeks ago. But the Dutch themselves have melted into the crowd, as it were. There is a lady called Lotte who's working at the Fish Shambles – she came with the refugees. Her husband is a fisherman and she's got work at the market there. Other than that, I've not seen any of them in months now,' Peggy added conversationally.

Peggy allowed Charlie to bring the launch all the way around the island, and she showed him the harbour entrance with its chain ferry. She pointed out the small Royal Navy base at the marina as they passed and showed him the Harbour Heights Hotel up on the hill where they were often asked to collect passengers from or deliver cargo to.

'You may as well take her all the way back into the quay, now, Charlie. You'll see the main channel markers here, and then heading west around the docks, that's the way up to the RAF base where all the non-civilian flying boats are based, and from there on to the Wareham Channel where you find the mouth of the River Frome. That takes you all the way up to Wareham.'

Charlie was very interested in the way to the River Frome and told her that sounded like a lovely place for a day out on a boat.

* * *

Once back on the quay, and after he'd helped the ladies to secure the launch, Charlie went home for his dinner with Mrs Rogers, and agreed to meet Peggy outside the pottery at two o'clock for their driving job. But first he would have to go inside to meet Rose Stevens.

'You must be Charlie Edwards,' Rose said with warmth as he opened the door to the security offices on the first floor of the pottery. He realised now that he'd seen and admired the dark-haired Rose around the quay before, and he thought her beautiful, but in an unreachable way that he couldn't explain. Not like friendly, chirpy, blonde-haired Peggy.

He lowered his eyes now as he greeted Rose with deference, and pulled out his identity papers.

'Thanks, Charlie, just take a seat and I'll get your employment documents organised. We need an account of everyone who passes in and out of the BOAC offices and boats here, just to keep us all on the safe side, you see,' she explained kindly and sat at her desk to begin the paperwork.

'So, Pat – Miss Foster – tells me you have quite some experience working on boats?' she asked as she worked, as if to make small talk, but Charlie knew this was part of his interview process.

'Yes, I've always been on or near the water. The docks in London on the river Thames, and several other ports around the place. I can handle a launch no problem at all, as I believe Miss Symonds will attest,' he offered politely.

'Oh yes, Peggy's very happy to have you around to help. And can you drive a car?' she asked more pointedly with a glance at his left leg.

'I can't I'm afraid, not with this weakness. It's my left leg that's dodgy, you see. But I'll be glad to help with the loading and unloading.'

'That will be very helpful, thanks, Charlie. Here you go – you need to keep this pass on you at all times while you are working with us, just in case you're ever called on to prove your employment status. And also because some of the passengers we have on the flying boats are of the more diplomatic kind,' she added meaningfully.

'Of course, Miss Stevens. Glad to help.' He hesitated at the door and Rose looked up enquiringly.

'Is there something else, Charlie?' she asked.

'I'm just wondering what I should tell them at the docks. Will you be needing me for long?' he asked tentatively.

'Oh, right – sorry Charlie. Consider yourself permanently full-time on the BOAC staff and, if I were you, I would tell them at the docks that you've been asked to work for us as we need your skills. The pay will be a little higher than they give you, I'm sure,' she said.

Charlie was glad of the extra money, of course, but the big win for him was time on the water, which after just one morning had made him feel much more like himself again. He was so buoyed up by the change in events of the last two days that he whistled to himself with something resembling joy as he walked back along the quay. He'd almost forgotten what that felt like, with all the loss this war had brought him. His time in Poole was going very well indeed and he knew he'd found the place where he could settle and start again.

12

POOLE – JULY 1998

By the time they boarded the bright-yellow ferry from the island to Poole Quay on the mainland, the early-morning rain had cleared and there were even a few patches of blue sky showing between the clouds, so Rebekah showed Paul up to the top deck where they could take in the full view of the harbour. He pointed out where he believed the runways had been set out for the flying boats during the war, and she showed him where his hotel sat, high on the hill, looking straight out towards Brownsea Island.

'Why is the island called Brownsea, do you think? The sea in the harbour isn't particularly brown,' Paul said.

'Interesting question, and it has nothing to do with the colour brown. The archaic name for the island and the castle was Branksea, and with the Poole accent like it is, I think the locals must have gradually morphed that into Brownsea. But even Branksea apparently wasn't the original name and may have been a variation on the Old English *Brunoces*, which means Brunoc's Island. It's been an important place for over a thousand years, when some monks built a chapel and hermitage. Language has changed a bit since then,' Rebekah explained.

'It sure has, and that makes sense. I'm glad to hear you're so interested in the history,' Paul said with a smile.

'What do you need to do first, when we get back to the quay?' Rebekah asked him. 'I'm free as a bird all day, and as long as I get back home before the last ferry this afternoon, with some groceries to eat for the week, I can fit around you.'

'To be honest, I think the first thing I should do is drive up to the hotel, have a shower, and put on some fresh clothes. These ones will need peeling off me soon,' he said with complete innocence, then blushed when Rebekah laughed and looked away.

Paul had left his car parked near the shore so they strolled that way along the quay and past the old lifeboat museum, and then Rebekah showed him the way to drive through Poole Park to get to his hotel. In the two years since she had been in Poole, Rebekah had mainly lived on Brownsea Island. But she had arrived with all sorts of local knowledge that her neighbour – whom she still sometimes thought of as 'Aunty Pig'– had shared with her over the years, and she had set about discovering all the places she had recommended.

Rebekah had spent her first few nights after she had arrived in Poole staying at the Harbour Heights Hotel herself, before finding a somewhat more economical option until the ranger's cottage became hers. She had hired a car for her first couple of weeks, intending to buy one. But when she got settled on the island, she realised she would hardly need one. And as her life centred around Brownsea, Poole Quay, and one or two other places she could easily reach on a bus or train, she hadn't missed it yet. But those first two weeks with a car had been helpful in learning her way around, at least.

'Watch out as we go under this little bridge here, Paul. It's tiny and only fits one car at a time. Slow right down and check there's nothing coming the other way,' she said, and he nodded his thanks.

'This is certainly a different route to the main road. Is it much faster?'

'Not really, especially as we have to slow down through the park. But I love the scenery this way, and I always think a journey – however short and necessary – is better if you can take the scenic route, don't you?'

He said that he did. Though for someone who usually drove around London, she guessed it wasn't often a luxury he could enjoy.

At the hotel, she hesitated, wondering if she ought to wait in the car. Suddenly, it seemed strange to assume she should follow this man she'd known for less than twelve hours up to his hotel room. Twelve hours. But it felt more like twelve days already.

'Come on up and enjoy the view while you wait, Rebekah. It really is wonderful,' he said without a hint of embarrassment or any inuendo intended, and a sixth sense told her she was safe.

The room was quite magnificent – definitely a more deluxe version than the one she had stayed in, this one being more of a honeymoon suite than a simple room. The picture windows were full of Poole Harbour. She could see lots of recognisable details on the island, as well as all the way across the harbour to Studland and beyond. Rebekah pointed out Corfe Castle to Paul.

'Is it somewhere I could visit?' Paul asked. 'I've seen it and wondered how to get there. It looks a long way from here.'

'Oh yes, very easy to visit. The best way from here is to go across the chain ferry and through Studland. It makes for a beautiful day out. It's owned by the National Trust too, just like the island. Do you have membership?' she asked.

'No, but I'm really starting to think I should. There are so many wonderful places to see once you get out of London. It's well worth the cost, I'm sure,' he called as he went into his bathroom and shut the door. Rebekah took a seat by the window to enjoy the view and tried not to imagine Paul undressing in there or picture him when she heard the shower water running. Honestly, he was very friendly and kind but as she knew well, he was only here on business for one more day, and besides – as she had reminded herself every time she'd ever found feelings like these rising – she was better off alone. If only he wasn't so easy to spend time with. To chat to. To look at. She laughed at her own immaturity and tried to rein in feelings that were in danger of getting her into trouble, or leading her back to pain.

When he stepped out of the bathroom, she was relieved to see he had already dressed and she didn't have to face the reality of him wrapped in nothing but a white towel – an image she'd been somewhat too focused on moments before. He was instead wearing navy shorts and a pale-blue shirt and was rubbing his wet hair with the towel.

'I think I could look at this view for the rest of my life and never tire of it,' he said as he watched Rebekah gazing out of the window.

'It is glorious,' she said dreamily, finding it hard to take her eyes off the view of Brownsea from up here. Then she snapped herself back to the more pragmatic and sensible Rebekah. 'So, what do you need to do first, Paul? You mentioned some work at the pottery.'

He sighed. 'Yes, there is that. But it should only take me a couple of hours. And it isn't even midday yet. It's not exactly a beach day, but it isn't raining any more. Why don't we go for a walk along the beach at Sandbanks?' he asked her.

'That would be lovely. A good stretch of the legs and perhaps a cup of coffee somewhere.'

They walked down the hill from the hotel to Shore Road,

where the wide sweep of Whitley Lake lay bare to the low tide. Rebekah pointed out some of the birds she knew, having learnt of them in the hides on Brownsea Island. There were godwits, oystercatchers and curlews, she told him.

'We have a curlew back home in Australia too, which looks very similar, but they're only cousins. These ones don't holiday down under,' she told him.

'This bay must be very shallow, even when the tide is in,' Paul commented.

'Yes, it is. You probably wouldn't get more than waist-deep until you almost reach the main channel out there. But when the tide is in, this area is full of windsurfers. It's a great spot for them.'

They walked on past the Sandbanks Hotel and onto the beach, each taking deep breaths of the fresh sea air that came in on the breeze as they paused to take in the view of the expanse of beach to the left and right of them.

'Which way shall we walk? Left towards Bournemouth, or right and along the peninsula, down to the Haven Hotel at the harbour entrance? Lovely spot for a cuppa or even a glass of wine in the hotel if we go that way,' Rebekah suggested.

'That's me sold! Lead the way Haven-wards, Ranger Rebekah.' He grinned, and she laughed in response.

As they walked, Rebekah told him more about her childhood in Australia, and how the native wildlife where she grew up in Brisbane had inspired her to lead the life of a conservationist.

'But why learn all about Australian ecology and then come here to England? Do you have family here?' he asked, knowing from various of his historical studies how many Australians had British roots.

Rebekah flinched as the pain flared in the deep scars left by her father and then Andy. The idea of coming to Poole and Brownsea Island had begun in her innocent childhood, but the trauma caused by Andy's abuse had been the hinge on which her life had pivoted, sending her across the world to escape him and the memory of fear and pain.

'Not family, no. But my next-door neighbour grew up here in Poole.'

'But she's not here now?' he asked.

'No. She went over to Australia after the war and became like a grandmother to me as I grew up. We lost Peggy to cancer not long before I came over here to live,' she said.

'Oh, I'm sorry,' he said with such feeling that she paused to look up at his face. He had a kindness in his look, all the time, but at this moment, he seemed to be reaching out to her with his eyes. And she was grateful for that extra connection. She lived a lonely life on the island by choice, but this moment made her realise that perhaps it was a little too solitary.

And before she knew how she'd really begun, Rebekah was telling Paul all about Peggy, the neighbour who had helped her mum to raise her. 'She was there through the worst of my life, and the best of it. At my graduation ceremony from university – that's when I first realised something was wrong. That first hint that she wasn't as well as she normally would have been,' Rebekah said.

She told Paul how, at the ceremony beside the river on Brisbane's South Bank in the winter of '88, she'd first seen Peggy resting in the shade and feeling unwell, when normally she would have stood through an afternoon like that and loudly cheered her on.

Earlier, Rebekah had taken a few minutes, before she had to get gowned up and find her seat, to look at the little section of rainforest that had been created there on the banks of the Brisbane River especially for the world expo display. It was an amazingly good replica, with a running creek and sprinklers that made a realistic wet rainforest environment for the frogs, and the few minutes she'd spent there had helped Rebekah solidify her plans for the short break she had before she went off to start her new job in the new year.

Rebekah told Paul how she had always been hoping for a job in a national park around Brisbane – perhaps Lamington, in the rainforest she loved so much. But first, she had ended up doing some work on wetlands conservation right in Brisbane, at Boondall. And all of this was just a precursor to the big plan: the world-wide travelling plan. The plan to graduate, work hard, learn lots more about Australian ecology, save enough money to travel, then head off to England to learn about the ecology of the British waterways and woodlands, and specifically those in Poole Harbour and on Brownsea Island.

Ever since Rebekah had been a little girl and Peggy had told her stories of her life in Dorset – the harbour, the beaches, the limestone hills and cliff faces and especially the island – she'd dreamed of visiting. For the whole of her life, Brownsea Island had been owned by the National Trust and Peggy had helped Rebekah to stay up to date on the news of what was being done to return it to its natural state, after years of farming and then neglect. She had books and news clippings and photos that had been sent out by Peggy's friends and relatives, who were working on the island as volunteers. And when Rebekah discovered that the island had its own rangers, she was hooked on the idea of visiting and becoming part of the place of her dreams. But first, there had been qualifications to earn.

'After my grad ceremony, when I found Mum, I saw that Peggy was still sitting in her chair in the shade. She was holding out a small bunch of lovely native flowers – red callistemon and pink grevillea, yellow banksia and grey-green eucalyptus leaves – all wrapped in brown paper and tied with a raffia ribbon,' she said. 'I remember so many details that I hadn't realised were important to me, but Peggy and I shared such a bond over native flora. It was the only choice of flowers she could ever have made for me. I bent down to give Pig a hug and heard her wince slightly. I didn't know then, but I soon found out. She was already in the late stages of cancer.'

Rebekah walked on in quiet thought for a while, and Paul gave her the space she needed for her memories.

Up until then, she remembered, she'd never thought of Peggy needing a man in her life, but it had suddenly occurred to Rebekah that Peggy might have been better off with a partner to care for her. She'd had Mum, of course, and Rebekah was there through the worst of it, but she had realised at that moment how nothing was quite the same as a lifelong mate. She thought again now that though being a strong, independent young woman was one thing, old age and sickness was something else altogether. Rebekah wondered now, for the first time, if it weren't true that everyone needed someone to spend their twilight years with.

And now here was this strangely kind and warm historian: Paul. She knew she'd probably only have a few more hours of his company before he disappeared back to London, probably forever, but something in her heart said that was wrong. That couldn't be.

Within half an hour, they'd reached what Paul had assumed to be the end of the beach as they approached the rocks that were laid as a sea defence all around the harbour entrance and a gate into the hotel that was marked, *Private Property: Hotel Guests Only*.

'Do we need to turn back to reach the hotel from the road?' he asked her.

In return, she just smiled and winked.

'Follow me, if you're feeling adventurous!' she called as she climbed and picked her way along the rocks at the water's edge, looking back over her shoulder to check he was following her.

Rebekah nimbly led the way around the rocks beneath the wall that surrounded the hotel, and past a couple of fishermen who stood with lines taut in the rush of the outgoing tide at the harbour entrance. When she reached the metal ladder that led up the wall to the front of the hotel, she checked that Paul was still with her. She was surprised to see he'd paused and was studying one of the stones that made up the rock wall, so went back to see him.

'Look at this, Rebekah! It's a whole hand, carved into the rock,' he said as he felt between the fingers of the huge print that must have been carved in the stone right here. She reached his side and explained.

'There's a face over there too, see? I'm not sure who carved them, or how long they've been there but this is Purbeck stone – quite easy to carve as the stonemasons of some of the country's finest cathedrals would tell you. If you'd had time to visit Corfe Castle, you'd see plenty of it there. The whole village is made of it. It's the prettiest place,' she said standing to wave in the general direction of the Isle of Purbeck. 'This is where you'd take the car across on the chain ferry, through Studland and on to Corfe.'

'Did anyone ever tell you that you'd make a good saleswoman, as well as a ranger? You're making it very difficult to leave Poole tomorrow morning and miss out on all this back in London,' he groaned.

'Actually, there's plenty of Purbeck Stone in London too, if that helps. There's even some at the Tower of London, I believe,' she said brightly before heading back to the ladder that rested against the wall and climbing swiftly up to the car park with Paul following on behind.

'Here we are: I give you the more conventional entrance to the Haven Hotel, though I must say I prefer our route for getting here,' she said as she led the way into the hotel foyer.

They ordered two glasses of wine from the bar and sat on the wide patio in the sunshine that had finally burned through the clouds.

'So that's Brownsea Island, just inside the harbour there?' he asked, pointing towards the castle that faced them and out in the channel.

'Yes, and just beyond the slipway to the chain ferry, at that jetty you can see, there's another ferry that takes this shorter route to the island. That's where most of the staff on the island catch the ferry,' she said.

'But you prefer the other ferry?' he asked, intrigued.

'They all have cars that they park here, and the *Enterprise* – that's the name of this ferry – is a much faster boat as the distance is so short. But as I don't have a car, and most of what I need to do is in Poole town centre, the *Island Maid* ferry to the quay suits me best. The only downside is that the last one of those runs at half past four in the afternoon,' she explained.

'And what happens if you miss that? Do you get stranded on the quay?'

'Hopefully not! There's another boat, run by the castle, called the *Castello*, which is bookable by castle guests and island residents like me. In the summer, it goes to and from Poole Quay several times a day. And I could always catch a bus or even a taxi round here and get on the *Enterprise*, which goes until late at night in the summer.'

Just then, a waiter walked by, his arms laden with plates full of divine-looking dishes of culinary creations.

'The food here smells wonderful. It will be one o'clock soon. Shall we ask for a menu?' Paul asked, looking around for a free waiter.

'It's a bit expensive actually, and I think you have to book for a meal,' Rebekah said hesitantly.

'Rebekah: I owe you for my night of unplanned accommodation on your most comfortable settee, the amazing meal you gave
me when I arrived in the middle of the night, *and* the perfect
omelette you cooked me this morning, not to mention the tour-
guiding so far today.' He held up his hand with mock severity to
stop the protestations she was about to emit. 'Please, it would be
my privilege to buy you lunch. May I?' he asked her as he caught
the eye of a waiter, who brought them each a menu.

Rebekah smiled her thanks and marvelled at how differently
this day was turning out from her usual Saturday plans: a visit to
the library to change her books, a quick dash around Sainsbury's,
a treat of fish and chips on the quay and then the ferry ride home
to Brownsea and Rose Cottage. As she sipped her wine, ordered a
luscious meal, and watched Paul watching the boats coming and
going through the harbour entrance, she decided one thing: it
was time to stop expecting anything to be normal, ever again.

* * *

Lunch turned into coffee and somehow time seemed to stay still,
while they'd been sitting there for well over two hours together,
talking, eating, laughing. Rebekah glanced at her watch as she
noticed the waiters seemed to be clearing up around them as all
the other lunch guests had left.

'Heck, look at the time! We'd best get a move on if I'm going to
get my groceries bought and make it onto that ferry home. And
don't you have work to do?' she asked him, feeling a little panicky
at how dependent she now realised she was on Paul to drive her
back into Poole.

Paul studied his watch and seemed to be mulling something
over. Rebekah saw him glance towards Brownsea and westward to
where she'd pointed out Studland earlier.

'You'll never make it, not comfortably, anyway,' he finally said, resting back in his chair and folding his arms decisively.

'What? Why not?' Rebekah cried, noticing the higher pitch in her own voice.

'We have a half an hour walk back to the hotel, then once we get into Poole, you won't have enough time to shop and do all your errands and still get back to the quay by half past four,' he explained.

'Oh, it's okay – I really don't need much and I'm quite good at flying around Sainsbury's in a hurry,' she spoke quickly, beginning to feel a little breathless now.

'And your library books?' he asked with an arch to his eyebrows that told her he was enjoying this. She had forgotten that she'd left them in his car.

'Ah, yes, I forgot about those. Oh, damn it. I really did want to change them,' she mused, biting her lip as she thought about it.

'I tell you what,' said Paul, folding his arms and leaning them on the table as he bent closer to Rebekah. 'Let's say we forget all about trying to make it in time for that early ferry. I'll help you get your errands done, and then we can spend the evening together. Have dinner somewhere. Perhaps even take a drive out to this castle and its village you think I should see. It will be light until nearly ten o'clock tonight. Then you can take the later ferry from here on the – what did you call it – the *Enterprise*? – and still get home to bed in Rose Cottage before you turn into a pumpkin.'

Rebekah realised she was staring at him with her jaw hanging open. His eyes were studying her face and she felt her lips tingle when his gaze lingered on her mouth, which she shut with a snap. Everything he had suggested sounded perfectly reasonable. And wonderful. But she had only met him fifteen hours previously. And was there something just a bit too close and personal about him wanting to spend so much time with her when he'd only just met her? What if he had that strange controlling gene she'd only seen too late in Andy?

She could just decline his lovely offer, ask to be dropped at the supermarket and let him drive away, never to see him again. Or, she could take a deep plunge and trust him. She felt the weight of two possible and polar opposite outcomes teetering in the balance, and took a deep breath before replying.

'You know, for someone whose Friday evening plans went so incredibly awry, your ideas for Saturday evening are pretty spectacular, Paul. Count me in,' she said with a smile, realising this was probably the most daring and trusting thing she'd ever said to a man before – particularly one she found incredibly attractive. There. She'd admitted it. He was divine to look at, and he had an easy way to him that made her feel like she'd known him for months rather than hours. She was loving every minute in his company.

'But we should still head off now, I think. These waiters are wanting a break before their dinner rush starts,' she said looking around the patio where they were the last guests remaining.

Paul went to pay the bill while Rebekah walked over to the *Enterprise* jetty to explain to the ferryman to expect her on the last ferry of the day at 11 p.m., if he didn't see her any earlier.

'Rightio, Bek,' said the boat's captain, who had always shortened her name without checking whether or not she approved – she didn't. 'And if you don't turn up for the eleven o'clock, what should we do? Don't want you stranded here, love,' he said, and Rebekah noticed that he was looking over her shoulder with a frown. She turned to see Paul approaching, tucking his wallet into his back pocket.

'It's all right, Bob, I'm sure I'll be here by eleven. And if I'm not going to make it, I'll let you know,' she assured him.

'Let's take the road way back to the hotel, shall we?' Rebekah suggested to Paul as they walked away from the ferry jetty. 'It runs all along the peninsula on the inside, so I'll be able to show you more of the harbour that way.'

Rebekah led the way down Banks Road and pointed out some of the most expensive property in the world. 'John Lennon bought a house for his Aunty Mimi just around the corner, you know,' she told him.

'That would have been a bit different from her place in Liverpool, I'm sure.'

'Apparently, John loved the peace and quiet here. And he was right, don't you think? It really is one of the most beautiful places in the world to relax,' she said.

'If you couldn't have your little cottage on Brownsea Island, then I suppose one of these mansions would do.' He shrugged and shot her a quick smile. 'But I much prefer the real deal. Your place is perfect.'

'Yes, if only it really was mine. It's just the accommodation that goes with the job, but wouldn't it be lovely to have a permanent home somewhere so magical as Brownsea?'

As they made their way out into the open of the peninsula road, the ferry to Cherbourg was chugging out of the harbour and seemed to tower above all the smaller boats around it.

'From what I've learnt about the flying boats that were here in the war, that ferry is charging straight down the main runway,' Paul said thoughtfully.

'Are you particularly interested in the war?' she asked.

'It's intriguing. I came here to gather information and sort through archives on the pottery, thinking it would be all about business transactions and staff members, but I had no idea what an important role the pottery played as part of the flying boat service during the war. Did you know that they used the Harbour Heights Hotel for their guests?' he asked and Rebekah shook her head gently. 'If they had to overnight before an early-morning flight, they'd stay at the hotel then be driven down to the marina at Salterns. Most of the male staff from the pottery were called up and went away to war, but some of the women were retained to work for BOAC – the British Overseas Airways Corporation. It became British Airways in the end.'

'Really? I had no idea about that part.' Rebekah was stunned. She knew that Pig had some memories of flying boats in the war, but Pig was just a fisherman's daughter. Perhaps she'd not known the full extent of this civilian service.

'Poole Harbour was one the first places in the world to be called an "Air*port*",' he said, with emphasis. 'Up until that time, the few planes there were in the 1930s were just based on random small landing strips around the country. But with the war and the sudden growth of the RAF fleet, all of those airstrips became RAF bases for the fighter planes and bombers, and the flying boat services were all moved from Southampton to Poole where it was thought it would be safer. So, for a short while, Poole Harbour was the only international civilian airport in the country – *port* being the operative word, of course, for the flying *boats*.'

Paul regaled her with the fascinating history he'd learnt all the way back to the hotel, where they picked up his car and drove back into Poole town centre again.

He found an empty space in the Poole Pottery staff car park.

'I'll go inside and see to a few things while you get your odds and ends done. Meet you back here about six o'clock?' Paul suggested. 'I'll leave this side door ajar, so you can just come up the back way to find me.'

Rebekah picked up the backpack that held her library books and headed up the High Street before she realised a flaw in their plan: she couldn't buy refrigerated groceries and have them hanging around for several hours in Paul's car while they went on a tour of the Purbecks. She glanced at her watch – 3.50 p.m. Just enough time if she was quick. She dashed around Sainsbury's and collected all the basics she might need for the next week, then hurried as fast as she could manage with her heavy bags back down to the quay. She reached the ferry just as the last passengers were boarding the final trip around the harbour for the day.

'Sorry, Phil, I've not managed my time very well this afternoon,' she explained to the ferry's deckhand. 'Can you please take these for me and get them into the Brownsea reception? There's a bag here that'll need to be popped in the fridge. I'll pick them up when I get home on the *Enterprise* later,' she said.

'Right you are, Rebekah, not a problem. Lovely evening. Doin' something nice, are we?' he asked with a smile.

'I hope so,' she called back over her shoulder. Relieved of the heavy grocery bags, Rebekah enjoyed the walk all the way back up the High Street to the library where she had just enough time to return her books and pick out a selection for the next few weeks: the latest *Harry Potter*, Helen Fielding's first novel – the serialisation of which in the national newspapers had been hilarious – and Thomas Hardy's *Wessex Tales*. Something fantastical, something to make her laugh, and some gritty Victorian realism set firmly in the heart of Dorset.

Rebekah made her way back to where she'd agreed to meet Paul at six o'clock and pushed open the door he'd left ajar for her. She found herself in a back corridor of the pottery offices. All was eerily quiet. The factory floor probably didn't operate on a Saturday anyway, but she knew the showroom and café did, as she'd been in there herself for a cup of tea several times, but they would be closed for the day by now. She made her way along the corridor in the rough direction she thought she might find Paul but was soon distracted by all the historical photos that lined the hallway. Some were in colour and showed the various pottery collection designs through the latter part of the twentieth century, but others were black and white.

There was one of the paintresses, all sitting in rows. Judging by their clothes, it must have dated from the 1930s. And then one caught her eye as it seemed to have nothing to do with the pottery at all. The photo had been taken on Poole Quay, and there were several women wearing dark uniforms of slacks and jumpers and matching caps with an insignia. A lone man was pointing out into the harbour and the women followed his gaze. It was obviously a staged photograph and looked to date from the Second World War. One of the women was strikingly beautiful. She had fair hair that curled under her cap, and high cheekbones. Something about her was familiar.

Rebekah read the inscription printed beneath the photo. The date was 1943 and it read:

Bosun Frank Hewitt points the way to a flying boat from Poole Quay, watched by British Airways Seawomen, Nora Bevis, Eileen Wigg and Margaret Symonds.

She wondered if Margaret might have been related to Peggy, but it was unlikely. The name Symonds was fairly common, after all. But the faraway look on that one woman's face – she presumed this was Margaret from the order of the names in the inscription – drew her in to the picture. Why did she not look as though she was giggling, as the other girls were? She was probably the same age, but something about her expression made her look older. Wiser. Deeper.

'Fascinating, aren't they?' said a deep voice that gently brought Rebekah back to the present.

'They're beautiful. And they must have been very skilled, too.'

'There's very little detail about them that I can find – and I've tried to look. Just their names and addresses, their roles, and their pay rates recorded in a random book I found. They weren't part of the pottery business, but the connection was strong between the pottery and BOAC.'

'It would be wonderful to find out more about these women. Who were they, do you think? And what happened to them?' she mused, but Paul had no answers for her.

Paul led the way up to the office along the corridor, where he was just packing up his things.

'I heard the door open and guessed it was you,' he explained. 'I just need to pack up and then we can set off. Did you get everything done?' he asked her.

'Yes, thanks. Even sent my groceries home on that last ferry to the island. What about you?'

'I think I've got as much sorted as I need to from this end now. I shouldn't need to come back here to the pottery to do any more on this job. Back up to London tomorrow, for me,' he said, then turned away from the desk and picked up his bag, addressing Rebekah as he straightened. 'So we have the rest of this evening for you to show me everything you think I should see.' He smiled.

'That's not very long to show you the best of the most beautiful county in England, but I do like a challenge. I would love to show you the other side of the harbour, and it's a perfect evening for a drive. We won't get inside the castle as we're too late, but we can drive around the Wareham way, have a walk around Corfe in the evening sun, and then have a pub dinner. We'll come home the Studland way to make it a circular drive and back over the chain ferry, then you can leave me in the safe hands of the captain of the *Enterprise*,' she explained as they walked out to the car.

'Captain Kirk? I've always wanted to meet him,' he said with a grin.

'Do you know, I've never even thought of that connection before! Now I'll never be able to think of Bob in any other way.' Rebekah laughed.

As Rebekah directed Paul along the quay, across the Hamworthy lifting bridge from one quay to the other, and towards Wareham, she relaxed into the delightful knowledge that she'd be with him for at least another four or maybe five hours. And, she thought to herself as she took a shy glance at him driving now, she was going to make every minute count.

13

POOLE HARBOUR – FEBRUARY 1941

As Peggy Symonds ate her crumpets and drank her tea with her family that Friday evening, the first dreary thoughts of doubt started to fill her mind. It had been almost a full week since she had seen Darrell Taylor at the dance hall last Saturday, and though she had been nursing high hopes of seeing him tonight, she began to wonder. Perhaps his non-appearance all week was not so much to do with the call of duty that had kept him busy. Perhaps he had been in Poole all along but had found another pub, with another girl to charm. She sighed deeply and looked into the fireplace flames, watching them flicker over the coals.

'What's eating at you, Peggy love?' asked Molly, who seemed to have turned a corner in the last few days and was beginning to glow, having got her appetite back.

Peggy, startled from her thoughts, took a moment to gather the worries tumbling through her mind.

'I had a lovely time with Darrell last Saturday, Molly. And I fully expected to see him again this week. I got my hopes up, and he's been nowhere. He's not "*mine*" as so many of the girls are saying. I have no rights to him. But I feel...' She turned her face back to the flames again. 'I feel as if I've lost something special. As if we really could have made a go of it, and now he might have gone off to find someone else. And I suppose...' she heaved a big sigh again '...I suppose I feel foolish for all that.'

'But Peggy, he's in the RAAF – he's busy and serving. You're just lucky he's based right here in Poole, and you're not waiting for him to come home on leave. I'm sure there's a reasonable explanation. Tell you what,' Molly added, brightening, 'let's go down to the Antelope together tonight and if he's there, he's there. If he's not, we'll have a nice cosy time together. I'm sure I could do with another pint of stout to keep my energy up for this one,' she said, rubbing her growing little baby bump.

The sisters put on their coats, and a little lipstick, and linked arms as much to stop each other from falling in the pitch-dark of the blackout as they did to keep each other warm and close. And soon they were outside the pub that they thought of as their local and pushing open the doors to reveal the humming mass of happy Friday-night chatter and laughter inside.

'You get the corner table, Molly; I'll go and fetch us a drink,' said Peggy, knowing full well that Molly would understand she needed to scan the room properly and look for Darrell. The pub was full of Friday-night locals, the fishermen, the wives, the BOAC pilots, some soldiers and sailors in uniform on home leave, and then, right at the last, she spotted a group in the back corner wearing the slightly different blue uniform of the RAAF.

'What'll it be, love?' asked the publican, waiting for her expectantly.

'Sorry, Jim, I was miles away. A pint of stout and a port and lemon, please,' Peggy said, reaching into her handbag for the coins to pay for her drinks.

'That'll be one and six please, Peggy love.'

Just as Peggy was about to lay down the coins on the bar, a

large, tanned, and hairy hand dropped one and six into the barman's hand.

'My shout,' said Darrell with a broad grin as Peggy looked up in surprise.

'Thank you! I...' For a moment, Peggy was lost for words, looking to the back of the room where Darrell must have appeared from and across to Molly who was beaming up at her. 'I thought I might have seen you again this week,' she added, looking up into the deep amber of his eyes that seemed to be drinking in the sight of her.

'I know. I'm sorry, Peggy. I was worried you'd think I'd left you all alone. I've not had a minute to get off. For some reason or other – that even we are not allowed to know – we've been on high alert all week, scouring the coast with double runs. I've barely slept, let alone had a night off to get out to see you. But I'm here now.' He smiled warmly.

'Indeed, you are. Would you like to join me and Molly?' she asked.

Darrell went to collect his own drink and then joined the sisters at their table.

Peggy caught him up on the activities in the harbour for the week, and the arrival of the welcome pair of hands in Charlie. And Molly listened in wonder as Darrell told them of an air-sea rescue they'd been involved in.

'We came across a ship that looked to be in trouble,' he explained.

'A Royal Navy ship?' asked Molly, desperate to hear any news of their brother, Samuel.

'No, this was a merchant ship – just as important with many sailors aboard, and not to mention the precious cargo she was bringing from America. We did a few circuits and once they realised who we were – which side we were on – they were waving for help. We landed and managed to make contact, fearful that they may have been hit, though they didn't seem to be going down. Turned out they had a man on board who was very sick. We got him aboard and brought him back here to Poole to the hospital, days earlier than they would have made it from where they were.'

'So, you saved his life?' asked Molly in awe.

'I think that was all down to the surgeon at the hospital, Molly. We were just the taxi service, in the right place at the right time,' Darrell said with the laid-back shrug of his shoulders that Peggy was becoming quite familiar with.

'So, if a ship was going down – hit by a torpedo, say – would you be able to rescue the men? How many could you take aboard a Sunderland? Surely, they're only built for two dozen or so passengers?' said Peggy, thinking of the hundreds who would be on some bigger naval vessels.

'Two dozen of your first-class types, yes, but we could probably squeeze in seventy or eighty at a push if they didn't mind being crammed in like sardines,' said Darrell with a laugh. 'Enough of my job, now, or I'll be getting myself into trouble! What have you ladies been up to while I've been busy?' he asked, and Peggy settled in for a relaxed evening with the man she was now assured was still very keen to keep up with her.

* * *

At ten o'clock, Darrell walked the two girls home.

'I'll see myself in, no need to rush,' said Molly with a wink to her sister, as she shut the front door quickly behind her, leaving Peggy on the doorstep with a face blushing crimson.

Darrell looked down the street and back to Peggy with a shy smile.

'We're so close to the water here. Does your house back onto the beach?' he asked, obviously keen to take the pressure off Peggy, who'd been left on the doorstep with him.

'Not exactly what you'd call a beach as this is a mud flat at low tide, but it is the shore of the harbour. Dad's fishing boat is kept just out there, and we have a tender pulled up on the shingle,' she said.

'Perhaps in the summer, we could go out for a little row one evening? I was in Plymouth last summer and the long, light evenings were glorious. This harbour would be beautiful for an evening row,' he said wistfully.

Peggy was lost for words for a moment while she thought about the loveliness of Darrell's idea.

'But do you think you'll still be here in the summer, Darrell? You may have changed your mind about me by then, anyway,' she added, feeling suddenly self-conscious.

'If I have my way, I'll be hanging around you for a lifetime, Peggy Symonds,' and while her mouth dropped open in astonishment, he lifted her chin with his finger, so tenderly, and bent down, kissing her lightly on the cheek. Peggy let out the breath she hadn't realised she'd been holding and saw the frosty air gather around them, realising how close their faces still were. She took a step back, and lowered her eyes a moment before daring to look him full in the face.

'I like that idea very much, Darrell Taylor. Let's hope summer comes early, shall we?' she said, daring a coy smile.

Darrell reached down and took her hand in his, stroking her thumb with his, and leant down towards her lips.

'May I kiss you goodnight, Miss Symonds?' he whispered.

'Yes please,' she said as she closed her eyes and waited.

The kiss, when it came, was the first real kiss of her life, Peggy realised later. She'd been out with boys before and had danced and let them walk her home. And several had kissed her good-night, but it had always been a rushed and harsh thing, prickly and tense. But this. This was something else entirely. Darrell's lips were soft against hers and touched her lightly, gently, again and again but slowly, like the lapping of a tiny wave on a shore, until she wanted more from him, and she found herself kissing him back, reaching up and pushing into him, pulling at his lips with her own.

He lightly touched one hand on her waist and the other cradled her head. He ran his hand through her hair, and she felt herself melting into him. He moved his hand to her back to stop her from falling away completely as she relaxed as if into a deep sleep. She placed her own hands behind his neck and felt the softness of his hair between her fingers and realised she was fully pushing her open mouth against his, searching him out and wanting him to search deep inside of her soul.

When she drew back for breath, she could not open her eyes and he held her steady as she swayed on the spot until she found her equilibrium and looked up into his warmly smiling face.

She beamed at him and reached up gingerly to touch his face.

'So this is what all the fuss is about,' she said dreamily and the dimples in his cheeks deepened.

'You'd best get inside, Peggy,' he said, nodding towards the front door. 'But I'm not working tomorrow. Can I call round in the morning? Perhaps we can spend the day together?' he asked, hopefully.

'I have a flying boat to meet in the morning, first thing, but I'll be done by about ten o'clock if you want to come by then?' she asked him.

He nodded his assent and bent to give her one last, brief kiss, pulling away and guiding her to the front door, which he opened for her, before she could protest.

'Don't want you catching cold out here, Peggy,' he said as he waved goodbye and walked down Ballard Road, back towards the quay.

'You two took your time,' called Molly with a hint of tease in her voice from the front room.

'Shush, Molly. Mother and Father will hear you, and what would they think?' Peggy giggled as she slumped into the fireside chair beside her sister.

'They already know. They've only been upstairs a couple of minutes.' Molly laughed. 'Don't worry, we all know how these things work,' she said, tapping her belly, and Peggy felt the heat of a blush rise from her toes to her ears.

'Oh, Molly, he is so lovely. And we're going to spend the day together tomorrow, too.'

'Of course you are, Peg. He is yours, like I said,' teased Molly as she stood to go upstairs to bed, kissing her fingertips and touching them to the photo of her husband that stood on the sideboard. 'It's about time we had some more good news around the place and I think that Darrell is just what you – and all of us – need. Sleep tight, my darling.'

* * *

The next morning seemed to take a lifetime to come around. Peggy usually slept soundly all night, but on this Friday night, she woke several times. Perhaps the moon was too bright, or the wind a little strong. Whatever it was, she woke often and excitedly thought morning had come already. So, when it was finally time to wake up, she did so with a start, feeling as though she was late. She dressed for work, and added a little makeup even though it was just a regular launch trip she was dressing for.

As Peggy approached the office to collect the launch key, she was surprised to find Charlie waiting for her.

'Good morning, Peggy.' He beamed. 'Miss Foster asked me to join you this morning so that Eileen could have the day off. She said it would only be a small run today and we could manage between us,' he offered.

Peggy was a little taken aback and realised that she'd entirely forgotten about the existence of Charlie since spending time with Darrell last night. But it was no problem. He'd already proved himself a fine boatman and all she was really focused on was ten o'clock and seeing Darrell.

Charlie impressed her with his skills again and managed to help with the mooring of the flying boat as well as bringing the launch alongside her and helping the passengers and crew off. They delivered them to Salterns Marina where a car to the hotel was waiting, and the crew took longer than Peggy liked chatting to Charlie about who he was and where he'd come from. She checked her watch repeatedly and was frustrated that they weren't going to get back to Poole Quay in time.

'Have you somewhere else to be, Peggy?' asked Charlie with concern as they set off from the marina and back towards the quayside.

'Yes, I'm meeting someone, and I don't want to keep them waiting,' Peggy replied.

'He's a lucky chap,' said Charlie coyly. And for the first time, Peggy saw Charlie as a man. Not just a helping hand, or strong arms, or a good boatman, but a man. A man who had apparently noticed her. Embarrassed, though not unimpressed that two men – handsome ones – had now taken an interest in her, Peggy just shrugged and tried to shake off the compliment.

'Tell you what, Peggy. If you're in a hurry, you just go on up the steps when we pull in, and I'll put the launch to bed. I'm quite capable, and I'm so grateful for the work. You go and meet your gentleman, and I'll finish up,' Charlie offered.

'Oh, would you, Charlie? I'm not quite sure if Pat would approve, but she's not there on a Saturday. Just nip into the harbour master's office and drop the key in when she's all secure, would you? Thanks so much,' gushed Peggy, thinking only of getting to Darrell and whatever fun might lie ahead today.

14

BROWNSEA ISLAND – JULY 1998

Rebekah finished her rounds of the bird hides that nestled in the woodlands on the edge of the lagoon, checking for any straggler visitors or detritus from the day's activities. She didn't want anything foreign to the natural landscape ending up in the lagoon, or anywhere else on the island for that matter. She recalled again the mantra from the Australian national parks back home: *take nothing but memories, leave nothing but footprints.* It was simple, but effective. Even something so ordinary and organic as a banana skin didn't belong in this landscape and shouldn't be left to rot among the leaf litter.

The birdwatchers had all left for the little quay to catch the last ferry off the island, except for those who were staying at the campsite or in the castle. The open-air theatre Shakespeare play was due to start in two days' time, so excitement was building, and the campsite was booked to full occupancy. The castle was expected to be heaving with private guests, too. This all made it much more complicated than usual to keep an eye on who was supposed to be on the island, and who should have left by now, and there were dozens of people from the Brownsea Open Air

Theatre company, known as BOAT for short, milling about on the Church Field. Rebekah stood for a moment and watched them all buzzing around busily in the afternoon sunshine.

The seating gallery was all set up, and the stage was ready, complete with theatrically roped curtains. Final preparations were being made to the set for *As You Like It*, and a group of actors was rehearsing a scene off to one side. Rebekah watched as she recognised the character of Rosalind in the act of revealing to Orlando that she was, in fact, the object of his admiration.

Rebekah sighed, and chastised herself for her gloominess over Paul. She was, after all, a confirmed bachelorette who had no intention of being roped into a relationship that might tie her down and hold her back, or worse – leave her black and blue and utterly violated. She still had plans: places to go, things to achieve, books to read. She snorted with mirth at her last thought and headed back towards reception to see off the last ferry and close reception for the day.

It had been almost five days since she had last seen Paul, the man she reluctantly admitted to herself now had become the object of her admiration after the blissful twenty-four hours she had spent with him last weekend.

Their evening out on the Isle of Purbeck had been pure perfection. The late-afternoon sunlight had been glorious and Rebekah had marvelled at the change in the weather from the gloomy rain when they woke up in the morning, to what had morphed into a beautiful summer's evening. They drove through Wareham to the village of Corfe Castle and parked in the National Trust car park, which Rebekah could use free of charge.

'Just another way to save money with the annual pass,' she had pointed out to Paul, who was already convinced he wanted to come back in the daytime to visit the castle itself.

'It's absolutely amazing – like something out of a storybook,' he said, gazing up at the perfect grassy mound with the remains of an ancient, fortified castle perched atop.

'It probably looked a bit better a few hundred years ago, before the roundheads destroyed the place in the civil war.' Rebekah laughed as she led him along the path and away from the castle. 'This is a circular walk, and it starts with a nice little hill climb up some steps. We'll be able to look back at the castle from the top,' she told him.

As they walked up the steep steps to the top of the hill, they chatted about the lives they each lived when they weren't being entirely spontaneous with a complete stranger in the Dorset countryside.

'So how often do you actually work in London, Paul, compared to time spent on little jaunts like this one to Poole?' she asked him, noticing how much more out of breath he was than her. An active life of constant walking in the outdoors really did pay off in fitness levels, she thought.

'It's probably about fifty-fifty,' he puffed. 'Around half my time, I'm based at home and lots of the jobs are within and around London itself, so there's no need to stay away. But then the other half are jobs that can be anywhere around the country, or some-times even abroad. I've been to Dorset several times before, but I've never seen so much of Poole as I have this time, thanks to you,' he said, stopping with his hands on his hips to catch his breath.

They had reached the top of the hill and, as promised, had a wonderful view of the castle from above, which looked even more complete from this angle. Rebekah pointed out to him where the original external walls were and the shape of the castle itself from the remaining ruins and foundations.

'I haven't been out here for ages,' Rebekah said. 'One of the downsides to not having a car is that I don't do these things as spontaneously as I'd like to. I could get here on the bus, of course, but it's not quite the same.'

'You drove at home in Brisbane, then?' Paul asked her.

'Oh yes – Brisbane is an impossible city to get around without a car because the areas are so huge. Public transport all works as if it runs on the spokes of a wheel – everything is fine if you want to get in and out of the city centre, but trying to get across suburbs is just about impossible without a car. The city bounds themselves cover over five hundred square miles, but plenty of my friends from university lived well outside that area and people commute into the city from as far as forty or fifty miles away. In comparison, just to give you an idea, the whole county of Dorset is about a thousand square miles in total. So, yes, I learnt to drive as soon as I could, back home.'

'I only ever use my car when I leave London. The Tube is so handy, and the traffic so bad, that there's really no point driving anywhere. But a drive in the country with good company? That's precious,' he said with a smile that reflected the warmth of the summer evening sun.

Rebekah felt her skin glowing and knew it was from more than the fresh air and exercise. As they walked on towards Brenscombe Hill, she pointed out the various islands in Poole Harbour, of which they had a virtual bird's eye view from this height.

'So somewhere across there is Rose Cottage on Brownsea Island, and beyond that, my bed in the Harbour Heights Hotel,' he said thoughtfully, and she briefly let her mind wander to what a night spent in his hotel room could be like.

As the walk route brought them back around into Corfe village, Paul admired the cute little thatched cottages – all made from Purbeck stone, as promised by Rebekah – and each sporting a remarkably small front door. They found their way into the

Greyhound Inn, Paul ducking under the low doorframe, and went through the stone-floored and timber-beamed main bar to the beer garden in the back where they could sit and look up into the ruined stone walls of the castle above them. They ordered their meals and drank deliciously cloudy Dorset apple cider while they waited.

'And when you're not busy doing historical, archival things,' Rebekah said, realising the cider had already affected her grasp on vocabulary somewhat, 'what else fills your time?'

She was expecting something to do with relationships and part of her was actually expecting the news that he had a wife and family in London. There was no reason why he shouldn't, after all. She was just a ranger whose door he had happened to knock on in the middle of the night, and no more than that. Just a bonus tour guide he'd spent the day with.

She froze as he studied her face and she felt the warmth of his eyes watching her. He picked up his cider and took a long draught before putting it down carefully on the beer mat, straightening it as he did so.

'I live alone in London. There's no one special in my life,' he said, and watched her to see her response. She smiled a little and nodded. She too lived a solitary life, with no one special. She knew exactly what he was telling her.

'But that doesn't mean I'm alone in the sad sense,' he went on. 'I keep pretty busy. Ah – here's something I haven't told you yet: I play violin,' he said with his eyebrows raised, expecting her comment.

'Really? Now that is something I would never have guessed. I'm not a bit musical myself, although I do love to listen. Do you play in an orchestra?' she asked.

'Regularly, I'm part of a small one yes: a chamber strings group. I'm one of the four violins. Nobody important,' he said with a wink. 'But occasionally, I join with others as and when needed, sometimes in a bigger orchestra or sometimes much smaller – just a quartet. So that's what generally fills my weekends and some of my evenings. And I practise several nights a week as well. I live in a detached house, so the noise doesn't bother anyone,' he added with a laugh, turning to thank the waitress who had placed their meals on the table before them.

'Did you study music as well as history, then?' she asked him.

'Yes, and no,' he said with a frown. 'I started a music degree – was accepted into the Royal College of Music in London, which was no mean feat. The audition process is one of the most rigorous in the world. And I studied hard for three years. But,' he said, with a deep sigh, and teasing his temples with his thumbs as if a pain lurked there, 'but in the summer holidays between my third and fourth years, my mum was diagnosed with cancer. I deferred my final year so I could spend more time with her.' He paused, but Rebekah knew there were no right words with which to fill the space.

'But she didn't recover. And afterwards, I just seemed to lose the joy, and couldn't find it again. Eventually, I had to choose something that I might make a living from, so I studied history, and here I am,' he said with a bright smile that belied the pain in his eyes.

'I'm so sorry, Paul. You've lost so much. But you didn't stop playing?'

'I did stop. For three whole years, I never picked up my violin. But then one day, I had just moved into a new flat, and everything was a mess. I had my violin in my hand, and before I realised what I was doing, I'd taken it out of its case, given it the tuning of its life, and was playing again. I'd grown rusty, naturally, but it all came back soon enough – as did the joy, at long last. But that took years.'

'You didn't want to go back and finish your music degree?' Rebekah asked, clearing her plate and taking a sip of cider.

'I did think about it, but by then I needed to concentrate on paying the rent and I just didn't have the time. But I was well enough regarded to wiggle my way into some community players' groups, and eventually into some more highbrow quartets and so on. But it is just for fun – I'm not considered professional, of course, without the degree and the status that comes with it.'

'And I suppose a violin is easy to carry around London on the Tube?' Rebekah asked.

'Absolutely. I'm so glad I'm not a double bass player – that's such a weight to heft around. You can't even fit it into a normal car.' He laughed.

'What's the next thing you'll be performing?' asked Rebekah.

'I'm doing a concert of the *Four Seasons* in a couple of weeks, just a smallish affair in some function rooms in Westminster,' he added nonchalantly.

'Oh wow! That sounds incredible to this little Australian,' she joked. 'How wonderful. I'm not at all arty but I do enjoy watching and listening to anything that anyone else does in the form of arts. And Westminster!'

'Yes, I suppose it does all sound a bit romantic to someone from as far away as Australia. But do you know, I was disappointed that my first university experience was only in Kensington? I grew up in Notting Hill and so I didn't even get to leave home to go and study. Most of my schoolfriends went further afield for university, and never lived at home again. I just caught the Tube in!'

'It all sounds like something from a very romantic movie script to me.' Rebekah laughed. 'Did you know we have Shakespeare plays on the island? They hold them every summer, and it's *As You Like It* this year. That's something of a romantic script too, I suppose.'

'Yes, I did see the set-up for all of that yesterday. Crumbs, was that only yesterday? It seems weeks ago now,' he said, confirming what Rebekah had been thinking all evening.

'They do a different play every year. Next Saturday night is opening night,' she added, but the moment the words had left her mouth, she regretted it. She felt that it sounded like she was asking him to join her, and she really didn't want to sound that forward. He ate on in silence for a while, catching up with Rebekah, and she would have given a ransom to know what he was thinking.

Eventually, she broke the silence.

'What time are you heading off to London in the morning?'

'I have to be out of the hotel room by ten, so the plan is to just drive home in the morning. I have a rehearsal at four in the afternoon, so I need to be back by then,' he said with a look that she took to mean he regretted it and would rather spend the day with her. She only thought for a second before launching out with her hopes.

'That's a shame. We could have come to see the castle tomorrow if you were free,' she said, wondering how fixed his 4 p.m. rehearsal was.

'So many things to stay here in Dorset for, but I suppose I'll just have to leave them for another time.'

Rebekah nodded, accepting that this was it. He would be travelling home in the morning, and she would likely never see him again.

She noticed a couple who were seated a few tables away. They sat opposite each other and as they ate, they continually but subtly touched each other. One would reach out to stroke the other's hand, or their knees would touch under the table. As they put down their cutlery, they reached across the table, holding hands. She watched Paul finishing up his meal and wondered what it would feel like to hold his hand. To have him reach out to touch her. She sighed. But she didn't want to be in a relationship anyway.

Paul put down his knife and fork and finished his cider. He glanced at his watch.

'Talking of the time, we should probably go and finish our walk and head back to the car park. How long is the drive home via the ferry?' he asked.

'Yes, we ought to get going. But the trip back will only take half an hour or so, depending on where the chain ferry is when we arrive.'

They walked through the village and around the base of the castle, then back to the car. The ride through Studland and to the chain ferry was strangely silent, considering the free and easy way they'd been chatting all day. Rebekah was not ready to say goodbye but didn't know how to tell him that. The ferry was waiting for them on the Studland side when they arrived, with plenty of room for them on board, so there was no delay at all. And in no time, they were on the Haven side of the harbour entrance, and Paul had pulled in beside the ferry jetty, with forty minutes to spare before the eleven o'clock ferry was due to leave.

'I can't leave you here in the dark on your own,' he said, concern in his voice. 'Will the bar still be open?' He glanced back towards the Haven Hotel. 'How about a nightcap?'

Even though the summer evening had been fine, the air was cooling fast and so they found soft armchairs in the lounge to relax with a cup of hot chocolate and a brandy each. Rebekah was burning to ask how she might contact him again, but fought with herself to keep quiet. She knew how off-putting she always found it when a guy seemed more keen on her than she was on him, and she did not want to be that girl.

And yet when the time came to walk back to the jetty, she felt his hand touch the small of her back lightly as he held the door open for her. The touch – the first time they had touched since that kiss on her cheek last night – sent a shockwave tingling up her spine that made her gasp. At the jetty, they stood face to face and both spoke at once when it was time to say goodbye.

'It's been lovely meeting you, Rebekah,' he said as she'd blurted, 'Time to be off then,' and immediately regretted it. He nodded, curtly, smiled tightly, and held a hand up to wave briefly.

'Thank you for looking after me so well, for saving me last night and for showing me around. I wish I could stay longer.' And then he was gone.

As Rebekah caught the ferry home to the island, went through the mundane business of collecting her groceries from reception, and trudged back up the hill to Rose Cottage, she couldn't shake the gloomy sense that she'd lost something precious. Lying in bed that night, recalling the last twenty-four hours of her life, she'd even begun to wonder if she could have imagined the whole thing.

And that had been five days ago. Now it was Thursday evening, and the routine of her week had made last weekend almost disappear, except for the sense in her soul there was something she was missing.

Rebekah checked that the last island visitors were ready to board the final ferry back to Poole Quay and watched the *Island Maid* ferry come into the little island dock, empty of passengers as expected. On Saturday night, this ferry would be full of playgoers on their way to the opening night of *As You Like it*.

After the last visitor was aboard, she turned back inside and checked the diary for the next day. Friday: Ben would be volunteering. Last Friday, with that unwanted hug, had been so awkward, and now she wondered if there was a way to avoid seeing him tomorrow. What if he started pushing for more? Perhaps he would bring her mussels again, or maybe a crab this time. *Full circle*, she thought, and found her thoughts drifting again to Paul when she heard a small movement behind her.

She turned and started as the embodiment of her imagination stood before her. Paul was carrying an old, brown, leather satchel, slung across his body, with a small wheelie suitcase at his side, the size you can take on board a plane. Big enough for a weekend away. He wore navy-blue shorts, a loosely buttoned, pale-pink, linen shirt, and tan-brown deck shoes. The whole impression gave off a mixture of tourist, travelling businessman and island hopper. He looked anguished as he waited for her to speak. She couldn't.

'Hello, Rebekah.' He paused. Still, she stayed mute. 'I bought two tickets to the play, just in case you might like to join me,' he said, motioning with his head in the direction of the Church Field where he knew the stage to be. 'And I knew I'd need some-where to stay, so I've booked the little Custom House cottage here on the island. Apparently, there was a last-minute cancellation, and I was lucky to get in,' he went on, waiting for her response. She still had no words. 'I didn't want to assume, you see,' he said, now looking for all the world like he'd rather be somewhere else. Anywhere else.

Rebekah watched the *Island Maid* chug away and looked back to Paul. All the words he'd spoken seemed to come through to her mind at once and she had to unjumble them before she could speak. And then she smiled.

'I didn't think I would ever see you again,' Rebekah said, beaming. 'I'm so glad you're here. There's something I forgot to do, the last time I saw you,' she said, and Paul crinkled his brow in confusion.

She took the few steps that separated them and brought her face so close to his that she could hear his breath. She reached up and, before she could change her mind, she took his face in her hands and stood on tiptoes to kiss him firmly on the mouth. His expression changed from anguished confusion, to stunned shock, and to pure joy in a series of exquisitely tiny movements. Rebekah pulled back, just a few inches, and searched his eyes for his response.

15

POOLE – MARCH 1941

Peggy could not help but enjoy the bounce in her step as she smiled her way in to work on the first Monday morning of spring. This past weekend had been a delightfully fresh start and she was breathless with excitement over what might lie ahead for her. The war clouds were still gloomy, and the night air was still freezing cold, especially out in the Anderson shelter. There were restrictions on everything from eggs to soap and even newspapers, and there had been another air raid last night, but the war could not steal from her the joy that she'd discovered in becoming Darrell's girl.

After she hurriedly left Charlie to finish locking up the launch on Saturday morning, she trotted back home and had a cup of tea with her mother and Molly at the kitchen table, then spent some time choosing what she ought to wear for her day out with Darrell. The choice was limited to three different outfits, but it still took her some time. She changed into her bottle-green day dress with the bow that tied at the neck, and pulled on warm, black, woollen stockings, sitting on the bed to buckle her more sensible brown shoes, in case of a long walk.

She almost ran down the stairs to open the front door when she heard the doorbell ring just after ten o'clock, her blonde curls bouncing all the way. Darrell had brought her a small bunch of primroses and daffodils, a bright gift of spring that shone like the summer sun that would be back in a few months' time.

'Oh, how lovely! Thank you, Darrell. Spring daffodils – I do believe these are the first ones I've seen. Such a sunny, happy flower, don't you think? Come on through to the kitchen and I'll put them in water,' Peggy said as he bent to give her a kiss and hand over his gift.

'Are your parents about?' Darrell asked, peering into the front room as he passed the door.

'Mother is out shopping, or at least looking to see if there is anything to buy, up the High Street, and Father is down the back on the shore, fiddling with the boat.'

'I should like him to know I'm here with you, Peggy. I'll nip out and have a word for a minute,' he said, pushing open the back door while Peggy filled a jug and arranged the pretty, yellow flowers, setting them in the middle of the kitchen table.

* * *

Once outside in the back garden, Darrell followed the little winding path past the rabbit hutch and through the gate in the low back fence leading onto the narrow, shaley beach, which was covered in upturned dinghies. A wooden frame stood covered in nets that were drying and a gull sat atop the frame as if to guard it, knowing the nets to be the bringer of all kinds of good food scraps to this little beach. The wind was chilly, but the sky was filled with white clouds and the sizeable patches of pale blue between them, not like the leaden grey blanket that threatened rain or snow and had seemed to be their permanent shelter for the past two months.

Darrell walked across the stony sand, crunching cockle shells beneath his polished, black boots, towards Mr Symonds, who was kneeling on the ground with a paintbrush in his hand, adding another layer of sky-blue paint to a small, wooden dinghy.

'Good morning, Mr Symonds, sir,' Darrell called brightly. Peggy's father looked up in surprise at being greeted so formally.

'Darrell, boy! Nice to see you. Not seen you down the pub so much this week, have we? 'Spect you been busy up there in your beautiful machine,' he said with a nod to the skies and just a hint of envy, or was it only admiration?

'We've been very busy this last week, but I do have the weekend off,' Darrell said, then hesitated, wondering if this was the segue he was looking for or if he was jumping the gun. Mr Symonds simply nodded and returned to his painting.

Darrell cleared his throat and took a step closer.

'Actually, it's about the weekend I wanted to talk. Well, not just the weekend, but some of what I'd like to do this weekend...' He faltered and saw the frown on Peggy's father's face. The old man must be wondering what this young idiot was twittering on about.

Darrell summoned the courage he knew he had aplenty when he needed it.

'I would like very much to take Peggy out with me. More often. To walk out with her, as it were. If you and Mrs Symonds were agreeable, that is,' he finally said.

Mr Symonds put down the brush, resting it carefully on the top of the paint tin, wiped his hands on his overalls, and stood up.

'I should think that would be all right, son. We saw you last night, of course,' he said with a wink and a laugh as Darrell turned a pale shade of grey. 'Our bedroom is at the front,' Mr

Symonds explained. 'And the wife don't sleep until the girls are indoors. She don't miss much, and had a peep out the window, when you two lovebirds was saying your farewells last night.' He chuckled.

Darrell winced and covered his face, but then laughed despite himself.

'I'll remember that, then. Thanks for the tip,' he said. 'No kissing on the doorstep from now on, sir.'

* * *

Back in the kitchen, Peggy had been watching him from the back window.

'What was all that about, then?' she asked Darrell as he stepped back inside.

'Just making sure the old man is all right with me taking you out, that's all. Seems he was expecting the question.' He laughed and explained to a very embarrassed young woman that their first kiss had been witnessed by her parents.

'Oh my word, I'll never be able to look them in the eye again,' said Peggy.

'I shouldn't worry. He seems comfortable enough with the idea.'

'So, what shall we do today, Darrell? Because I know one thing for sure: I'm not waiting here until Mother gets back in, now I know what they saw us doing last night!' Peggy said.

'What about that lovely castle over on the other side of the harbour – I've seen it's in ruins of course, from the air. But one of the lads said it was a nice place for a picnic,' said Darrell.

'Ooh, yes, I've not been to Corfe Castle in ages. Bit chilly for a picnic though. We could have a meal in the Greyhound and then go for a walk around the castle. It would be lovely and warm in the pub by the fire. There's a bus that goes around Wareham way we can catch,' Peggy said, reaching for her warm, black coat and the little hat she liked to wear on a slant.

Darrell took her arm and let Peggy lead the way to the bus station, where the pair boarded the green bus headed for Swanage via Wareham and Corfe Castle. They sat up the top, in the front seats for the best view, and ate a packet of humbugs that Darrell had pulled from his pocket when they sat down.

As the bus approached Wareham, Peggy noticed Darrell's interest in the town.

'We're coming up to the quayside soon, and if you look to your left, you'll see where the river meanders away down towards the harbour. There's a pretty little church you can see the tower of just through there,' said Peggy, pointing out the bus window. 'It has a square tower, like our St James's in Poole does, but this one is much older.'

Darrell nodded but his attention was on the boats moored up at the quay and further down the river. Within moments, they'd passed over the bridge and the river was out of sight again.

'And this is the River Frome, the one that has its mouth in the harbour, not far from our base in Hamworthy?' he asked Peggy thoughtfully, and she wondered why he seemed so interested.

'That's right. I could bring you up here for a jolly one day, perhaps, in Dad's dinghy, if you'd like that?' Peggy asked hopefully.

'How long would it take to row all this way? That would take hours, wouldn't it? Something like your BOAC launch would be better for the job, I'd think,' he asked.

'Row? Not likely!' Peggy laughed. 'I'd row you to Brownsea and back for fun, no trouble, but for a trip up to Wareham, I'd put Dad's Seagull on the back.'

Now he looked more confused than ever, and she laughed at the stupefied look on his face.

'Not a real seagull, silly! It's an outboard motor. They're made right here in Poole, you know. "The best outboard for the world" they say about them, and I have to say they are pretty reliable. A Seagull on a dinghy and we'd be up here to Wareham quay in no time,' Peggy said with confidence. 'Now that's something to look forward to for when the weather is a bit warmer, hey? A picnic on the river, just like Ratty and Mole in *The Wind in the Willows* – messing about in a boat together.' She beamed.

The rest of the journey from Wareham to Corfe was then taken up with an explanation of Peggy's favourite childhood book, which she could not believe Darrell had never even heard of, let alone read.

'Don't your Australian mothers read to you kids over there, then?' she teased him. 'I think we should slip a few good books into the cargo on one of the flying boats headed to Sydney to improve the education of those poor Australian children,' and she threw her head back to laugh heartily as he tickled her in a mock attack.

In the Greyhound pub, they ate their hot dinner of lamb stew and dumplings, with bread and 'butter' pudding to follow, and afterwards, thankful that the weather had stayed fine, walked up the grassy hill to the castle ruins where Peggy was pleased to show Darrell a glimpse of Poole Harbour from a completely different aspect.

Later that night, they walked hand in hand to the dance hall, and meandered home as slowly as possible afterwards, careful to say goodnight properly, well out of sight of Mr and Mrs Symonds' bedroom window. And on Sunday, he came to meet her after church and walked her home along the quay, where her mother asked him inside for dinner with the family.

In just two days, Darrell had become a firm favourite with the whole family and now, walking back into work on Monday morning, Peggy knew, without doubt, that her life had changed forever. And she was about to find out that her life would change in ways she could never have expected.

As Peggy dropped in to the harbour master's office to pick up the launch key, Patricia came out to meet her.

'Peggy, would you mind just stepping into the office, please? There's someone here to meet you. From London,' Patricia said with meaning. Peggy had never been asked to meet anyone from BOAC outside of those few people who were running the show here in Poole, and she wondered quite what this could be about. She straightened her cap and walked into the back office, fully expecting to meet someone else wearing some form of the BOAC uniform. But the gentleman who stood to greet her was in no uniform at all.

'Miss Symonds, thank you for coming,' he said brusquely as Pat left the room, closing the door behind her. 'Please, do sit down.'

Peggy sat in the chair opposite him, eyes wide in wonder.

'I'm sorry if this comes as something of a surprise, but the government has need of your services. I am about to share with you information that is top secret. It is not to be shared with a single soul outside this room – ever. I do not have to share this information with you, and if you choose, you may leave now and remain in blissful ignorance. However, the war office feels that you may be able to help us in a matter of extreme importance to the safety of this country.' At this, he sat back in his chair, folded his hands in his lap and watched her. Intently.

Peggy blinked, her mouth open, a feeling of utter stupefaction flooding her mind.

'I'm sorry,' she said at last, 'but who are you?'

'Oh, my apologies, Miss Symonds. I cannot tell you my full name, owing to the department for which I speak, but you may know me as Fletcher.'

She nodded dumbly. 'Thank you, Mr Fletcher. And what is this information you have for me?'

He continued. 'If we go ahead and I release this information to you, you will be bound for the rest of your life by the Official Secrets Act, and to that end, you would sign this document,' he said sliding a single piece of paper on the desk a little closer to her.

Peggy was stunned into absolute silence, and realised at length that her jaw was hanging open in a most undignified manner. She snapped it shut and stole a quick glance at the door, wondering what Pat was doing right now. Did Pat even know what this was about? Peggy thought. She looked again at the contract and back at Mr Fletcher.

'If I don't help, will people be in danger?' Peggy asked, eventually.

'Very likely, yes. And we believe that you can help us alleviate that danger and remove a problem that is a threat to the security of the nation,' he said.

'Is there any particular danger to me, or my family?' she asked, concern making her voice crack a little.

He thought hard for a few moments.

'I suppose it is possible, but I don't believe it very likely, no,' he said at length.

'Well, then, I cannot see any reason why I should object. If I can do any more than I already am doing to help us win this war and protect our nation, I can do it. I *must* do it, I think,' she said, quietly.

Mr Fletcher smiled slightly. 'Thank you, Miss Symonds – Peggy, may I call you Peggy?'

She nodded her assent.

Fletcher bent over the desk, took out his pen and briefly went through the legal requirements of signing the document that signified Peggy was now bound by the Official Secrets Act. Forever. And then he relaxed back into his chair a little and explained what he wanted of her.

'Let me explain the issue in clear terms, Peggy,' he had begun. 'A few days ago, we heard from one of our regular agents who operates here in the harbour – don't be surprised, Peggy, you will probably never find out who that is – that there is a member of BOAC staff who is suspected of not being exactly who he says he is. The information came to the operative from a woman working on the quayside here. She tells us there is a gentleman working on the launches who claims to be someone that he is not. We know him as Charlie Edwards.' Fletcher paused to take a sip from his coffee cup and allow Peggy to take on the information, which seemed so ludicrous, she almost laughed.

'Charlie seems perfectly genuine to me, sir,' Peggy said, feeling suddenly protective towards her new colleague. 'Surely this is a mistake?'

'It could well be, but there are a few things we would like to know. When he arrived here, Major Carter checked his papers in the usual way and nothing seemed amiss. But after we had received the alert that he may not be whom he claims to be, we put in some enquiries in the docks at London. It does appear that Mr Edwards' true identity is in question, and as we know that you are forming a friendship with him...' Peggy began to object at this presumption, but Fletcher simply held up his palm to her and continued, 'we need you to find out all you can about him. Get to know him – in every way. Become as close to him as you feel able, and get to the bottom of this for us.'

'But, you can't mean that I should be seen to be courting Charlie, sir?' she pleaded.

'Is that too much to ask, do you feel?' he asked.

'I am already courting an airman from the RAAF. What on earth will he think of me?' She felt tears beginning to prickle her throat.

'Miss Symonds, ask yourself this: if you are able to help your country uncover a spy, and possibly save every one of your fellow Englishmen from the threat of Hitler, is it too much to ask that your love affair with a visiting airman might be put on hold? Hmm?' His tone was demeaning as well as demanding, and Peggy knew that she was fighting a losing battle. He did not care if she lost Darrell because she was saving her country. She would simply have to trust that all would be well. Trust and hope.

* * *

As Peggy walked across the quay towards the launch that morning, she prayed that this nightmare would be over soon.

'Morning, Peggy,' said Charlie cheerily when he met her at the launch. 'You're looking very well today. Have you had a nice time with that young airman of yours?' he asked, and she started a little at this question – too personal for Charlie to ask his new superior. Suddenly, everything in Peggy's world had changed. Was Charlie who he seemed to be? Was anyone she knew in Poole to be trusted? She had to question everything. Report everything. Trust no one.

'Yes, thank you, Charlie. And what have you been up to?' she asked, just a little more curtly than usual.

'Nothing much. Just pottering about,' he replied absently.

'We've a busy day ahead today. We're taking the crew and passengers from the *Clare* into Salterns Marina and then running back to the quay where we will be picking up some VIPs from Major Carter at the pottery. They'll have come in direct from the night train, apparently, and we are needed to drive them up to the Harbour Heights Hotel. There are three people and each needs to be in a separate car, for some strange reason,' Peggy told Charlie as they set off towards the main runway.

After the launch trip was complete, they walked down to the pottery where Rose Stevens stood waiting for them beside two cars.

'You and Charlie are to take one car, Peggy, and I'll take the other. Major Carter has gone ahead to the train station in his private car. We will meet him there, then we'll take the three passengers separately to the Harbour Heights Hotel,' Rose explained.

'Who are they, Rose? This all seems like a lot of trouble.'

'You'll see,' Rose replied with a face that told Peggy she was in for a surprise.

She thought again about her mission, and wondered if Charlie should even be here, as new as he was to the team, though she was determined to prove Fletcher wrong about him.

'Do we need Charlie too? I'm sure there's plenty of work for him to handle on the boat and I can drive quite well on my own,' she offered.

'It will be good for Charlie to see some more of what we do, Peggy. No problem to have him along with you,' said Rose lightly.

Peggy sighed deeply, feeling the weight of her new knowledge.

When they arrived at the train station, Major Carter was talking with a very recognisable figure. Peggy couldn't believe her eyes.

'Is that...? It can't be,' she said in awe as a familiarly stooped figure in a long coat, a bowler hat and smoking a cigar shuffled from the platform and into the back of Major Carter's car. Another vaguely familiar gentleman was directed to Rose's vehicle and a third, whom Peggy did not recognise at all, was led towards the back seat of the car she would be driving. Peggy sat in the driver's seat and Rose ducked her head into the window and spoke in a hushed tone, giving Peggy the only information she was going to get.

'You'll recognise the prime minister, who is going with Major Carter, Peggy, and I'll be taking General de Gaulle. Your passenger is Mr Menzies, the visiting Australian prime minister, but it is enough to call him "sir",' she said, then disappeared back to her own vehicle. Peggy was so stunned, she wondered if she would remember how to drive.

'Women drivers, hey?' Mr Menzies asked in a tone and accent that was instantly recognisable to Peggy, having spent so much time with Darrell.

'Yes, Mr Menzies, sir, I'm afraid so. They've issued us with all the right moving parts to operate a clutch successfully,' she said, biting her tongue the moment the words had left her mouth. But she had nothing to fear, and her passenger laughed heartily, understanding her sense of humour perfectly as she set off. Charlie remained silent in the front seat, seeming even more stunned than Peggy by the presence of international dignitaries.

As the motorcade drove away from the station, and everyone's eyes had been on the VIPs and the cars, nobody noticed the lone man who stood leaning against the wall of the train station, his hat pulled low and his face hidden as he held his cigarette close. He watched them leave, then checked his watch and walked off into town quickly.

When they arrived at the Harbour Heights, and she and Charlie stepped out to help with the doors, she heard the unmistakably French accent of the leader of the Free French, General de Gaulle.

'Goodness gracious, Rose, whatever is going on?' Peggy whispered when the gentlemen had been ushered inside the hotel. Peggy was stunned to think that she, a simple fisherman's daughter from Poole, had just been in the presence of the prime ministers of England and Australia and the man who ought to be prime minister of France.

'We have no idea, Peggy – ours is not to wonder, just to do our bit with the passenger services, be they by land, sea, or sky. Now remember, both of you: you've seen nothing and no one of any interest, rightio?' Rose asked them, tapping the side of her nose. 'Loose lips and all that.'

'No problem at all, Rose. Passengers is all they are, just like the others,' said Charlie confidently. Peggy simply nodded, with an expression that showed exactly how stunned she was, and why she could not speak, and now she wondered how on earth she was ever going to keep this quiet from Molly and her parents. And Darrell.

Later that night, after the day that Peggy knew had changed her life forever, she poured herself a cup of tea and took it upstairs to her room where she sat at her dressing table and stared out of her small bedroom window, which looked over Poole Harbour and towards Brownsea. She thought about the danger there was to each one of them all the time that Hitler was at large. Her brother Samuel, Molly's husband Bill, Darrell – all of them. If there was a risk that there might be a spy in Poole, she had to do everything in her power to stop them. And she knew, then, that she had the strength to do it.

16

BROWNSEA ISLAND – JULY 1998

Rebekah would never forget her first kiss with Paul. She had reached up to his lips on pure instinct, and with no thought process whatsoever. She had no expectations. But what happened next would explode sensations and desires she hadn't even imagined could still linger within her, after the hell she'd been through with Andy.

Paul stood perfectly still, allowing her to hold the kiss for as long as she wanted. But when she pulled away, after what seemed a lifetime of connection, and looked into his soul for his response, he kissed her back. He dropped the satchel on the ground beside him, gently rested his hands on her shoulders, and bent down to touch his lips against hers, lightly at first.

But when she sighed, there was a hint of a groan in her voice, a sound that opened the floodgates for Paul. She had stepped back and found herself leaning on the wall and he'd pushed forward, kissing her with an urgency and strength of passion that spoke of nearly lost chances, and hope found again. And when he finally pulled back and they eased apart, Rebekah felt as though the last five days had simply melted away.

'Welcome to my island,' she said with a cheeky smile, and led him by the hand through reception to where he could collect his keys to the cottage for the weekend.

'You've chosen the cutest little cottage to stay in,' she said, after explaining to the accommodation manager that Paul was a friend of hers. 'It was only an office and a couple of storerooms back in the day when it operated as a Custom House, but now it's a tiny studio cottage with a little kitchen and bathroom. It's perfect for one or two people for a few nights,' she explained.

'Apparently, I was very lucky to get in on a cancellation at such short notice, as it's always booked out for months ahead,' Paul said as Rebekah unlocked the front door for him. 'Oh wow, look at that view!' he cried, dropping his bag and walking straight to the picture window.

The cottage looked out onto the Haven side of the harbour entrance, and the water was busy with yachts and motorboats coming and going. The chain ferry across to Studland was on its way back and one of the huge cross-channel ferries was out in the bay, approaching the harbour entrance. Just outside the front door was a little table and two chairs, perfect for an evening meal with a glass of wine.

Rebekah still held the keys and watched as he took it all in, waiting for him to make the next move. He spun around, as if reading her thoughts.

'Rebekah, do you have plans for dinner tonight? I've brought food. And wine. And if you'd like to join me, that would be wonderful,' he said, watching her face eagerly for her response.

Rebekah had about a thousand questions. When had he decided to come back to Poole? Why hadn't he been in touch earlier, if he'd been thinking of her? What would he have done if his presence had been unwelcome? Did he have work to do at the pottery, or was this trip just about seeing her? And, would she be sleeping in her cottage or his tonight?

She must have paused for a few seconds longer than he expected, because the eagerness in his look turned to anguish once more. She reminded herself to speak, and made a mental note to stop doing this to him.

'Sorry, Paul. What was the question?' she said, trying for a light and cheery smile.

'Would you have dinner with me tonight? Here? Please?' he asked, sweeping his arm around to take in the kitchen, the dining table, and the outdoor setting beyond the picture window.

Rebekah eyed his simple luggage and complete lack of grocery bags with a frown. Either he was into minimalist food or something was missing. 'Where's the food you brought?' she asked, wondering if he'd accidentally left something on the ferry.

'Ah, yes – I should check on that. If everything went to plan, then this fridge should have everything we need,' he said peering behind the fridge door and then holding it wide with an exultant grin on his face.

'Voila!' he said with a flourish. The fully stocked fridge was bursting with fresh produce, wine, milk, juice, pastries, and some paper-wrapped parcels that most likely contained meat or fish.

'How did you do this?' she asked, incredulous.

'Magic,' he said, with a laugh. 'Well, not magic exactly, but it did take some effort: I learnt last weekend that your friends on the ferry don't mind carrying the odd bag or two of groceries, and I knew I wouldn't have time myself. So, I made a few phone calls, and here we are. All organised. And I have to say that, so far, everything is going very well indeed.'

Ten minutes later, they'd agreed that Rebekah would go home to shower and change, swapping her somewhat muddy workday ranger's clothes for something a little more suited to dinner, and come back to the cottage for seven o'clock.

On the walk up the hill to Rose Cottage, Rebekah felt like skipping and couldn't wipe the smile from her face. Just an hour ago, she'd been lamenting the fact that she would never see him again, and now Paul was right here on the island and cooking her dinner.

When she opened the front door, Rebekah was surprised to see an envelope resting against the wax-covered wine bottle she used as a candelabra on the dining table.

She frowned, wondering what it might be; the staff from reception had access to the spare set of keys to the cottage, but nobody usually came in here without mentioning something to her, and her mail was generally kept for her at the office. The envelope was marked simply in a neat hand, *For Rebekah* on the front, with no markings on the back. She tore the envelope open and found inside one ticket to the opening night of the play. There was a piece of notepaper, folder into four, attached to the ticket.

Dear Rebekah,

I wanted to ask if you'd like to come with me, but I didn't want to come across as pushy, so here is a ticket for you. I'll be there too – but no pressure. Just enjoy the play.

From Ben, with love. xx

'Oh Ben,' she said and bit her lip. He was such a sweet guy, and there was nothing wrong with him. It was just that she wasn't interested. She realised now that she'd thought she wasn't interested in anyone, but Paul had changed all that. And now that she thought about it, Ben seemed to bring her a gift of something or other nearly every week, and had been doing so all summer. And he'd worked out what she liked, what she wanted. He even knew that she would want to see the play, but wasn't interested in a date. She rubbed her eyes and pinched the brow of her nose, sighed, and dropped the note and ticket on the table.

Right now, she had a date with someone she very much wanted to see, much more than Ben. Someone she'd been longing to see for five days now.

She took off her boots and went upstairs, dropping all her dirty clothes on the bathroom floor and stepping into the steaming shower. She felt sure that she had never led Ben on. She was just friendly with him, as she was everyone else. It wasn't her fault that he'd seen more in their friendship than there really was. Ben was a nice guy. Quite nice-looking. Kind. Helpful. He'd grown up here in Poole and made his life here, and there was nothing wrong with that – she doubted that if she had grown up here, she would ever have left either, but... *But what, Rebekah?* she asked herself. Ben was not Paul.

Paul had come into her life with excitement from that first knock on the door last Friday night. Paul was from far away. He was a talented musician. He was deep. He had something attractive about the way he didn't try, and he was spontaneous. He excited her. Rebekah sat on her bed, towelling her hair dry, and reached into her drawer for underwear but her hands found a book resting on the bedside table first. She dropped the towel on the floor and found she was holding her copy of *Far from the Madding Crowd*. She turned it over and reread the blurb of the book she'd read dozens of times now. Was Ben her dependable Gabriel Oak and Paul her dangerous Frank Troy? Ben was certainly stable and predictable, whereas Paul was new and exciting. And, just like Bathsheba, she didn't need either of them. But, despite the risks she knew so well from her past experiences, something inside her wanted the thrill.

Rebekah chucked the book on the bed and scoffed at herself for being so ridiculous. Gabriel and Frank were nothing but fictional characters and Paul was the only man whose absence had made her feel sad. Ben... well, it was rough for him that he was attached to her, but she would have to help him deal with that. Right now, she had a date with a man she hoped very much to be seeing a whole lot more of.

As Rebekah approached the front door to the Custom House cottage just before seven o'clock, she paused against the castle wall to smooth the blue dress she'd chosen, which had ridden up as she'd walked, and changed her flat walking shoes for the sandals with little heels.

At the front door, she dropped the walking shoes to one side and knocked. When Paul opened the door, his face lit up like the sun, and all the cloudy doubts blown in by Ben's gift wafted away on the breeze.

'I brought you this,' she said, holding up a chilled bottle of Chianti. 'I know you have plenty of wine here, but it didn't feel right to arrive empty-handed.'

In reply, he took the wine in one hand, and Rebekah's hand in the other, pulling her gently over the threshold and into his arms for a kiss it seemed he had been waiting hours for.

'Hungry?' he asked her, when they finally pulled apart.

'Strangely, yes. Though I would like a lot more of that later.' She giggled.

He served them salmon, cooked with spinach and potatoes, and set with a cream and egg sauce, topped with melted cheese, and then to follow he produced individual chocolate mousse bowls, unashamedly bought ready made from Marks and

Spencer's. They sat outside on the little alfresco setting for dinner, enjoying the warmth of the summer evening, and moved indoors to the settee that faced out to sea through the picture window for dessert, which he served with coffee. Rebekah rested against the arm of the sofa with her feet tucked beneath her and, after she'd finished her coffee, accepted his offer of another glass of wine.

'So, you've heard every single detail of what I've done since you last saw me, Paul, and now you know everything I've been thinking about,' she said with a teasing smile, alluding to the fact that she'd told him, without holding back, how much she'd been missing him. 'But what have you been doing? When did you decide to come back?' she quizzed him.

'I decided to come back at approximately three minutes past eleven last Saturday night, as I was watching the ferry take you away and back to the island,' he said.

'But you didn't watch me go; you walked off to your car,' she said, bemused.

'I did go back to my car, you're right. But I moved it just a little way around the corner. I got out again and watched your ferry leave. And as you left, I knew I had to see you again. I drove back to the hotel and went up to my room, poured myself another drink and sat in that window looking out across the blackness of the harbour to the few twinkling lights on Brownsea Island. I waited until I saw a set of lights high on the hill go out, and I knew you'd gone to bed. I pictured you sleeping. I regretted the kiss goodnight I hadn't given you, and I knew I had to come back. I even thought about not going home on Sunday morning, you know,' he said.

'Really? Would you have come back onto the island?' she asked, setting down her wine and leaning towards him.

'I might have done. I didn't check out of the hotel until the last minute, and I drove down to the Haven and watched the island ferry come and go a few times. But the longer I watched, the more I doubted myself. I had no way of knowing if you wanted to see me again, and I was terrified that if I just turned up, you'd be embarrassed. It could have been really awkward.'

'You would have made my day if you had come over, you know?' she said.

'Yes, I understand that now,' he said, reaching out to stroke her ankle. She put her hand on his and squeezed it gently. 'But last weekend, it was all so strange, so unexpected. I've never done anything like this before, Rebekah, not with anyone. So, I drove home, unpacked my bags, sorted out a few papers from the week's work, and then went off to my rehearsal at four o'clock. And while we were practising, I was reliving our walk and the dinner and how I had told you all about the violin and my mum, and everything. And I just wanted to be with you again. And I carried on working, eating, sleeping, rehearsing on Monday, Tuesday, Wednesday.

'This morning, I woke up thinking about the island, and the play this weekend, and about you. And something just clicked. I decided I was coming and made all the phone calls I needed to make, while I packed a bag, and closed off a few loose ends. I explained to my client that I needed to go back to Poole to see to a few more artefacts at the pottery – and I do, in fact – but the only thing I really wanted to do was to see you. To find out. To hear from you if I have any kind of a chance.'

Rebekah watched him as he fought to control emotions that were clearly bubbling just under the surface of his very calm and smooth veneer. She slid off the sofa and knelt on the floor in front of him, taking both his hands into hers. The light had grown dim inside the cottage, apart from the warm glow of the candles he'd lit and the twinkling reflection of the harbour lights that played on the whitewashed walls. She took a deep breath.

'Paul, I should probably tell you that before I met you last Friday night, the last thing on my mind was ever getting into a place where I let a man in so close that I made myself vulnerable. I've been hurt very badly by a selfish bastard who thought he could control me. And I felt stupid for falling for it, even though I grew up watching my mum live alone after she'd been through the same thing. Both she and Aunty Peggy survived quite well without a man in their lives, so I've been trying to work out what it is you've been doing to me. It's strange, but I need you to know that I've been willing you to come and step back into my world, with almost every step I've taken since I saw you last Saturday night. I don't understand this at all. I'm really not good at relationships, and thought I would never welcome one again, and yet I've never wanted anything more than this. I'm frightened, because I'm probably going to get this wrong, but I'm choosing to believe that this is a good thing. And I trust you. Do you understand what a big thing that is for me?'

Paul reached out and stroked her face, gentle as a feather, and seemed to be peering deep into her soul, as if his gaze might find her scars and heal them.

'Rebekah, I promise that I will never do anything to hurt you. Thank you for trusting me. I won't let you down.'

She responded by falling towards him and kissing him hungrily. 'I don't know what you've done to me.' She laughed, and his smile broadened, deepening the crinkles around his eyes, which glistened now. 'But whatever it is, I don't want it to stop.'

He squeezed her hands tightly and bent down to kiss her again, until she pulled back and stood, still holding his hands.

'It's getting late,' she said, looking at the clock on the wall. 'I think we should be getting to bed.'

He gave her a confused look, as he too glanced at the clock. It was only half past nine, and whilst the mid-summer sun had just set, there was still plenty of light in the sky.

But in response, she simply smiled, and led him towards the soft and welcoming bed that was snuggled at the back of the cottage.

17

BROWNSEA ISLAND – JULY 1998

Rebekah tried hard to stay nestled in the delicious dream she'd been having. The details were already flying away like a will-o'-the-wisp, something she could sense and almost see but was unable to grasp fully. There was joy and comfort and a delicious sensation of coming home, and of rest and the feeling that all her happy nerve strings were being strummed and plucked by the skilful fingers of a harpist. She could smell coffee and hear the sounds of someone moving about and then the other nerves all electrified and jumped into action: she was not alone.

She opened her eyes wide and found herself staring unexpectedly at a blank wall she didn't recognise. Spinning over in the bed, under the voluminously fluffy, duck-down quilt, she saw where she was, and her dreams and memories became one. She had not dreamt the wonderful night she'd just spent in this cottage, in this bed, with Paul. Her new lover. She chuckled and then gasped as Paul came around the corner from the kitchen, carrying two mugs of tea and wearing – nothing.

Last night, she'd barely taken the time to think about how he looked naked. The urgency with which she had decided she needed to take him to bed had shocked her almost as much as it had him. And what had followed was a night of divine sex and whisperings in the dark.

She sat up and pulled the sheet up to cover her a little, feeling ever so slightly more self-conscious of her nakedness than Paul did, obviously.

'Good morning, my lovely,' he said as he put the tea mugs on the little bedside table and sat down beside her, reaching in for a kiss. He gently lifted his forefinger to her brow and brushed a stray strand of hair out of her eyes, tucking it behind her ear, before stroking her cheek, her neck, her collarbone and then her breast. She shivered and sighed, closing her eyes and waiting for more, but he stopped and reached for her hand instead. When she opened her eyes, she gave him a look that she hoped encouraged him to keep going.

'But I'll make you late for work, Rebekah. I don't want to get you into trouble,' he whispered, kissing her neck, her ear, her cheek. She glanced at the clock. It was 8 a.m. already. She groaned. The boat of other staff would be arriving at half past eight, and she really needed to be out of here and up in her own cottage by then if she wanted to avoid them knowing exactly what she'd been doing last night before she'd had chance to consider it fully herself.

'You're right. I really don't want to be here when the others arrive. They could almost see me in bed through that front window if they were looking for me from the boat.'

Paul sat in the bed beside her, and as they drank their tea he held her hand tenderly and stroked her with his thumb.

'Coming here last night was the best decision I've ever made in my life,' he said and leant across to kiss her on the head.

'I actually think the best decision you've ever made was lying down in the heather last Friday afternoon and falling asleep there so that you became marooned on my island and I had to rescue you from the killer midges in the middle of the night. Not exactly a best decision in the traditional sense, I give you that, but it had a magnificent outcome.' She laughed, and he laughed with her.

'I have food for breakfast, but I think we slept too late for that,' he said sadly.

'We did. But I have a morning break around 11 a.m. I could come and see you then, if you're happy to wait and call it brunch?' she said, looking to him hopefully.

'Brunch with you would be perfect. I'll be waiting.'

After she'd dressed and had risked one last long, amazingly wonderful kiss, just inside the door of the cottage, she put on her walking shoes and scampered up to Rose Cottage feeling as sprightly and excited as the red squirrels always seemed. Everything looked fresh and the weekend ahead was now full of thrilling possibilities. She opened the front door and went to run upstairs for a quick shower and change into her ranger's uniform, when she caught sight of the ticket and note on her table where she'd left them the night before. Ben. She had to face Ben today, and she was going to have to be firm. But his sweetness, she knew, was going to make it difficult. *Rip off the sticking plaster fast*, she told herself. It was the only way.

At the island reception, all was normal for a busy Friday morning in summer: the staff and volunteers all arrived on the first boat from Sandbanks, and shortly afterwards, the *Island Maid* arrived from the quay, full to the brim with happy day-trippers. There were families with children – all tucking into their sandwiches before they'd even got off the boat – couples wearing serious walking gear who were obviously intent on covering every inch of the island in one day, and seniors who wanted a gentle stroll, a look in the visitors' centre and a lovely lunch in the café in the shadow of the castle.

Rebekah busied herself at one of the ticket stations, giving every new arrival a beaming smile and a warm Brownsea Island greeting.

'Hi! Welcome! Have you been to the island before?' she asked as she got the till ready to take the fee.

'No, first time today for us, and we're hoping to see our first red squirrels.'

'Ah, lovely, well you're going to have a wonderful day. And are you members of the National Trust?' Rebekah recorded their membership number and gave them a receipt for the ferry ride, handing the visitors a map of the island and a ferry timetable.

'There's a perfect place to spot the squirrels just along the path before you get to the church, but they might be a bit shy today – we have a lot of visitors for the play, you see, and they don't like too much company. Plenty of places for picnicking wherever you like,' she said with a nod to the big picnic bag the gentleman carried over one shoulder, 'and one of our volunteers will be taking walking tours on the hour between ten and three, from just in front of the visitor's centre around the corner.'

'All sounds wonderful – thank you.' The couple beamed as they made their way through reception and Rebekah greeted the next family.

'Hi! Welcome! Have you been to the island before?'

Once the whole boatload of visitors had been welcomed, Rebekah left the other staff while she went to start her ranger rounds, checking in first at the hides beside the lagoon. There were already a number of birdwatchers taking up positions and she watched as a kingfisher swooped from a low tree branch across the edge of the lagoon to snap up a dragonfly. Next job was a hike out to Maryland where she needed to check on the number of rhododendrons and meet a representative from the

Dorset Wildlife Trust who was bringing over some workers next week to continue clearing the area.

By the time that was done, it was 10.40 a.m. and she still had a solid half an hour's walk to get back to the cottage by the quay. She set off at a brisk pace and then, when she knew nobody was around and she wouldn't cause any alarm, broke into a trot, laughing at herself and the urgency of getting back in time for her brunch date. Just as she passed the visitors' centre, she saw the 11 a.m. walking tour setting off, and realised that one of the ticket staff was leading the tour and not Ben, who was the volunteer rostered on for today. She thought for a moment about stopping to ask if anyone knew where he was, but decided to leave it for later. She ducked into the small staff lunchroom and explained to her team that she'd be having her break with a friend who'd made a surprise visit to the Customs House Cottage.

'Not a surprise to us, Bek,' said Luke with a wink. 'The fellows on the *Island Maid* let us know – they brought him here last night?' he continued as she felt her jaw hanging open. Of course. They would have been watching – and they'd brought his groceries over earlier – and they must have seen them kiss on the quay when Paul arrived. So, not such a well-kept secret after all. Everyone who worked on the island probably knew by now that Rebekah had spent the night in the Custom House Cottage with a man named Paul, who'd come down from London yesterday. She couldn't think of anything to say – and asked herself if there was anything she needed to say anyway. She just nodded and turned to leave.

'Shame for poor Ben, though,' Luke continued, and Rebekah stopped in the doorway, looking over her shoulder.

'Ben?' she asked.

'Poor lad'll be beaten up over it I 'spect. Still, your choice, Bek,' he said in his thick Dorset accent, and in every way made her feel as though she had deliberately chosen to break the heart of someone whom she had never intended to encourage.

'Where is he, by the way?' she asked. 'Wasn't he rostered on today?'

'Called in sick. Probably just 'ad a few too many down the Lord Nelson last night,' he said in a way that Rebekah knew was probably meant to reassure her that she wasn't to blame, though it had the opposite effect.

She just nodded curtly in reply and went off to find Paul, rapping the door twice and then opening it and going straight in.

'I'm so sorry I'm late,' she said, noticing it was now twenty past eleven. 'Sometimes, things on this island just don't go to plan in the usual way you might expect for some other jobs,' she explained.

'That's okay. I put it down to island time,' he said with smile. 'I've warmed some pastries, and also made up some hollandaise sauce. Do you like eggs Benedict?' he asked as he switched on the coffee machine and poured two glasses of orange juice.

'Oh, yum! Sounds like a feast, and yes, please, I love eggs Benedict, but I only have half an hour to spare,' she said, anxious that she might spoil his plans.

'That's okay. The time-consuming part is done. Carry these things to the table, would you, and I'll poach the eggs. Help your-self to a pastry.'

* * *

'Mmm, delicious – thank you,' Rebekah said as she wiped her mouth and swallowed the last of the delicious cup of coffee he'd made her. 'So, what are your plans for the rest of the weekend? You did say you have something else to do over at the pottery?'

'My plans are to spend every single moment possible with

you,' he said, with a smile that shone from his eyes and made her sigh. 'But I do need to go to the pottery as well. They've discovered an old filing cabinet in a storage room that no one realised was there. They think it could have been hidden behind their archive shelving since the war. It looks to be some staff records, but some of the names don't tie up with any others we've found so far,' he explained.

'That sounds interesting. I'll be busy here now until around five o'clock, so you could go over this afternoon on the half-past-twelve boat and come back on the half-past-four one, if that would be long enough? That way, we can be as free as we like all day tomorrow, until the play in the evening of course,' Rebekah said.

'Sounds perfect. That should be plenty of time. And I already know what I'd like us to do tomorrow,' he said and grinned.

She questioned him with her frown.

'Can we spend the day at Corfe Castle – I mean in the castle itself, not just the village?' he asked and she had to laugh at his almost schoolboy eagerness to see the ruins.

'That's a great idea. You have your car here, I assume?'

'Yes, I left it parked in one of the staff spaces at the pottery – very convenient.'

'That's fixed then. I'll see you tonight,' she said and kissed him goodbye as though it was something she'd been doing for decades, rather than hours.

* * *

By the end of their Saturday morning exploring the old castle, and after a bracing afternoon walk from the perfectly horseshoe-shaped bay of Lulworth Cove and across the cliffs to Durdle Door and back again, it seemed Paul was falling head over heels in love with Dorset.

'This place is just magical, Rebekah,' he cried as he stood on the clifftop admiring the gorgeously turquoise waters that crashed relentlessly below the white limestone cliff face. 'I can't believe I've never explored around here before. There is so much more to see!'

'Exploring the world does that to you, I've found,' she said as they started walking again. 'It's a bit like reading; you think that if you read all the books – you know, all the great works of literature, all those ones on the big lists – then you can tick that off: job done, books read. But it's not like that at all because every book you read opens up another world of books and authors to discover. Travel and exploring is the same, for me; you go to see a place so you can say "been there, done that", and all that happens is you discover at least another ten places there are to see with every new discovery. It's infuriating and wonderful, all at once,' she said and laughed.

'So, tell me: where else do you want to go? What else do you want to see?' he asked her.

'Oh, everywhere. I've only really discovered a small part of Dorset while I've been in England and there is so much more – fishing coves in Cornwall, Dartmoor in Devon, and the Peak District in Yorkshire is stunning, so I hear, and that's just a few spots in England. And then there is all of Europe too – Paris, Venice, Barcelona, Switzerland. I only just dipped my toes into everything that Queensland had to offer before I left and came here, but I did get to see some of the best National Parks – rainforests and reefs and wide, sandy beaches that go on forever,' she said wistfully.

'I should like to see Australia,' he said.

'I'd love to show you, Paul. I know you'd love it.'

* * *

That evening, back on the island, after they'd covered themselves in mozzie repellent and taken umbrellas in case of an evening shower, they took their seats on camp chairs and unpacked a picnic of cheese, grapes, crackers and a chilled bottle of Champagne to enjoy as they watched the play which, as usual for B.O.A.T., was brilliantly performed and delivered. In the interval, Rebekah saw a few of the other island staff and chastised herself for only now remembering that Ben would have been hoping to see her. She saw him in the distance and paused to summon the courage to do what she knew she must.

'Ben!' she called and watched his face light up when he saw her walking towards him. 'I'm glad you're feeling better – I heard you were a bit under the weather yesterday?' she asked and saw him flinch. 'Thank you for the ticket. It was very kind of you, but I actually already had one and I'm here with a friend. Well, more than a friend, really,' she said making sure to wave in the direction of Paul who had his head stuck in the programme as he sipped a glass of wine. 'I wasn't able to get in touch to let you know, and so I gave the ticket to Luke – who was glad of it. I hope that was all right?' She realised that she hadn't given him a chance to object, but it was done. The poor guy did look crestfallen, but this was one of those occasions when it was better to be firm and fast. It wasn't fair for him to think he had a chance, and she wished now she'd realised earlier that his gifts and attention were about more than mere friendship.

'Who is he, then, Rebekah?' Ben asked pointedly, frowning in Paul's direction. 'I've never seen him before, and I've known you for over two years now.' The comment hit like the barbed tail of a stingray and knocked Rebekah's confidence down several pegs.

'He's a friend from London,' she said, realising as soon as the words left her lips that Ben knew full well that she had exactly zero friends in London. 'I haven't known him long, Ben, but his name is Paul. He's a historian working at Poole Pottery, and he and I have become close. Very close,' she said, hoping that would be the end of it.

'So, he's a boyfriend then?'

Heck, would he not let it go? Who did Ben think he was anyway: her big brother? Her protector?

'I know it's none of my business, Rebekah,' he said as if he'd just read her mind, 'but the thing is, I like you. I like you a lot. And I thought... I had hoped...' He stopped and waved his hand dismissively and took a deep breath, looking up to her with a tight smile. 'It doesn't matter. I just hope he makes you happy,' Ben said and walked away. As she watched him go, she couldn't help think of Farmer Oak and wonder whether she'd just waved security and stability goodbye for the sake of fun and excitement that was more thrilling than any she'd known before.

She walked back to Paul and sat down, taking the refilled Champagne glass he offered her.

'Who was your friend?' he asked casually, and the word made Rebekah think deeply. She mulled it over for a few moments before she answered.

'He's one of the volunteers here on the island and he's been bringing me presents – he brought the mussels we ate last Friday night – and I haven't realised until very recently that he thought we could be more than friends. But I don't know him. Not really. I've known him to speak to for two years, but I don't fully *know* him, not like I know you,' she said, frowning as she tried to understand it herself just as she was explaining it.

'Oh, you mean in the biblical sense?' he said with a wink and an actual nudge in her ribs, making her laugh at herself.

'No! I mean in the friend sense. I've only known you a week,

Paul – with a very unwelcome gap in the middle – but it feels as if we've been friends forever, doesn't it?' she asked him, turning to look him full in the face.

'Yes. Yes, it does,' he said carefully, taking a sip of his Champagne and reaching out for her with his spare hand. 'I can't really remember a time when I didn't know you were here, to be honest. And I want you to be my friend, always.' She leant in to kiss him and then he added, whispering wickedly into her lips, 'With some extra delicious benefits.'

* * *

On Sunday morning, they lay in bed facing one another and trying to make plans. Paul had to get back to London that afternoon for his regular rehearsal, and he had a solid week of work ahead of him, as well as mid-week rehearsals for his concert in Westminster next Saturday night. And Rebekah would be doing what she did day in and day out on the island home that she considered her own slice of paradise. But first, this morning, Paul had to spend another hour in the pottery collecting things before he left.

By the time they'd finished breakfast, there was a plan: Rebekah would go with him to the quay, wait while he finished at the pottery, then she'd take him on a walk through the old town to show him the back streets of the quay, the old church of St James's, Market Street, and the Guildhall. They would have a walk in the park, and lunch on the quay, before he drove back to London, and she fetched some groceries and went back to the island.

An hour later, she was relaxing in a chair in the Poole Pottery offices, while Paul was sorting through some files he'd just hauled up from the basement storage room. He was wrangling them into a briefcase when he groaned aloud.

'What's the matter?' Rebekah asked him.

'I've left some behind. These are some extra personnel files we found from the war years and they were in alphabetical order but I've only got A to N here. There must be more, looking at the number there are here, though many of these names are unfamiliar. I haven't seen them on any other lists of Poole Pottery staff, but I need to look into them, all the same.'

'I'll go back down and fetch them if you like – I've nothing to do and you're busy,' she said and kissed him on the head before she trotted down the stairs. She paused in the corridor to look again at the mesmerising face of the beautiful Margaret Symonds in the old photograph that she'd been fascinated with the weekend before. She was a stunning woman, with curly, fair hair and eyes that stared straight into the lens of the camera with the boldness of a supermodel. There was something so familiar in Margaret's looks, too.

Rebekah found the storeroom, and the filing cabinet Paul had mostly emptied. At the back of the bottom drawer, there were a few more suspension hangers and in them she found folders that were labelled with surnames from Osmington to Young. These were the missing ones. She pulled them from the drawer and fanned them out as she walked up the stairs and then something caught her eye that stopped her dead. One of the files was labelled:

Symonds, Margaret – B.O.A.C.

Rebekah knelt on the floor right where she was in the middle of the corridor and opened the file. Inside was a copy of the same photograph that was on the wall just a few feet away, and papers relating to the employment of Margaret as a seawoman working for BOAC – the British Overseas Airways Corporation.

Margaret had lived in Ballard Road, which Rebekah knew was only a few metres away from where she stood right now. The details said she was a seawoman employed to operate a launch, carry out sundry driving duties, and there was a red rubber stamp with the letters *OSA* on the bottom of the page, dated March 1941.

Rebekah gathered up the papers and took them up to Paul.

'I've just found something really interesting here,' she said, kneeling on the floor beside him and putting the other folders down.

'Oh, great thanks – you've got the rest of the alphabet.'

'Yes, but like you said, I don't think they are all pottery personnel. Remember that photo we were looking at of that gorgeous girl in the corridor downstairs – the black and white wartime picture?'

Paul nodded. 'Marion or someone, wasn't it?'

'Margaret – Margaret Symonds. Well, here's her file, and she didn't work for the pottery; she worked for the flying boats.'

'That is interesting – I thought all those papers were held with British Airways. They shouldn't still be here. Let's have a look.'

'She was a local girl – very local. Do you know what "OSA" stands for?' she asked him, holding out the paper with the rubber stamp to show him.

'Goodness gracious, do I ever!' he said and carefully took the folder from Rebekah's hands, as if he were taking a precious and delicate artefact. 'It stands for Official Secrets Act,' he explained. 'This woman was involved with some very sensitive information during the war,' he said, scanning the document and noting the date, 'and right here in Poole, so it seems.'

'Wow! I never knew Poole had anything much at all going on in the war – apart from the refugees they had on the island, of course. I've heard about that bit of history, and the fact that Maryland Village was used as a decoy for air raids.'

Paul flicked over a few more papers and then an envelope fell from the folder and into Rebekah's lap beneath him where she knelt on the floor.

'Oh, sorry, I dropped something,' he said as Rebekah picked it up. She read the inscription on the front and frowned up at him. Rebekah showed him the envelope and he read the inscription out loud.

'Flight Lieutenant Darrell Taylor, care of RAAF 461 Squadron, RAF Hamworthy, Poole.' He flipped it over and read the back. 'To be given to Flight Lieutenant Taylor in the event of the death of Peggy Symonds of 11 Ballard Road, Poole. Peggy? Who's *Peggy* Symonds? Isn't this the file of Margaret... oh wait... of course,' he said, slapping his forehead with his palm. He looked up to explain to Rebekah what he'd just realised and saw that she'd gone such a pale shade that she was almost grey.

'What is it?' he asked, putting down the folder and cupping her cheek. 'What's wrong?'

'Peggy Symonds. Aunty Pig,' she said and laughed. 'This is unbelievable, Paul. Peggy Symonds was the name of my neighbour in Brisbane, the one who taught me all about Poole, and the harbour and Brownsea Island. Peggy grew up here. But why is this letter in this person Margaret's folder? What did Margaret have to do with Peggy? Was Margaret a sister to Peggy, do you think?'

'No, I don't think that at all. I think that Margaret *is* Peggy. It's a strange thing with old names, and particularly from that era. People were named something quite formal-sounding, like Margaret, for instance, but were always known as a more relaxed nickname. Peggy is a common short name for Margaret. It probably started with Maggie, Meggie, then Meg which easily becomes Peg, Peggy,' he said and then realised she was not listening to a word he said.

'Peggy – my old, kind, spinster aunty Peggy – worked on the flying boats in this harbour, and signed the Official Secrets Act? She was involved in top-secret activities during the war? That can't be right. She was just a simple woman, who loved to bake, and care for other people's children, and feed the birds,' she said, incredulity in every word.

'People can have all kinds of dark histories. You'd never imagine some of the stories I've uncovered.' He paused before going on, his thumb tucked under the seal of the letter.

'Wait a minute,' she said, sorting through the file for the photo of Margaret again. She studied it carefully. 'Yes, I can see it now – this is Peggy! My Aunty Peggy, when she was young and *very* beautiful. Wow. And so, who on earth was this Flight Lieutenant Darrell Taylor?' asked Rebekah.

'Shall we find out?' he asked, ready to rip open the letter, the secrets within having been sealed for over fifty years.

18

POOLE – MARCH 1941

When Charlie woke the next morning, the smells and sounds that attacked his senses took him immediately back to the Blitz. Even inside his small bedroom, with the window firmly shut against the cold March night air, he could smell smoke that must have come in through the chimney to the little fireplace that had been, and was still, unlit.

The all-clear siren had been sounded some hours earlier, but now there were whistles, and the clanging of the fire-truck bell, and men shouting from all directions. And yet, Charlie thought with an emotionless snort of dry humour, here he still lay: alive, surviving, alone.

When he reached the bottom of the stairs, still pulling the straps of his braces over his shoulders, Mrs Rogers came in through the front door in a flurry.

'Oh, there you are, son! Did you stay up there all night, you fool? You might have been killed, you know? I was down in the public shelter and had visions of you crushed beneath the rubble of this place,' she said admonishing him and yet the love and concern for him flowed like rivers.

'I slept so soundly, I didn't hear the sirens, Mrs Rogers,' he lied easily. 'But all's well, as you see,' he said, holding out his arms and grinning. 'Here I am, all in one piece.'

She had moved into the kitchen and lit the range, and began to heat a kettle for tea, then mixed up some oats with water and a little milk, setting them on top to begin simmering. He stepped outside the back door and made his way to the shared outhouse, where, thankfully, there was no queue this morning. The smoke was thick and the air still full of the sounds of panic, but from this perspective, he couldn't see any buildings that were damaged.

'It was a bad one, then, was it?' he asked his landlady as he took a seat at the kitchen table and gladly drank the cup of tea she placed before him.

'The island took a lot of damage last night, and I'd say there's nothing left of Maryland this morning, looking at the flames going up over there. So sad, you know, that mad old woman taking over and throwing us all out. I grew up there, with all my brothers and sisters. Went to school in the little village, and Sunday school in St Mary's Church too. My father was a farmer on the island, as was his father before him,' she said. 'Still, we must be grateful that Brownsea Island is doing its bit to protect us all now.'

Charlie had learnt that the area of Brownsea called Maryland Village had stood empty of all but ghosts ever since Mrs Bonham-Christie had bought the island and ordered all the inhabitants to leave in 1927. She turned the island into a nature reserve of sorts and after a dreadful fire in 1934, she had not let a soul visit the place. But the defence forces had decided to set up the village as a decoy for bombers, and flares were lit all over Maryland, attracting the attention of the Luftwaffe away from Poole and Bournemouth – and particularly the munitions factory on Holton

Heath between Poole and Wareham – while the towns on the mainland were protected by blackout.

'There must have been a few places hit on the mainland too, going by the sirens and shouting I can hear outside. Can't see any damage near here though,' Charlie commented and he started to blow on the bowl of hot porridge he'd been given.

'Yes, there's a few places hit around West Quay Road, and I hear that Parkstone took quite a lot of damage, and even some places at Canford Cliffs. They're saying it's the worst air raid we've had here so far. Usually, it seems they just drop their bombs off here on their way home from the other cities, but this time it was more of a direct attack, so they're saying,' she told him.

Charlie ate on in silence as he thought about the VIP guests who had spent the night up at the Harbour Heights Hotel. What would happen to Britain's chances if Churchill were taken out, let alone De Gaulle and Mr Menzies, all at once? It didn't bear thinking about. And had the whole raid been meant for them? He glanced at his watch and, thanking Mrs Rogers politely for his breakfast, Charlie set off on the short walk to the harbour commissioner's office where he was due to meet Peggy for the first trip of the day.

* * *

Peggy didn't know how long she had stayed at the back fence watching the flames and smoke billowing out from Maryland Village on Brownsea Island. The Symonds family had spent most of the night in their Anderson shelter and with nothing but harbour waters between them and Brownsea, the noise of the bombs that fell there through the night had been terrifying. Several times, Mrs Symonds had shrieked in fear and Peggy was certain that their house, or at least one very close by, must have been hit. But in the smoky, hazy light of dawn, after the all-clear had sounded, they had crept out and been amazed to discover not one house within sight had been hit. After a subdued and sleepy breakfast at the kitchen table, she had taken a last trip down the garden to the outhouse, and had become transfixed, watching the fires rage on the island.

But now she must draw her strength, from those deep reserves she was discovering inside that she never knew she had before the war, and get on with the day. She looked to the north, towards Hamworthy and the RAF base where she knew Darrell would be. There were no smoke plumes in that direction, thank God. She sighed and turned on her heels, heading back into the kitchen to collect her bag and gas mask before trotting off down the road towards the quay, calling a quick cheerio over her shoulder as she left. Her dad was staying home today, as the smoke on the harbour made fishing too difficult, and her mother needed him close for her nerves' sake.

Peggy saw the smoke coming from over near Holes Bay, probably on West Quay Road. As she was passing the pottery, she was busy looking out across the harbour to Brownsea again when Rose Stevens ran out and called her name.

'Peggy! Can you stop in here for a few minutes, on your way, please?' Rose called.

Peggy looked at her watch. Still fifteen minutes before she was due to pick up the launch key, and plenty of time before she had to be at Salterns to pick up the guests from the hotel and take them out to board their early-morning flight.

'Morning, Rose. How did you and your sister sleep last night?'

In reply, Rose just grunted and made a face.

'Enough said. Must be tough for Daisy, getting so well on with the baby as she is. But at least the two of you have your shelter to yourselves. There are four of us crammed into ours and poor

Molly is not one to suffer in silence! It's like a game of hide-and-seek in the cupboard under the stairs.' Rose managed a smile at this, though Peggy could see she had something important on her mind.

'Major Carter would like a word, if you don't mind, please Peggy. Just this way,' she said, leading Peggy into the offices of the major who was responsible for Field Safety in Poole Harbour.

'Ah, good morning, Miss Symonds,' the major said as he stood to welcome Peggy with a businesslike handshake. He indicated she should take a seat, and Peggy was surprised when Rose sat down beside her as well. She was too stunned to make any small talk and simply waited for him to speak.

'You'll be aware of my new position since the war – that I'm responsible, as part of the British Army, for the security of Poole Harbour and surrounds, especially as relates to the BOAC flying boat services.' He said it as a statement of fact. There was no room for Peggy to claim she had no knowledge of the fact, and so she simply nodded in response.

'You will also be aware, as part of the fleet of staff who took part in the transfer, that three very important dignitaries were spending the night at the Harbour Heights Hotel last night,' he said with meaning and he leant towards her, resting his forearms on the desk as he did so.

'Yes, sir, I am aware. Very important dignitaries indeed,' she said.

'Quite so. And you will also be aware, as are we all, that last night Poole was targeted by the Luftwaffe in what was the most extensive air raid to date?'

'Yes, sir. It was a terribly rough night,' she said.

'The thing is, Peggy, we want to be sure you understand the very serious nature of the secrecy needed around our guest lists. We are reminding all the staff, individually, that nothing of the business of BOAC must ever be repeated outside of our own circle. Our nation is depending on this. You understand me?' he asked with a very firm tone.

Peggy took a few seconds to think about the conversation she'd had with Fletcher, just yesterday, and how much further up the pecking line Fletcher must be than Major Carter. Did the major even know of Fletcher's existence? Possibly not. But of one thing she was sure: they were all in grave danger while Hitler was still at large and there was a possibility of spies in Poole.

'Yes, sir, I understand you perfectly. Mum's the word,' she replied.

As Peggy left the pottery, and stepped back outside into the smoky gloom caused by the bombs of the Luftwaffe planes dropped on Poole overnight, and probably intended for Churchill, de Gaulle, and Menzies, she knew that she would stop at nothing to protect them all from any spy that might be leaking secrets to the enemy. But she was utterly convinced that Charlie was not that spy.

19

POOLE – JULY 1998

Rebekah sheltered from the surprisingly hot sun, under a big shade umbrella. The outdoor table rested on the old cobblestones that created the apron in front of the Custom House Bistro on Poole Quay. A waitress had taken their order for lunch and Paul was at the bar, buying two glasses of wine. Rebekah held the letter in one hand and traced the feathery handwriting with her finger again. The script, as was often the case from this era, was not easy to read, and took some concentration, besides which the paper was yellowed with age.

My dearest Darrell,

If you are reading this letter, then I am so terribly sorry for your loss. But I promise you it is my loss too. As I write this, you might think nothing more of me than I'm just a girl you met in a pub; a girl you went out on a day trip with. But, for me, I want you to know that I want this to be more. I barely know you, Darrell, and so this is so strange to put into words, but at this moment, I hope to spend the rest of my life in your arms. I hope that this terrible time of war will end, and that Hitler can be stopped and driven back. I hope that peace, and sense, will prevail. I hope for a time of plenty: of food, and homes, and work for all. For a time when we can sit in the sun and enjoy life together. But, if I have my way, you will only be given this letter to read if I have lost my life before you in these dark days.

I will not have told you why I am behaving so differently at this time; why I am spending less time with you and more time with others – with one other in particular. You may even believe that I don't love you with the same passion you do me. I will not have told you, because I am not allowed to. I have signed the Official Secrets Act and have been engaged in an important espionage mission. Even now, in death, I am not allowed to share the details with you.

But I need you to know this, Darrell – I will love you, and only you, for all eternity, and I will see you when you get here. I will be waiting for you.

With all my love, forever,

Peggy

Rebekah looked again at the inscription on the front, and the intriguing message on the back.

Flight Lieutenant Darrell Taylor, care of RAAF 461 Squadron, RAF Hamworthy, Poole.

'To be given to Flight Lieutenant Taylor in the event of the death of Peggy Symonds of 11 Ballard Road, Poole,' she whispered to herself. And now the idea struck her that this letter was private, and only ever meant for the eyes of this Darrell Taylor. But Peggy was gone now, and couldn't be hurt by this intrusion on her privacy.

Since they had first read the letter earlier that morning, Rebekah had been stunned by the idea that her dear old Aunty Pig could have been involved in some kind of espionage work during the war. The idea was so incredible, it seemed impossible, until she thought about how little she knew of Peggy's life before Rebekah was born.

Peggy had shared lots of details about the harbour, about Brownsea Island, of Poole and its buildings, of birds, and of fishing and growing up as a fisherman's daughter. Rebekah knew that Peggy had left England and arrived in Australia on a flying boat, but that was it, and she'd never thought to ask if there was more to the story. And now Peggy was gone.

But did this Darrell Taylor know about this? Peggy had survived the war, and so this letter had never needed to be delivered to him, whoever he had been. It must have just stayed here in this file and been forgotten. Did he ever find out what it was that Peggy had been doing, and what, exactly, was that? The letter gave no details, except of the undying love she had for Darrell, an idea that seemed so surprising when she thought of Peggy who had seemed to be so happy with her life as a spinster.

If Rebekah could find this Darrell now, would all this be a shock to him? Could she risk upsetting a man who might have left all this in the past as his history, just to satisfy her piqued curiosity?

'You look like Atlas,' said Paul as he sat down and placed two glasses of chilled rosé on the table. Rebekah noticed the condensation forming on the outside of the cold glass in the summer heat of the day. Then she registered what he'd said.

'Atlas?' she asked with her face screwed up in confusion.

'With the weight of the world on your shoulders – like you have some very heavy thoughts to think about,' he said, gently.

'I don't know about heavy – but they are certainly consuming. I'm trying to decide whether or not to pursue this Darrell and pass on the letter. I have no idea who he is, or if he is even still alive, and I wouldn't want to upset him or his family,' Rebekah said. 'But what if it is a message he needs to receive?'

'What about your mum? Might she know something about it? She knew Peggy for much longer than you, and adults often share things they don't let the children know about,' he offered.

'True. I should ask her. I'll call tonight when I get home,' she said, glancing at her watch and working out how long she would have to wait before her mum would wake up on Monday morning in Australia.

The waitress delivered the large pizza they'd ordered to share with the insalata caprese that Rebekah had chosen from the menu. The mozzarella was deliciously soft and creamy, and the tomatoes so ripe that they made her taste buds sing.

'Mmm, amazing food. This was a wonderful recommendation. Perfect for such a beautiful day,' Paul said as he devoured his plateful.

'It has been a beautiful day. And incredibly surprising.' She referred in part of course to the discovery about Peggy but also to the lovely walk they'd taken and the history Paul had taught her. She had thought to show him the old buildings of Poole, and was amazed that he knew so much of the history already. He taught her about how important the Newfoundland cod trade had been to Poole's wealth, and also the connection with the flying boats. Apparently, some of the first international flights from England to New York had started in Poole. The route took them through a stop in Foynes, Ireland, and then on to Botwood in Newfoundland, before stopping in Montreal, Canada, and from there to New York.

'Those trips were taken in one of the Short Brothers C-class flying boats – a sister to the craft that were used by the RAF, and which, presumably, the RAAF – and this Darrell Taylor – flew from Hamworthy,' he explained.

'What a glamorous way to travel, stopping for overnight stays in hotels along the way and in a plane with plenty of room to walk about in-flight, or lie down to sleep if necessary,' Rebekah said, remembering the cramped cattle-class economy flight she'd come to England on, though she had at least had a three-day stopover in Rome, which was a lovely distraction along the way.

'Have you flown back to see your mum since you came here to work on the island?' Paul asked.

'No, not yet. I've been here for over two years and I'm probably due a trip soon. I have plenty saved up as I find I don't have much to spend my wages on, especially as my accommodation is part of my salary deal.' As Rebekah sipped her wine and watched Paul while he looked out across the quay and over the harbour to the island she now called home, she allowed herself to hope he might stay in her life long enough fly with her back to Brisbane one day.

When their meal was over, they said farewell, with a definite plan for the following weekend. Neither was prepared to part without knowing exactly when they would be seeing each other again. They shared phone numbers – including the number to Paul's new Nokia mobile phone – and the next weekend was plotted out: Rebekah would travel up to London on an evening train on Friday, and stay with him for the weekend in London, going to watch his strings concert in Westminster on the Saturday night. Then she would catch the train back again on Sunday evening. Two whole nights and days together in London, with a classical concert thrown in. And they would talk on the phone each night.

That evening, Rebekah sat in her favourite window seat with the cottage's portable phone by her side. She had a lot to tell her mum. She had heard nothing about Paul, and it was important to Rebekah that she let Mum know she had met someone who had fast become very special to her. And she wanted to ask about Peggy, and if Mum had ever heard about the existence of this Darrell. But she needed to go about it the right way. At ten o'clock, she dialled the number. It would be seven o'clock the following morning for Mum and Rebekah knew she would be up and about, enjoying the cool winter morning in Brisbane.

As she'd suspected, Mum was awake and busy, and she asked Rebekah to wait as she seemed to be giving instructions to a yardman about chopping some wood ready to burn in the pot-bellied stove that evening.

'It's a chilly one here today love, only eight degrees when I woke up! I had the fire burning last night, but it's still plenty warm enough in the middle of the day. What's it like with you there at the moment?' her mum asked.

'Lovely summer weather today, actually, top of around twenty-four degrees at lunchtime. The beaches must have been packed out,' she said and shared a laugh with her mother that the Brisbane winter midday temperatures were roughly the same as the English summer ones. 'Talking of summer, I'm hatching a plan that I might come over for Christmas this year. It'll be three years since I left on New Year's Eve,' she said.

'That would be wonderful, love! How long would you be able to come for?' she asked.

'I've got plenty of leave allowance, and winter is the best time for me to get away, so I'd like to make it a month if I can. That ought to be possible. Might as well make the most of the flight once I've paid for it,' she said. 'And I have a bit of a project to work on while I'm there too,' she added, looking for a way to introduce her main reason for the call.

Of course, introducing this Darrell Taylor character to the

conversation, and the discovery she'd made at Poole Pottery about Peggy, also meant sharing details about Paul, who he was, and how they'd met. And before long, she realised she was telling Mum that she'd found someone who could turn out to be quite significant in her life.

'All sounds very romantic, darling. So, how did the two of you meet then?' asked Mum, making Rebekah think fast on her feet. She couldn't exactly tell her mum the truth: that Paul had knocked on her door in the middle of the night, and she'd let him sleep on her settee. She'd be horrified at Rebekah's lack of security-mindedness!

'He was visiting the island, and we got chatting. One thing led to another and I showed him some of the sights of Poole. We just hit it off from the start. It's strange,' she mused. 'I feel like I've always known him though it's only been a couple of weeks,' she said, stretching the truth since it was no more than eight days now. 'And one of the lovely things is that it's just so comfortable being with him, even if we aren't doing anything special or even talking.'

'That is a very good sign, love – the best of friends are content just to be with each other, without any effort at all,' she said, and Rebekah wondered how her mother had become so knowledgeable about good, lasting relationships all of a sudden.

'But this news you tell me about Peggy in the war – goodness me, I've never heard anything about it at all! And, like you say, it is quite possible that this Darrell is still alive and doesn't know anything about the letter,' said Rebekah's mum.

'Perhaps if I do come to visit at Christmas, I could spend some time searching for him, Mum. He was in the Australian Air Force, so there is every chance that, if he survived the war, he went back to Australia afterwards. With Paul's knowledge and access to census data and detailed military records, I might manage to find him that way,' Rebekah suggested.

'That's a good idea, love. And if you bring your Paul with you, we'd love to show him a proper Aussie Christmas!'

As Rebekah hung up the phone, she leant on the windowsill and stared out at the pines swaying in the evening breeze, a little confused at Mum's use of 'we'. Of course, Rebekah and Mum would love to show Paul a Brisbane Christmas, but Mum seemed to be suggesting there was another person around. Strange.

She could hear the sounds from the outdoor play coming up the hill from the Church Field, and somehow Paul's face formed in the middle distance before her, as if in another dimension, close enough to see but too far away to touch.

The idea of taking Paul with her to Brisbane as early as Christmas had not even crossed her mind when she'd been thinking of it earlier. But now that her mum had posited the idea, it sounded like the most wonderful plan. But she'd only known him a week. She couldn't possibly ask him to go on a trip around the world in four months' time, could she?

* * *

The following Friday night seemed to take a month to arrive. Rebekah had phoned Paul, or he had phoned her, every evening and she'd repeatedly run down the battery on her portable phone by lying in bed and talking with him until she was virtually asleep. It was almost as good as having him there. Almost.

When she caught the afternoon ferry off the Island on Friday, she carried just a small backpack and an overnight bag, and once she'd landed on Poole Quay, she walked the short distance up the High Street to Poole train station.

Rebekah watched the countryside zoom by in the summer

evening sunshine until, over the next two and a half hours, the scene gradually morphed into the built-up areas on the outskirts of London. As the train approached the city, it slowed and she began to peep familiar landmarks, spotting the tower of Big Ben in a short gap between buildings. At Waterloo station, she walked with her neck stretched, in awe of the architecture of even the most commonplace building as a train station, and so, not looking where she was going, she bumped into Paul before she'd even seen he was waiting for her at the end of the platform.

He laughed and picked her up for a tight hug and a kiss, before taking her hand and leading her down into the Tube and on to his home in Notting Hill.

'Wow, I didn't know you still lived so centrally,' she marvelled. He opened the front door of the very narrow-looking terraced house and led her through the lengthy hall to the kitchen and dining room at the back.

'This is the house I grew up in. After Mum died, and we'd got through the initial stupor of grief, Dad took up work that kept him travelling. I think that was his way of dealing with it: while he was away from home, he could imagine she was still here, waiting for him.'

Paul made a pot of tea and heated the soup he'd prepared for them to share for supper. While Paul was busy in the kitchen, Rebekah studied the photos on the mantelpiece, and noticed how old they were: Paul as a baby, with two charming-looking parents; Paul graduating in cap and gown with just his dad by his side.

'So, he lives here with you now?' she asked when he carried the tea to the table.

'No. He never came back to live here permanently again. He was spending a lot of time working in the north, and while he was there – years after Mum died – he met a lovely lady, Suzanne. They're married now and he lives with her in York. She has three grown children, and I don't have any brothers or sisters, so Dad, in his ever pragmatic and practical way, decided to simply sign this place over to me, so it would always be mine. Blended families can be a shocker when it comes to wills and inheritance, you know,' he said, casually taking a big bite from a chunk of buttered, crusty bread he'd torn from the fresh loaf on the table.

'Gosh, that was incredibly generous of him. And kind,' Rebekah added.

'It was. And he is. And it's so good to see him happy now, so contented. You mentioned you'd like to visit the Peak District the other day? Well, that's only an hour's drive from where he lives in York. He and Suzanne spend their time walking their dogs on the Yorkshire Dales – beautiful countryside. He took early retirement, and it looks good on him.'

Rebekah glanced around the room again. The furnishings were classy, but busy, and didn't seem in keeping with a young professional like Paul. There were some gorgeous silver candelabras atop a very shiny, black baby grand piano, and an elaborate crystal vase overflowing with beautiful silk lilies on the mantelpiece in front of an ornate mirror, doubling the effect of the flowers. The living room had a Queen Anne-style bureau and the fireside chairs looked as though they could have come from Windsor Castle. It was beautiful. But it wasn't Paul.

'So, the house is all still furnished as it was when you grew up, then?' she probed.

He sighed and made a face that showed her he wasn't happy with the arrangement.

'Don't remind me! At first, I didn't want to change anything at all because of Mum – this is all her work, all her style, you see? But she's been gone a decade now, and Dad's not lived here for almost as long. The house has been entirely mine for over five years, but somehow I've never known quite what to do.'

The busyness came from a mixture of styles and colours, Rebekah realised. Removing some of those and picking one main colour and style would have the effect of enlarging the spaces and simplifying what the eye dwelt on. She'd never had her own place to decorate, but loved the way Rose Cottage was sparsely furnished, mostly white with a small splash of new spring green in places, as if the cottage had taken its lead from the woodlands outside. Spending her life looking at what nature had done so marvellously and beautifully well without the help of mankind, gave her a good eye for what worked with interior decorating too.

'I could show you some ideas if you like,' she offered. 'I have a few interior design magazines at home that could help.'

'That would be super, thank you. I've no idea where to start and I'd love your help,' he said, flashing her that sunny smile she loved.

* * *

The next day, he took her on a whistlestop tour of the sights of central London, before they headed to Westminster for the pre-concert rehearsal. Rebekah went alone for a tour of Westminster Abbey, while Paul was rehearsing, then she walked up Horse Guards Road, alongside St James's Park, passing the Churchill War Rooms, and crossing The Mall on her way to The British Academy for the concert. She couldn't help thinking again about Peggy, and whatever it was she had been involved in during the war along with so many incredibly brave, ordinary, everyday people who had bought her the freedom she enjoyed today. Rebekah prayed a silent prayer of gratitude for the liberation their efforts had won.

At the British Academy, Rebekah was ushered to the seat Paul had arranged for her in the upstairs Music Room and waited in the distinguished quiet for the concert to start, taking in the splendour of the highly decorated walls and ceiling.

When Paul walked out with the other musicians to take his place, she almost gasped aloud at the effect of a dinner jacket and bow tie on the body she had become very familiar with by this stage. 'Dashing' didn't quite cover it, and she couldn't help a smile of delight when he spotted her in the audience and winked. But once he took his seat and began to play, all his attention was caught up in the music, and Rebekah soon found herself floating along on the joy of the journey. She was familiar with all the melodies but had never known classical music well enough to name any of the pieces she might have heard. From this night on, at least, she thought, she would always recognise Vivaldi's *Four Seasons*, and the programme helped her understand which season was which.

As they walked home from the Tube station that night, he listened shyly as Rebekah told him everything that was wonderful about her evening.

On Sunday, they decided to make the most of the continuing beautiful blue sky summer weather, and Paul packed a picnic hamper, which they took to Hyde Park. He spread the picnic blanket out on the lawn beside the Serpentine and they lay in the sun, soaking up the warm rays.

'You'd never do this in Brisbane, you know,' she told him as she collected another round of cheese, smoked salmon, and soft bread from the food laid out beside the hamper. Paul was in the process of pouring them both a glass of wine.

'Why ever not? Surely you must have more sunny days in Brisbane than we ever do here?' he asked.

'Oh, we do – it's sunny virtually every day of the year. But the sun is so hot, you'd be mad to lie out in it like this. You'd burn in no time – even with plenty of sunblock. Slip, slop, slap – that's the only way to deal with it if you absolutely have to be outside, or at the beach.'

He frowned, waiting for an explanation.

'It stands for "slip on a shirt, slop on some sunblock, and slap on a hat!"' she told him.

'But you do go out in the sun?' he asked.

'Oh yes, all the time! Australians do as much as they can outdoors. But we just choose to be under shade where we can and avoid being out in the direct sun between eleven and three, if possible, particularly in the middle of summer.'

'And that's at Christmastime, right? That must be so strange,' he said.

'Not strange to me at all. Christmas carols are sung outside, just as they are here, but in the heat of a steamy, sub-tropical night. On Christmas Day, we set up tables and chairs underneath the mango tree in the backyard, cook a barbecue, eat cold cheese-cake and pavlova for dessert, and go for a swim in the pool after we're sure we won't sink from all the food,' she said, laughing.

'All sounds wonderful, Rebekah. Must be hard for you getting used to an English Christmas.'

'Not really, no. The English Christmas suits England and the English weather. The Aussie Christmas suits Australia.' She paused for a moment and decided she had found the right time. It was only two weeks since she'd met him, but this felt so right.

'Actually, Paul, there's something I wanted to ask you about Christmas.'

'Hmmm, what's that?' he asked casually, lying on his back with one arm under his head.

'With what we discovered about Peggy, and now we know my mum can't help at all, I really would love the chance to go to Bris-bane to see if I can find this Darrell. Before it's too late, you know? And, I think I mentioned the other day, I haven't been home for nearly three years now and it might be nice to have a Christmas in Brisbane.'

'That sounds lovely. And I can certainly get started on the research to see if we can find where Flight Lieutenant Taylor ended up, after he left Poole – hopefully tracing him to an address in Australia. And the holiday sounds like a great plan. You seem to work pretty hard on that island of yours and don't get to take much time for yourself. A holiday at home would be a good thing for you to look forward to,' he said, barely opening one eye.

'Well, I was thinking we could make it something that we could both look forward to,' she said and waited.

He opened both eyes and turned to look directly at her.

'How could I look forward to losing you for a month and not being able to see you, knowing you were on the other side of the world from me?' he asked, reaching out to take her hand.

'That's my thought exactly. So why don't you come with me? To Australia – for a holiday. I could show you Brisbane, and my favourite national parks. We could go to the Great Barrier Reef. Have you ever snorkelled?' By the time she'd asked him about snorkelling, he was sitting bolt upright and looking at her with the most divine look of excited anticipation in his expression.

'You'd like us to plan a holiday together? To Brisbane?' he asked, and she nodded. 'Rebekah, that is the most wonderful idea you've had in the whole fourteen days and...' he checked his watch, '...thirteen and a half hours since I first laid eyes on you. You're a genius!' He paused to lean across and kiss her, taking the time to cup her cheek in his hand and stroke her tenderly with his thumb. 'And yes, please, I'd love to!'

20

POOLE – MARCH 1941

Peggy had thought, in the few moments she had taken to consider what could be so important that she might be expected to sign the Official Secrets Act, that she was going to be asked to become a regular driver for the VIP political leaders visiting Poole Harbour. Or perhaps she was even being asked to become an air stewardess and fly with them – an idea that thrilled her to the core. That she might be asked to take part in what was essentially a spy role would never have occurred to her. Didn't they already have agents for that? What could she do that was so important to the country? She had asked these and many other questions in the moments after Fletcher had explained the problem to her.

And now, early on the day after the most awful bombing raid Poole had suffered so far, she was about to find out more detail. As she'd arrived for work that morning, Patricia had told her there was a new plan for the day. She was to go home, change out of her uniform and go directly to the train station where she would catch the eight o'clock train to Waterloo Station in London. She was to walk from Westminster to an address in Whitehall, where she would meet with Mr Fletcher.

The look on her face must have told Pat that Peggy had a thousand questions, but Patricia just held up her hand.

'Peggy, I know it's all strange. But the instructions have come from the highest level of government. You just have to do as you're asked.'

Peggy was grateful that her family were all still in bed when she went home, and nobody noticed her changing into her best dress, hat, and coat, and heading out again. On the train, she'd thought of little except Darrell and how this new role might come between them.

Once the train neared central London, Peggy had been horrified to witness the damage to the buildings around her, the sandbags, the gaping holes where homes had once stood. There were fire trucks attending to fires that still burned from raids the night before, and yet, amongst it all, women still walked out with their prams to fetch food for the day, children played in the streets, there was a semblance of normal life.

Once she reached the address in Whitehall, just a short walk from the Houses of Parliament, she was ushered down a series of corridors before she came face to face with Fletcher again. He reminded her of the serious nature of the mission she was being tasked with and updated her on the events of the night before.

'As I explained, Miss Symonds, we believe that Charlie Edwards is not who he says he is. We now think that he may be a German spy, and that he sent information to the German forces yesterday about the whereabouts of the VIPs you were involved in transporting. The air raid last night could have been meant to wipe them out, all three. Thankfully, the decoy on Brownsea Island worked a treat. The village of Maryland is probably smashed to smithereens this morning, but the Harbour Heights Hotel still stands, and our leaders live on. And today, they will fly to a secret destination for diplomatic discussions with other countries, just as they planned to do.'

Peggy was astounded at the local knowledge Fletcher had and wondered how much time he had spent in Poole before she met him. Had someone been watching her as well?

'Goodness gracious! But what exactly am I to do?' Peggy asked, bemused by the whole situation. 'I'm just a launch operator; I'm not a trained spy. How can I help?'

'Today, you will receive some basic training, and we have one or two helpful articles to give you that all our operatives carry. Essentially, though, we want you to carry on doing exactly what you do with Charlie by your side, but we need you to listen. To get closer to him. To get as close to him as you possibly can, Peggy,' said Fletcher with great meaning in his eyes and tone. 'Become so close that he thinks you're his girl, if necessary.'

Peggy's mind and heart reeled as she realised the full extent of what Fletcher was asking her to do. She was being asked to put Darrell completely aside, and strive for a relationship with Charlie so deep that he would confide all his secrets to her. The idea churned her stomach and she felt her heartbeat quicken irregularly as panic at losing Darrell almost overcame her.

'I can see that this is asking an awful lot of you, my dear, but you must remember how much is at stake. Find out anything you can about this "Charlie" and tell us everything you learn. You'll be shown today how to write telegrams to us in code that we will understand and that will seem quite ordinary to others. And remember, we don't know yet that he *is* a spy, and there may be a perfectly reasonable explanation for the discrepancies in stories. Last night's raid could have been pure coincidence. But the more information we have on him, the better.'

By the end of the day, Peggy had been shown some basic self-defence techniques, was issued with a small pistol and taught how to use it, and learnt an elementary code system for her telegram missives back to Whitehall, and a phone number and code to use for emergency calls. Fletcher had explained to her that once her mission with Charlie concluded – whatever that looked like – she might be asked to take some more thorough training and continue in the same line of work if she wished.

On the train home that evening, Peggy's mind swam with new information and ideas – things that had never occurred to her before in her predictable life in Poole, on the shores of the harbour. She was still utterly determined that this new line of work would not cause any tension between her and Darrell, but was beginning to wonder quite how she would manage that. As the beautiful English countryside sped past the carriage window, she remembered the devastating destruction she had seen in and around London. The whole population were, every one of them, living on the edge, nobody knowing if a bomb with their name on it could fall at any time.

And now she was putting herself directly into the path of danger. Much more danger. Keeping an eye on Charlie was one thing, but looking for a German spy who might be lurking, waiting to kill in cold blood the very leaders they all depended on – that was something else altogether. A mind like that would not hold back from eliminating her, in any way necessary. And what if the worst happened to her, and she never had chance to let Darrell know how she felt about him? He was bound to start doubting her once she spent more time with Charlie, and she had to let him know, even if she died, that she loved him.

Peggy pulled out the notepaper she'd been given in Whitehall earlier that day, and began a letter to Darrell. She would ask Rose to keep it filed away somewhere safe, just in case she lost her life to this mission. She searched her heart for the words to write, and began.

My dearest Darrell,

If you are reading this letter, then I am so terribly sorry for your loss...

When she arrived home, she had been expecting to have to explain her day but found, strangely, that everyone seemed to know where she'd been – although everyone believed a lie. Her family had been told by Rose Stevens that she'd been to Southampton for the day for some urgent training on the Solent regarding BOAC work. The next morning, she learnt that Rose had been told this by Patricia, who had also advised Nora and Eileen the same thing. The intricacies of the lies that she was already involved in amazed and horrified Peggy in equal amounts, and she longed for the simplicity of her life a few days earlier.

The presence of the pistol that she carried in her small kitbag seemed to make it much heavier than it really was, and Peggy imagined everyone would be able to sense it even if they never saw it.

Patricia gave her the rundown for the day's jobs, as if nothing in the world was different.

'Now, Peggy, Charlie will be waiting to meet you at the launch, and you'll be picking up some passengers at Salterns Marina and taking them out to the Clare this morning.'

Peggy stepped out into the spring March air. It was beginning to feel quite a bit less chilled even at this early and dark hour of the morning. April was only days away now, and though the days were growing slightly longer, the mornings were still terribly dark owing to the war-time one hour advance that was in place the year-round to increase productivity. But in a few weeks' time, on May the 4th, the clocks would spring forward another hour for British summertime. Then the evenings would be wonderfully long, and the blackout would hardly be a problem at all.

Peggy marvelled at her ability to be distracted by such things, considering the enormity of what had transpired over the last two days. She was practically a spy now, and sworn to secrecy her whole life through.

Peggy still couldn't imagine there was anything untoward about Charlie. He seemed such a nice chap, happy and helpful, and kind. He was a gentleman. But Peggy also knew the woman who had reported on Charlie, and trusted her as well. No, she realised. She really didn't know any of these people at all well and they could be anything other than what she believed them to be. One thing was sure though – Charlie definitely had a history of working on boats. Of that she was certain. His skills spoke for him in that regard. As she approached the Custom House steps where the launch was tied up, she saw Charlie ahead of her. He had already collected the key and was working with Nora to get the launch ready.

Once on the launch, and carrying out her normal duties, Peggy had the strangest feeling. Nothing had changed, in essence. This was the same launch, and the same crew she'd been working with for a couple of weeks – Nora for much longer, of course – and they were taking the same route she'd taken dozens, or even hundreds of times before. Yes, she had been in the presence of Churchill just two days ago, and he could have been dead by now, and that was a little jarring to the nervous system. But it was more than that. It was the sense that she was changed now, that everything about the way she would behave from this point on was tainted by this new role. She watched Charlie without watching him. She listened to him without looking as though she was listening. She saw him as another creature entirely. And she wondered if that was really fair.

What if his story was true, and this was all just a mistake? Would she be able to go back and see him the same way again? But then again, what was his story, really? Did she even know?

They pulled into the jetty at Salterns Marina, collected the small party of passengers, delivered them to the waiting flying boat and towed it out to the start of the number-one runway. Everything went like clockwork, just as it always did. And nothing was said that could possibly give away where these passengers were headed – even Peggy had no idea of their destination, and she heard that neither did the stewardess. The details were being kept secret from even the pilot until he was in the air. But Peggy still watched Charlie like a hawk and started to plan how she might get closer to him to learn more about him.

Peggy remembered the way Charlie had complimented her, and made her feel as though he would have liked to have had a chance with her if she hadn't already met Darrell.

Darrell. How was she supposed to get closer to Charlie without offending Darrell? She absolutely could not risk their budding romance, yet now she was sworn to secrecy. But so was Darrell, she suspected, being part of the RAAF. He wasn't allowed to tell her too much about where he'd been or what he'd been doing. Could she say something vague, and just ask him to trust her? What man would agree to that?

'Penny for your thoughts, Peggy?' Charlie's voice broke into her mind's wanderings like the sharp point of a knife. She felt as though time stopped then, for an indefinite period. She seemed to have enough time to think through all the possible ramifications of what she was about to say, accept the outcome, compose her answer, and begin the play-acting role of a secret spy, all in the time it took for her to draw breath and turn to look into Charlie's face.

'I was just thinking how unusual this all is, Charlie. Meeting three such important people, then the air raid the other night, and now seeing these passengers off to who knows where on this very secretive flight. These are strange times we live in, don't you agree?' she asked him.

'It certainly is peculiar. Imagine them trusting us – simple boatmen as we are – with the job of protecting such important characters. I'd have thought they'd need, at the very least, an army or navy escort,' Charlie said thoughtfully.

'I wonder why they travelled with BOAC, rather than on one of the Sandringhams at the RAF base?' Peggy asked, thinking out loud as much as asking Charlie. She was surprised when he answered.

'Perhaps they thought it less of a safety risk this way. I would think any enemy attack would be directed at the defence bases and transports, rather than civilian ones, wouldn't you?'

'I suppose so, if they know where to find them,' Peggy answered, as she slowed the launch on the approach to Poole Quay. 'Here, Charlie – you take the helm from here. You're more than confident,' she said stepping back and giving him room. 'Tell me again where it was that you got your experience with boats. You're so confident with this launch, I'd hazard a guess you've handled plenty like her before,' Peggy said, encouraging him to talk about himself.

She noticed that Charlie hesitated for a discernible moment before he answered.

'Mostly on the docks in London, but before the war, I spent some time on the continent too.'

'And where's your family? Are they in London?' she pried, and this time, she saw his face twitch with something like pain, or hate, or possibly even regret.

'I don't have any family any more, Peggy. The war took them all. The war's taken all I had left that was precious to me,' he said, avoiding her question in a way that made it impossible to probe any further without offending him.

He brought the launch in to the quay and Nora and Peggy worked to secure it, while Charlie shut down the engines. The three of them walked over to the offices to return the key and look at the schedule for the rest of the day.

'You all get an early dinner break, today,' said Patricia as she checked the flying boat itineraries. 'There's nothing due in now until four o'clock, and Rose doesn't even have any driving jobs for you today.'

Nora took no time at all to act on the good news and head home to her mother, looking forwards to a hot dinner and an afternoon tending the vegetables in the garden before coming back on duty again. Peggy looked at her watch and made a proposition to Charlie.

'Far too early for me to go home, Charlie, and I don't expect your landlady will want you hanging around under her feet while she cooks, either. Why don't we pop into the pub for a quick drink before dinner time?' she asked him, knowing full well she was pushing into unusual territory. She would never have dared asked a male workmate for a drink before this morning. What other new and strange behaviours might this peculiar mission lead her into? Peggy wondered.

* * *

Charlie bought a pint and a half of beer and carried the two glasses over to the table in the back corner of the Jolly Sailor where Peggy waited for him. She had suggested the Jolly Sailor, but he said he'd preferred this pub, and seemed to be glancing around him looking for someone he either did or didn't want to see, Peggy thought as she watched him. She tried again to find out a little more about how he spent his time when he wasn't working.

'So, with no family here, Charlie, and living in digs as you do, how do you spend your free time?'

Charlie looked at her with a confused expression and she tried again.

'What do you do to relax, I mean? I have my parents and sister, and the garden to tend, and there's always something to be doing on a boat with my dad,' she prompted.

'And you spend a bit of time with that airman, too, I've noticed,' he said with a sideways glance in her direction. She knew he was really asking her what she thought Darrell would think of her spending time with Charlie in a pub, in the middle of the day, alone.

'Yes, that's right. The Australians seem to have made the Antelope their Poole local, and that's where my family goes most often,' she said, trying to generalise her attachment to Darrell as being to the whole of the Australian Squadron. 'I've danced with them all, Charlie. I'm nobody's girl in particular,' she lied and was shocked at how easily it slipped off her tongue.

By the time Peggy walked home alone for the hot dinner that awaited her there, she had learnt that Charlie spent most of his spare time thinking of his late wife and child who had both died in an air raid, and he had readily admitted that he had spent some time somewhere on the continent before the war. And even though she had been tasked with finding out if Charlie might be lying about any of his past and could in fact be a German spy, she still found that hard to believe and dearly hoped she might be able to prove otherwise. But when she thought of her brother and Molly's husband and the peril they faced at the hands of the Nazis, she was reminded how important it was to do everything possible to eliminate the enemy. Whoever he was.

One other interesting thing she had learnt from Charlie was that he now lived with a Mrs Rogers in Blue Boar Lane, but this was probably not new information to Fletcher. However, what neither Charlie nor Fletcher knew was that Mrs Rogers was the widow of one of Peggy's mother's cousins. This gave Peggy a clear line to finding out more about Charlie without him even knowing.

As she opened the front door at home, the welcome aroma of oxtail soup greeted her and she could hear her family already gathered in the kitchen.

'Sorry I'm a bit later, Mum. I was catching up with Charlie, our new hand on the launch,' Peggy explained. 'Did you know he is boarding with Aunty Joan?' Peggy asked her mother.

'Our Barry's Joan, you mean, down Blue Boar Lane? That poor woman's had such a tough life, you know. Well, I'm happy for her that she's able to get boarders in. That'll help her make ends meet,' Mrs Symonds said as she ladled out the soup and Molly sliced and buttered some bread to go with it.

'Once this war is over, and I move out with Bill and this little one, you'll have a room here you can let out to a lodger, Mum. And perhaps our Peggy will be making a home with an Australian airman we know,' Molly said with a wink.

Peggy smiled at the idea but was keen to turn the conversation back to the task at hand. She already feared that the happy ending she'd so easily imagined just days ago might never come to pass. She didn't need reminding of it now. She had to stay focused on the mission.

'Do you see Aunty Joan to talk to very much, Mum? It's just that me and the other girls would be interested to know a little more about Charlie, working with him as we do, and what with him coming from out of town. He doesn't seem to have any family to speak of,' she said.

'You're not a bit sweet on him then love? I thought Darrell was the one who'd caught your eye,' Mrs Symonds said.

'Not me, Mum. Nora is a bit keen though. But she's shy, and would rather know a bit more about him before showing him any signs,' Peggy said, thinking on her feet.

Peggy knew this was all she needed to say to prompt her mother on her own mission of investigations. Anyone who came from out of town and was entering the world of her girls and their friends was to be treated with suspicion, and Mrs Symonds would dig out any information there was to be mined on Charlie's story.

After lunch, Molly helped their mother with the washing up while Peggy went outside to help her dad with some work in the vegetable garden, which was beginning to really take off now that spring was advancing. There were pea sticks to put in and seeds to sow at their bases, carrot and radish seeds to sow, and tomato and lettuce seedlings to plant out. The leeks were coming along, and there were some new potatoes to harvest already. As Peggy gently felt for them in the soil under her gloved hands, she could almost taste the rich butter they used to melt lavishly on these delicious morsels, back when butter was freely available.

'When this war is over, Dad, and we don't have to live under rationing any more, I'm going to buy a pound of butter, and a pound of sugar every single time I go to the shops, just because I can!' she said with longing in her voice.

Her father laughed heartily, but the look he gave her showed her he couldn't agree more.

Peggy rested for a while and leant on the back fence, looking across the harbour. The flames on Brownsea Island had died down somewhat but there was still an awful lot of smoke coming across the water.

'Strange to think how close all those bombs were to us the

other night. The decoy over there seems to be working well,' she mused.

'It certainly is. Sad to sacrifice the village, but better that than the lived-in homes here in town,' he said, and Peggy was grateful afresh for the pragmatism that had grounded her as she had grown up. She went back to her planting, resting on her knees not far from her dad, thinking all the while.

'Dad,' she said at length, 'I was given an interesting task this morning. I can't tell you or anyone else anything about it, naturally, but I'm worried about Darrell.'

'Why would you be worried about that strapping lad, love? I'm sure he can look after 'isself.' Her father chortled.

Peggy smiled, belying the anxiety that was growing inside.

'I have no doubt he can look after himself perfectly well, Dad. I'm just worried about what he might think of me. I'm going to have to spend some time away from him, because of work, and... it is going to seem... as if I were growing cold on Darrell. And I'm not! I think he's the loveliest man I ever knew, and I'm worried he might get the wrong idea. That's all,' she said, wondering if she was digging herself a hole that it might be hard to climb out of without using the details of her mission as rungs on the ladder.

Mr Symonds stood up, brushed the soil from his knees and hands, and perched against the fence, taking a good look at his daughter.

'Peggy, you're a bright girl. You always have been capable of anything. If you've been trusted with a job that you can't share with any of us, then it's an important one, and one I'm sure you will do very well. Darrell is an intelligent man, Peggy. Explain to him what you've said to me, and I'm sure he'll understand,' he said, patting her on the arm and bending back down to the rows of new plantings. 'Come on, Peg. These vegetables won't plant themselves.'

After the work was done, and their tools and hands all scrubbed clean alike, Peggy and her dad went back inside for a welcome rest and a cup of tea. Peggy had been thinking about how she would talk to Darrell and what she might say, but she still had a knot of worry in her stomach about carrying a secret that could mean some people – Darrell especially – might think less of her. She would look for a chance to see him again, and soon, to show him how much she cared for him.

21

BRISBANE – DECEMBER 1998

Rebekah leant against the airplane window, peering eagerly at the beautiful landscape below. They'd crossed landfall somewhere near Darwin several hours ago and the rugged red landscape of outback Queensland had gone on, and on, and on, without a cloud in the sky to break up the view. She glanced back at Paul, who was dozing with his earphones in. If he slept much longer, she was going to have to wake him up so he didn't miss the view of the coastline from this glorious height.

She'd grown used to watching him sleeping, and sharing all the little moments of life with him. And though she had never expected this, Rebekah couldn't imagine a life without Paul beside her. They'd spent virtually every weekend together since July, either in Poole or in London, and occasionally further afield, even taking a weekend trip to Paris in the autumn. She'd bought herself a mobile phone too, so they could stay in contact wherever she was, especially as she was so often outdoors and away from a desk. And now they were on this journey together, home to Brisbane.

The air stewards started raising all the window shields and

bringing out the breakfast trolley. Soon, the general hustle and bustle of the plane, or perhaps it was the smell of coffee, roused Paul from his long and much-needed nap. He'd barely slept at all from London to Singapore, and so he'd caught up on the Singapore to Brisbane leg of the journey.

'We're over Queensland now, babe,' she said and couldn't help but do a little jiggle of delight, she was that excited. Once the coast came into view, she swapped seats with Paul for a while so he could see the gorgeous turquoise colour of the ocean, and the insanely large areas of completely unspoilt beaches.

'I can't wait to get down there and explore it all with you. You're my perfect tour guide – and have been since the moment I met you,' he said, kissing her hand.

As the plane dropped altitude over Brisbane, Rebekah just about squealed as she saw the Story Bridge over the Brisbane River in the city centre, and the newer, bigger Gateway Bridge much closer to the airport. The flight path took them out over Moreton Bay and she showed him some national parks that were easily identifiable from the air: Moreton Island and North Stradbroke Island, two of the largest sand islands in the world. Then the plane dropped low over the water and as they headed towards the runway, she showed him the mangroves that made up an important layer of the ecosystem all along the coast wherever there were mudflats. She gripped the armrests as they bumped in to land.

* * *

'Rebekah!' she heard the familiar voice of her mum cry, as they pushed their luggage trolley out through the frosted glass sliding doors to the arrivals lounge. Rebekah left Paul with the trolley and ran to throw her arms around her, not realising until this second how much she'd missed the feel of Mum's hugs.

'Oh, let me get a good look at you, love! Your hair's grown so long!' cried her mum as she held Rebekah out at arm's length again. 'And this must be Paul,' she said reaching out both hands to pull Paul into a hug too.

'Hello, Mrs Martin. Lovely to meet you,' he said with his broadest and most handsome grin, Rebekah noticed, although he was looking about as smooth right now after this long-haul flight as he had done the very first time she'd set eyes on him – exhausted, unshaven, and in need of a good shower.

'None of this formal business please, love; I'm just Helen to my friends,' Rebekah's mum told Paul warmly.

At home in Barrawondi Street, they settled with coffee and cake on the back deck, and both enjoyed wonderfully long showers and dressed into cool linen clothes, much better suited to the humid heat of a Brisbane December. Feeling refreshed, and ready for the adventure ahead, Rebekah had started with a walking tour of the backyard, showing Paul the red bottlebrush, the gigantic gum trees, the yellow grevillea, and explaining to him where the incessant shrill sound was coming from.

'That's the cicadas. They're a flying bug that comes out of the ground in the hot, humid weather, and some of the Australian cicadas are among the loudest in the world,' she explained.

'I don't doubt that for one second.' He laughed, just as a flock of rainbow lorikeets chattered overhead and landed in the bottle-brush tree to eat nectar from the red flowers hanging there.

'This place is absolutely alive with wildlife, Rebekah – and this is only your back garden.'

'You should wait until you see Pig's garden – I mean the garden next door that used to be Peggy's. She's been gone longer than I have now, but from what I can see, the new owners have kept it just as it was when we planted it together.'

She took him to the front of the house, and they leant on the side fence so Rebekah could explain everything to him. She told him how, back before her graduation morning, she and Peggy had decided to transform the barren and often dusty front yard of her place into a haven for indigenous plants and wildlife. She'd been freshly inspired by the rainforest at South Bank that there would need to be water, and frogs – a kind of mini billabong as a home for insects and skinks. They had planned for as many native flowering trees and shrubs as they could fit into the sunny sections, to draw the honey-eating birds, and she had made contact with a man who could provide them with a small hive of native stingless bees. And in the shady area underneath the front deck of the house, around the damp edges of the billabong, they had planted a young, shade-loving tree fern.

Now, just three years later, the little pond was alive with frogs and insects, and the trees had grown to at least triple the height they'd been when she last saw them. The tiny black bees were busy among the flowers, and there was even a water dragon resting under the cooling fronds of the tree fern.

'Peggy and I planned it all together. Well – she actually let me do all the planning, and she did as much of the work with me as she could manage. But it was a real joint effort,' she said with a pleased sigh.

'It really is something, and quite different from most of the plain lawns I can see up and down the street. I wonder who moved in who is just as keen on the garden as you were?' Paul asked her just as Helen came along to join them.

'That would be Tim,' she said, and gave a little nervous cough. 'Tim's been living here for two years now, and he and I have become quite close friends. Actually, he's coming over for dinner tonight,' she said, looking as shy as a young girl.

'Mum? What kind of friends?' teased Rebekah, but her mum just walked away chuckling.

'Well, I never thought I'd see that happen,' whispered Rebekah to Paul. 'Mum's always been so independent, and happy with it just being the two of us.'

'Was she really happy with that arrangement do you think? Or was it just the way it had to be while you were growing up?' asked Paul, wrapping his arms around Rebekah's waist as they watched Helen disappear into the house.

* * *

That evening, Paul and Rebekah shared a wonderful meal with Helen and Tim from next door who, it was obvious, spent a lot of time here with her mum. He was kind, and helpful, and looked at Rebekah's mum as though she was the most wonderful thing in his life.

Rebekah took the chance to talk with her mum as they were fetching the dessert from the kitchen.

'Tim is lovely, Mum, and I'm very happy for you both,' she said.

'Steady, love, we aren't getting married or anything.' Helen laughed. 'But he is wonderful, I know. It all started when I needed a hand to chop some wood for the fire – as clichéd as that sounds – but I never have been able to handle an axe, though I can do pretty much everything else for myself. And then we got chatting about caring for that wonderful native garden you and Peggy created and the rest is history,' she said as they went back to the dining table.

'Actually, we probably should talk about Peggy, Mum,'

Rebekah began, and she and Paul updated her on all they had discovered so far about Peggy's interesting life in Poole, and the whereabouts of this mysterious Darrell Taylor.

Paul had used some of his knowledge and contacts to trace what had happened to him, and found that he'd returned to Australia after the war but left the air force, working instead on commercial airlines, and particularly the flying boats that operated right here in Brisbane, out at nearby Redland Bay.

'He is still receiving a Defence Force pension, and lives in a retirement village down by the water. We have a phone number, but haven't called yet,' said Paul. 'We don't want to alarm him, and he might be upset to have old memories brought up again.'

'Why don't you write a note and deliver it to his mailbox? Leave your phone number, and ask him to call you if he would like you to visit?' offered Tim.

After dinner, before they went to bed, Paul and Rebekah wrote the letter to Darrell together, telling him about the letter that had been found addressed to him and kept in Poole for over fifty years.

'I have the perfect place to take you for a day trip tomorrow, and we need to catch a ferry not far at all from Darrell's address, so we'll drop this off on our way,' Rebekah said.

That night, they were asleep by nine o'clock and awake the next morning before dawn, thanks to the jet lag kicking in, but that was a perfect start to the day trip Rebekah had planned for them. They made up a sandwich picnic bag, and added a couple of bottles of chilled beer with some frozen cooler blocks and, borrowing her mum's car, Rebekah drove them south, over the river, and out to Cleveland. They found the retirement village, and posted the letter to Darrell, hoping they would get a reply soon. From there, they drove to the car barge to North Stradbroke Island.

'This is one of the islands you pointed out from the plane, isn't it? Quite a bit bigger than Brownsea, I think,' Paul commented, and she laughed.

'Brownsea is a speck on the map compared to Straddie. It's an island with a lot of Aboriginal history – Minjerribah, in the traditional language – and you're going to love the scenery. If we were here in winter, we'd be able to spot humpback whales breaching on the ocean side of the island, but I'm hoping today for wallabies, turtles and dolphins at the very least,' she said as she drove the car off the barge at the end of the trip across Moreton Bay to the island.

'And I'm keen for you to get your feet wet in the Pacific Ocean, too,' she said as she parked the car at the gloriously unspoilt Cylinder Beach, named for the perfectly formed surfing waves that crashed onto the shore.

Rebekah taught Paul how to apply sunblock the Aussie way, and they stepped quickly across the baking-hot, silky white sand, and slipped into the refreshing, crystal-clear water that glittered in the sunlight. They jumped over and swam through the surf until they were deep enough to float on the waves as they came in.

'This is a delectable and rather tiny bikini,' Paul said, hugging her near-naked shape to him as they floated in paradise. 'I'm quite fond of the way the weather here dictates clothing that shows me your gorgeous skin, so much of the time,' he said, and she turned round to encircle his waist with her legs and kiss his salty lips. But, in closing her eyes for a moment, she'd taken her attention off the waves and didn't see what hit them. They tumbled in the surf, and came up gasping for air, with sand in their hair, feeling like they'd had a round in a salty washing machine.

'I can't believe the power in these waves!' gasped Paul, coughing as he wiped sand and saltwater from his eyes.

'Sorry, I should have warned you how strong it is – and this is not exactly what we would call big surf. But I'm sure it's more than you're used to in England.' She showed him where the freshwater showers were at the edge of the beach, and then they relaxed in the shade of the grassy picnic area to eat their lunch, the cool beer soothing their salt-washed throats, then they lay in the shade from a whispering she-oak tree, enjoying a few minutes' siesta time as the whispers soothed them to sleep.

'This is a wonderful start to our holiday, Rebekah. What a glorious place. Tour guide extraordinaire, as always,' he said sleepily, raising her hand to his mouth so he could plant a kiss on each of her fingers.

'There's much more to come after lunch,' she said, turning to her side and draping an arm over his chest, revelling in the prospect of a whole month spent together. 'Wait until you see the gorge we're going to walk. It's too beautiful to describe.'

The gorge walk proved to be an even bigger hit with Paul than had the beach, and Rebekah was not surprised. She never failed to be amazing by the clarity of the waters, the colour of the most pristine Ceylon sapphire. They crashed and foamed relentlessly into the gorge, worn away by the same action over millennia, oblivious to the changes that humanity wrought on the world around the island. She had spotted turtles floating at the mouth of the gorge and they'd leant over the railings to watch them dive and disappear into the deep. Then, as they stood to admire the beauty of the unspoilt beach that swept away into the far distance, they spotted a pod of dolphins surfing in the waves.

That night, she dreamed of surfing with dolphins, and swimming in the peaceful silence of the sparkling waters beneath the waves, where the sunlight shone through the water like raining diamonds. When she woke in the cool of the dawn, a flock of kook-aburras laughed at the morning, and she turned to Paul's sleeping face, wishing he'd been awake to hear it. There would be others. But they were only here for a month, and then they'd be back in England, on Brownsea, which she loved, and he in London, which she knew he was beginning to love less. Rebekah wished she could bottle the glorious nature of Australia and take a little home, to pour into the bath on a cold winter's night and bring herself back here.

She chuckled at the idea but couldn't lose the feeling that by gaining the joy of living on Brownsea – and ultimately meeting Paul – she'd lost so much by leaving behind the Australian land-scape and weather that she loved so much. She wouldn't change anything, she realised, but there was an acceptance of loss to be considered even in what she had gained.

The next morning at breakfast, Paul and Rebekah showed her mum all the documents in the folder that they'd found on Peggy.

'Are you allowed to have these with you?' Helen asked. 'Shouldn't they be in some official records somewhere?'

'By rights they should be, yes, but where we found them, they had no business being. So nobody is missing them. In time, I expect I'll get them sent to the British Airways archivist, if they think it worthwhile. But we're not hurting anyone by having them here. And besides, the whole problem is that these papers really don't tell us anything,' Paul explained.

'We want to give the letter to Darrell Taylor, Mum. It was written for him – and was meant to be given to him on Peggy's death, which it seemed she imagined was going to occur during the war. So, now she's gone, we're doing the right thing by deliv-ering it. And I'm hopeful he might have some clues about exactly what she got up to during the war, and whether they had any relationship afterwards.'

'Whatever it was she did, you can bet she did it with gumption,' said Helen, as she got up to answer the phone.

She came back a few moments later looking stunned.

'It's for you Rebekah – a Mr Darrell Taylor,' she said with meaning, and Rebekah had to stop herself running to the phone.

When she came back to the others, she was glowing.

'He wants to meet us. He was shocked, but he remembers Peggy very well, and is interested to read the letter. We're invited to go there today for morning tea.'

22

POOLE – MAY 1941

Charlie had half undressed himself for bed, but had ended up lying on his back, hands behind his head, staring at the ceiling where, by some strange work of magic in his mind, he could see the face of Peggy Symonds. He had a bubbling feeling in his chest and a sensation on his face that seemed to come from his ancient past. He was smiling. Not just trying to smile, or putting on a smile for effect, or smiling to be polite. He was smiling because he felt happy.

For the last six weeks, a delightful change had come into his life and he had begun to form a strong friendship with Peggy.

He had always been fond of her and had often complimented her on the expertise with which she handled the launch, and she'd accepted his praise as any other colleague would. But one day, she seemed to be smiling so sweetly, and chatting so freely with him that he'd dared to compliment her on how pretty she was looking. No one could have been more surprised than Charlie when she responded by giving him a coy smile and thanking him. Charlie had heard that she was already firmly attached to one of the Australian airmen, but she seemed very open to spending more time with him.

And so they had begun to spend some time sharing drinks together, and he would occasionally walk her home. She had asked him if he might be going to the dance one Saturday night and with all his soul, he'd wished he didn't have this stupid limp, but he couldn't possibly go dancing. He would look a fool, and make a fool of Peggy too, which was worse.

Instead, he suggested they go for a picnic, and she had the most wonderful idea of taking her dad's dinghy out across the harbour.

As he lay there that night thinking of the day he had spent with Peggy, he was in awe of the way his heart seemed to have made room for her. His dead wife still had her place in his soul, but now there seemed to be another space just the right size for Peggy to fill. The idea of Peggy and her lovely smile, her bouncy, blonde curls and her merry laugh filled him with a joy he could not explain. He wondered if he should be prepared to explain his feelings to his wife. What would she think of him? But it was now almost exactly a year since the day she had died and the rough journey that grief had taken him on, though a steep and winding path, seemed to be dwindling now. He shook away his darker thoughts and took himself back to the happy moments of this picnic day.

They went ashore on the little beach near the ruined pottery on Brownsea Island – risking both the wrath of Mrs Bonham-Christie who had banned all visitors, as well as that of the army that patrolled there, manning the bomb decoy site. They drank a flask of hot tea and ate the oatmeal and syrup biscuits she'd made from a recipe she said she had learnt of lately from a friend. He became jittery about them being caught, and he was sure that Peggy had noticed his

unease though she said nothing of it. They left and motored across
to Arne instead. She'd suggested a walk, and he went for a little way
before tiring with his limp, so they'd lain in the late spring sunshine
on the heather, watching and listening for the many different birds
that flew overhead and hopped around the heathland.

And when it was time to go home, he'd sat in the stern of the
dinghy and taken the tiller of the Seagull engine and watched her
as she sat in the bow, her blonde curls blowing in the breeze and
her fingers trailing in the water. And he had started to hope that,
perhaps, she could be his.

Today was Sunday, and tomorrow they would be working
again together on the launches, and perhaps driving up to the
hotel. He didn't mind what the work entailed, he realised, as long
as he could be with Peggy.

As he settled to sleep that Sunday night, Charlie worked hard
to scare off the visions of war that troubled his mind and was
determined instead to think on the pretty face of Peggy Symonds.

* * *

'Thanks for coming in, Peggy. I've told Patricia that you won't be
on the launch as planned this morning as we have some paperwork to catch up with,' explained Fletcher, after calling her into
the back office on her arrival at the harbour master's office the
next morning.

'So, it's been over a month and I know you've been spending a
lot more time with Charlie than just at work. Do you have
anything to share with me?' Fletcher asked, pouring coffee for
himself and offering one to Peggy too.

'I think there might be something in the claim that he is not
English, and he openly admits to spending some time on the
continent before the war. He can't – or won't – give me any details

about where he is really from. He says he had a wife and daughter who died in an air raid, but he won't say where. I tend to believe him, though something isn't quite right. It could have been London, or almost anywhere else in Europe, but he won't give me any details. He is still grieving, but he keeps his heart to himself. I'm a little worried that he might be falling for me, if I'm honest. My mother is a cousin to his landlady, and all she could learn is that he is an honest, polite, hard-working young man. He is making Mrs Rogers' life easier just by being there with her sons away,' Peggy reported.

'Well, you'll need to keep trying. You may have to get very close to him – see if you can get him to slip up and mention his late wife's name. You'll have to work out how to extricate yourself from the friendship you've developed with him, in your own way, when the time comes,' Fletcher said, as if this was the most matter-of-fact thing in the world. But Peggy's heart was breaking over the rift she knew was already developing between her and Darrell.

After the working day was over, and Peggy had eaten dinner with her family, they'd all gone out to enjoy the warm, light evening with a walk along the quay, which had, inevitably, led them into the Antelope for a drink.

The delights of being able to enjoy the evening in daylight and without the hassles of blackout, brought the community together in a way that was not too dissimilar to their past lives, back before the war began. All except for the masses of uniforms everywhere, of course. The pubs all along the quay were busy with locals and visiting soldiers, sailors, and airmen alike and all were relaxing in the warm, evening air.

Peggy hadn't seen Darrell for a week and although she had been doing her best to explain, she felt sure that Darrell was growing more and more suspicious. Even though the mission that

Fletcher – and the British Government – had charged her with was far from over, she was determined to try and spend more time with Darrell again, and reassure him of her affection, and she was hoping to see him tonight. She was looking around the faces in the pub, eager to see him, when she felt a tap on her shoulder.

'Looking for Darrell, are you, love?' she heard an airman say in that now beloved Australian accent. 'He's just gone out, down the lane.' He nodded in the direction of the pub's side door. 'Didn't know you were coming, I expect. You might catch him if you run,' he added touching his cap and heading back to his friends at the bar.

Peggy went out into the evening air, which was beginning to grow dusky with pink in the sky to the west. There was no one in this lane at all and she wondered if she'd been led astray, but went out into the main street to see if Darrell was nearby. Just as she reached the corner, she saw him disappear into another lane opposite. She followed, quietly, checking over her shoulder in case she too was being watched. She got to the end of the dark lane that ran between the terraced houses where Darrell had disappeared and looked out to her right, towards the quay, but he wasn't that way.

Just as she was deciding to give up and go back, a hand was clamped over her mouth and an arm wrapped around her waist and she was pulled quickly backwards into the lane and held tight against the body of man. Her instinct was to scream but the shock had paralysed her, and her mouth was tightly clamped anyway. She shut her eyes and concentrated on taking deep breaths to calm herself. *Stupid, stupid girl*, she thought, *running about in and out of dark lanes alone in the evening. What did you expect?* And then he whispered her name.

'Shush, Peggy love, stay calm, it's me,' cooed Darrell as he spun her around to face him. Peggy began to cry then, with relief, but he put his fingers to her lips and squeezed her tight.

'You must stay quiet, Peggy. Shush,' and he held his hand up to indicate she must stay exactly where she stood while he moved towards the corner again. Peggy nodded, mutely, and she heard a new sound, a foreign sound. Darrell was peering around the end of the lane and Peggy could hear two voices, speaking in another language – German, she presumed, by the sound of it. They were arguing, and their whispered, spitting tone suggested words of hate and anger, though she didn't understand a word.

One of the men began to cry and his tone changed to one of pleading, and then a pair of footsteps ran away. Darrell still stood frozen with his hand up to stop Peggy from moving, and then she heard the second man sniff, and seem to take a moment to calm himself, before he walked away fast, but not running. She recognised something in the uneven rhythm of his footsteps on the pavement.

Then, at last, Darrell came back to face her and breathed a great sigh. She questioned him with her eyebrows, and he nodded.

'Come on, Peggy, it's safe now. Let's take a little walk. There are some things I need to explain,' he said. 'And I'm sorry for frightening you back there, but I had to stop you. Who knows what might have happened to you if you'd walked into the middle of that argument.' Darrell led her gently with a tender hand at the small of her back. Once out in the open, he checked to see that nobody had noticed them leaving the dark lane and offered her his arm.

'Who were they, Darrell? I wish you'd let me see. And what was all that about?' Peggy asked. She held her bag close to her, feeling for the weight of the pistol and knowing she would have used it if necessary.

'Did you not recognise either of the voices, Peggy?'

She thought about it for a moment before replying. She knew exactly who one of them was, but was not about to tell Darrell she recognised the voice of the man she'd been getting to know very well just lately.

'One of them had something familiar to it, but I don't even know what language they were speaking. Were they German?' she asked, feigning innocence.

'That is the big question I'd like to know the answer to. They were speaking Dutch, but they said the word *Deutsch* several times, and *Deutsch* is Dutch for German,' Darrell said, and he waited.

Peggy couldn't decide if she was thrilled to have Darrell's help, or angry that she hadn't realised he had been following Charlie too. Either way, she now wished the ground would swallow her whole. She had to think fast to keep her secret under wraps.

'And I know exactly what you've been doing, Peggy, giving me the run-around with him, and I couldn't have you getting about with someone that nobody knows anything about and not keep an eye on you, could I?' Peggy was horrified to realise she'd been that obvious, and had to make a snap decision to put Darrell off the scent.

'I don't know what you mean, Darrell. Charlie is a lovely young man and we share a working relationship. Yes, I've spent a little time with him lately, and what's that to you?'

She saw him smart at her words and pieces of her heart fell to her feet and smashed there on the pavement.

'I see. Well, Peggy, I really thought we had something, but it seems you're keeping all your options open.' He sighed and took a few steps away, stooping to light a cigarette and then turning back to her sharply.

'Whatever you're up to, you should know this. Yesterday,

when you were out all day, I spent a little time watching this other bloke, the one who was holding up our Charlie here. I think his name is Klaus – and he may well be German. He keeps a rough old dinghy on the shore at Hamworthy Beach, not far at all from the RAF base. I've seen him come and go several times. He seems to head off towards the mouth of the river. And your mate Charlie went that way once too, you know.'

Peggy was genuinely shocked.

'Really? What would Charlie want up the River Frome? And what boat did he take?' she asked.

'None other than your prized BOAC launch,' said Darrell with an arch look.

'What? How? When? On his own?' she demanded in rapid fire, standing up straight and turning to face Darrell straight on.

'Oh yes, that was quite a while ago now, long before you started spending so much time with him. There's something up that river that interests the pair of them. They're not English, they're hiding something, and I'm going to find out what it is.'

Darrell went on to explain what he'd seen yesterday while she and Charlie had been enjoying the most delightful day of picnicking, when she had been supposed to be spying.

He had followed the other man across the lifting bridge to Hamworthy and to his dinghy on the beach, where he'd left, as usual, and headed off up towards the mouth of the river.

Earlier today, on this Monday afternoon, Darrell had watched as Charlie was accosted by this same mystery man who, after an argument, seemed to have showed him some papers. The two had tussled there in the darkness of the lane but the stranger had run away, leaving Charlie looking for all the world like his life was over.

Peggy thought on her feet fast.

'Darrell, this is ridiculous! Charlie is just a boatman about whom we all know very little. He's a very pleasant man, and he doesn't need you chasing him around, just because you're jealous,' she said, managing to sound more exasperated and less desperate than she really was.

'All I really set out to do was protect you, Peggy. I just found a few interesting titbits of information along the way. And I think the attention you've been giving him has distracted him to the point he's not noticed that I'm keeping an eye on him. But there's definitely something fishy about this pair.'

'Darrell, I really think you're being a bit extreme. Everything will look more natural in the daylight tomorrow,' she said, trying to appease him.

Darrell stared at her hard for a few moments before seeming to make a decision. 'Come on, then, it's time I was getting you home to your parents. They'll have wondered what happened to you,' Darrell said as he took her hand. The air between them was cold as frost, though, and Peggy ached to be able to tell him the truth.

They walked home in the peace of the moonlight, hopeful that it was to be a quiet night, with no air raids. The weather was soft and warm, the night was clear, and a million stars sparkled above them. Peggy chose to forget, for this precious moment, the troubles of the war and this strange double life she had begun to live.

At the front door, Peggy kissed Darrell and held him close, mustering all her energy to try and appear calm, all the time knowing that she had to take control and work out what Charlie was up to.

'So, you're spending your days with him, and kissing me goodnight now? What will your Charlie think of that, hey? You're going to have to choose, Peggy. You can't keep us both hanging on,' he said, shuffling his feet in the gravel as he looked down.

'Darrell, I don't know what you mean. I'll see you again soon,' she said, keeping her voice calm and even despite the turmoil she felt inside. Hopefully, it would only be a couple of days before she could explain everything to him. Darrell left to go back to the RAF base, and she went inside, closing the door slowly behind her.

She went through to the kitchen and sat quietly at the table, knowing her family were already upstairs in bed. She stayed as still as one of the bollards on Poole Quay for ten whole minutes, listening to the sound of her own breathing and giving Darrell plenty of time to get up to the lifting bridge and over it to Hamworthy before she set off. Then she crept out the back door, through the garden, and along the beach until she made it onto the road in front of the lifeboat house. She kept her head down as she walked quickly along the quay, thankful that the pubs had all closed for the night and most people were at home by now.

When she reached the Fish Shambles market, she ducked quickly into the end of Blue Boar Lane, checking over her shoulder that nobody had seen her. She found Mrs Rogers' home, and then, looking up at the one upstairs window facing the street, took a punt that it would be Charlie's. If not, she would have to think fast to find some reason she might have for getting Aunty Joan out of bed.

Peggy picked a couple of small pebbles from the ground and threw one at the window. When there was no response, she threw the second. A moment later, the window opened to reveal the puzzled face of Charlie Edwards. She held her finger firmly to her lips before he could speak and signalled to him to come downstairs.

As he opened the front door, hastily pulling his jacket on, Peggy looked from one end of the lane to the other and decided the back way would be safest from prying eyes. She did not speak, and would not permit him to do so until she had led him well away.

'Peggy, what on earth is going on? Are you in some kind of trouble?' he asked, full of concern.

'No, Charlie, I'm fine. It's you I'm worried about.' She turned to face him fully, looking him square in the eye and taking a deep breath before she fired her first shot. 'Had any more conversations in Dutch lately?'

He visibly reeled and now it was Charlie who looked furtively over his shoulder. Seeing that they were still alone, he took her elbow and guided her along the lanes until they reached the church yard. They sheltered on the dark side of the church, not that there was ever really a light side in this blackout. The only sound at this midnight hour was a nightingale that chirruped prettily from one of the chestnut trees in the church yard. Peggy turned to face Charlie and spoke under her breath.

'Who are you, Charlie? And who the hell is Klaus?' she demanded.

He sighed deeply and, rubbing his face with his hands, he slid down the wall and crouched on the ground. Peggy sat beside him.

'I am Charlie now, Peggy. This is who I want to be. But Charlie is not who I was. My name is Hans Meyers, and I am Dutch. I came from Rotterdam. My wife, Katrijn, and baby girl, Anika, were killed by a German bombing raid that butchered them and all of the beautiful city, and I fled here, to Poole, as a refugee,' he explained. 'This injury to my leg, it is not from my childhood. The damage was done in the same air raid that killed my family.'

'But, you said you'd come from London. And when you speak to me, you don't sound Dutch at all,' she said.

'I did come from London just before I met you. I was here in Poole, at first on Brownsea Island and then in the town for a few weeks after I arrived. But I could not get work. Everyone thought I was German here, and people were unkind. So, I left and went to London where I could get lost in the crowds. I learnt to speak like a Londoner, and I found work in the docks there. But it is not a friendly place, and I was lonely. I wanted to be here, by the sea, where I feel more at home, and where I left my boat.'

'And Klaus? Is he a friend of yours?' she demanded.

'No! I barely know the man, and he is not good news, Peggy. He hitched a ride with me when we fled Rotterdam, and I don't trust him. He's trying to blackmail me to give him information about flying boat passengers, but I won't do it,' Charlie said.

'Blackmail you? What with? What does he have on you?'

'I can't tell you – it's nothing really – something personal. It doesn't matter to anyone but me,' he said.

'And where is Klaus now? If he is causing some kind of trouble, then we need to get him picked up. Is he Dutch? Or is he German?' she asked.

Charlie shrugged his shoulders slightly a pulled a face. 'He's Dutch. Like me,' he said at length.

They sat in silence for several minutes while Peggy decided what to do.

'I have to report you for not being who you say you are, Charlie, but I believe you. I believe you aren't a threat. But this Klaus – him we must find and have arrested. Do you have any idea where he is?'

In reply, Charlie simply shook his head.

Peggy sighed deeply. 'The best thing we can both do now is go and get some sleep. We'll deal with all this in the morning. Come on, help me up,' she said reaching up her hand to him as he stood.

They walked back to Blue Boar Lane in companionable silence.

'I thought it was going too well,' Charlie said at last.

'The way you've deceived us all, you mean?' she asked with a cynical tone.

'No. I mean the way you seemed to like me so much. I thought we had something good, Peggy. But I was wrong. Nothing good is ever going to happen to me again,' he said despondently.

'Don't say that,' she said, feeling suddenly guilty for having led him on. 'I'm sure everything will turn out all right, Charlie. You may not be who you said you are, but you aren't the enemy, and you aren't a German spy. Things will be okay, again, I promise,' she said, and despite a little voice that warned her against it, she reached up and kissed him on the cheek in farewell. 'Get some sleep and I'll see you tomorrow,' Peggy said as she slipped away, home to her own bed.

* * *

Sleep, when it came to Charlie, was deep and dark and he sank into the rest it brought as though he hoped never to wake again. He dreamed they were walking along the beach, hand in hand, and Hans found a perfect place to lay down the picnic blanket in the shelter of the dunes. He helped Katrijn to sit down and then unpacked the picnic basket, making her a plate with freshly baked bread that he tore apart, a hunk of cheese and some sliced ham. He poured her a glass of wine and then one for himself and together, they drank. She sighed and looked out to sea and then her smiling face shone as she turned to face him again.

'This is a good place to celebrate,' she said.

'I have always loved it here. My mother and I used to come here when I was much younger, after we first arrived,' he said wistfully. 'But what are we celebrating?' he asked her.

'The news that you are going to be a father, Hans,' she said, her laugh a tinkle and her face aglow with joy.

To begin with, it was as if he'd not heard. As if she'd spoken some strange, ancient language that sounded somewhat familiar but with words and phrases he couldn't quite place. And then the realisation filled his soul with wonder. He reached out to grasp her in his arms but before he could get to her side, he woke up and saw nothing.

Waking fully from his dream, he realised he wasn't on a beach at all, but in bed in Blue Boar Lane, and Katrijn was dead, and so was their baby, and now Peggy knew his secret and all the happiness he had begun to feel was over. It was all over. Charlie pulled the pillow over his head and prayed for death, his hatred for Klaus growing stronger by the second.

* * *

As she finally crept to bed that night, and undressed in the dark, Peggy felt angry with herself for allowing things to get this way. How had Darrell managed to tail Charlie, and discover what he was up to, when she'd been spending so much time with him for that specific purpose? What kind of a useless spy did that make her? She sat on the edge of her bed and took the small pistol from her handbag, turning it over so the steel gleamed in the moonlight that shone through the window into the dark room. She wondered what Charlie would have thought if he knew she'd been carrying it with her whenever she was with him.

She tucked the pistol under her pillow and lay down on the cool sheets, and before she closed her eyes, she knew that tomorrow would be different. She could explain that while Charlie was really called Hans, he was not the spy Fletcher believed him to be. Tomorrow, she would contact Fletcher, explain what she knew, find Klaus, protect her country, and save her relationship with Darrell.

23

POOLE – MAY 1941

Charlie sat on the edge of his bed, rocking back and forth and holding his head in his hands. How had it all come to this? Just a year ago, his life had ended when the Germans took his wife and baby from him in the bombing of Rotterdam. The flight to England had seemed the only way to survive and, to begin with, it had appeared that Poole would be a good place to make a new start.

His short stay in England as a refugee had not gone anything like he had expected; although, he thought again now wryly, he had barely had time to consider the idea before he'd fled Rotterdam, and his soul had been in tatters. It still was. He could have laughed if he wasn't already crying. Back then, after he'd been allowed off Brownsea Island, he had stayed in Poole for just a few weeks before he found the intense scrutiny from the locals about his life in Holland to be too much to bear. His Dutch accent sounded German to them, and where was his family? A lone man with no wife or children, and an accent that sounded distinctly like the Hun meant he was treated like an outcast at best, and an enemy at worst.

The first time he'd tried to buy a beer in the Poole Arms on the quay, it had ended with him being asked to leave, after the local fishermen had been muttering and murmuring in his direction. So, he had upped and left, and made it to London where it was easier to hide. He found a small room for rent not too far from the river Thames, where he liked to walk and listen to the sounds of activity on the water. It hadn't taken him long to find work on the docks; a man who could handle a boat like he could was always wanted on the water, despite his pronounced limp and the way it slowed him down.

He chose not to speak unless absolutely necessary and soon learnt how to mimic some of the locals and the way they spoke, hiding his origins as much as possible. London was where he had holed himself up and let the second wave of grief wash over him. With each nightly air raid, in what he now knew had come to be called the Battle of Britain, he refused to leave his bed, almost willing the bombs towards his roof to knock him into the next world where Katrijn and Anika waited for him. Time after time, he asked himself what foolish whim had made him run from Rotterdam. Why hadn't he just lain down and died there with his girls? Or been a better husband and father, and got them out of there before the city was destroyed by Nazi bombs? Hans hated his own body for its natural instinct for survival. But he continued to live on, existing, and the longed-for end never came.

But everywhere in London, it was hard to explain why he wasn't in uniform. Even those with obvious injuries still wore their uniform and played some part, however small, in the defence of the nation. One night, in a pub around by the docks, he'd overheard a young man talking about the injuries he'd got on the beach at Dunkirk, and how he would never be allowed to fight again, but could still do his part for King and Country. The young man now wore the uniform of the Home Guard and stayed in London to help wherever he could – however he could.

Hans realised this was his way out and so he lied about where and when he had injured his leg, worked on honing his accent to sound more naturally English, and become someone else instead: an injured Englishman from London. But then he had decided to return to Poole. He'd left his boat there and though it had since been used by the navy and taken to Dunkirk to help with the evacuation, he had hoped to retrieve it, presuming it had come back in one piece. He had thought he might be able to travel westward to another English port, and maybe even sleep aboard the boat that held such precious memories of Katrijn. And the bigger problem, as Klaus had reminded him so forcefully today, was that he'd left his German identity papers on board the boat.

Hans had travelled back to Poole by train, looking every bit like an Englishman in his Home Guard uniform, and when he stepped off the platform in Poole, before going to find the lodgings with Mrs Rogers, he went into a pub for a beer. This had been his first chance to hear his new English accent practised in public where nobody could possibly recognise him as the Hans who had arrived on Poole Quay as a refugee last year. Hans Meyers had chosen his new English name, Charlie Edwards, because it sounded so perfectly British and friendly to his ears.

He changed his story to say he'd had the limp from childhood, to help avoid details about where and when in the war he'd been injured.

Back then, when he first arrived in Poole last year, he'd spent a few weeks boarding with a family in Denmark Road, a little way from the centre of things around the quayside. Then he'd left for London, telling the family he'd got a job working in the docks on the river Thames. As it turned out, he did spend a little time working for a haulage company, unloading and reloading barges.

He'd stayed away long enough, he hoped, for everyone in Poole to have forgotten the faces of the Dutch refugees.

Meeting Peggy had changed everything. He had been relaxing into this new and beautiful friendship with her. Peggy, the wonderful woman who had welcomed him, shown him kindness, and had seemed to be giving him every reason to believe they might have a future together.

He hadn't thought it would ever be possible, but he knew the feelings that were beginning to grow were the seeds of love. He would never stop loving Katrijn, or grieving her loss, but his heart had made room for Peggy too. At first, he had thought she had already been tied to that Australian, but then it seemed that she had time and eyes only for him. Yet, how could he ever have a loving relationship with a woman like Peggy when she hadn't even known who he really was? It was all bound to come out some time. And now it was over.

Charlie lay back on the bed and stared at the images of his life that seemed to flash across the dark ceiling: a life with Peggy, and a life without her. Was there still a chance to save it? To hang on to this new possibility of happiness? He had two choices. He could either let Klaus threaten him and wreck his chances of a new life as Charlie, or he could deal with Klaus and move on. Perhaps once Peggy vouched for him, and explained he was not a threat to England, he would be allowed to carry on here in Poole as before. The spark between him and Peggy was real. He knew that, and she'd confirmed it tonight with that tender kiss on his cheek.

He sat up, knowing at once that he had to go and deal with Klaus before morning. And he knew exactly where he would be hiding.

* * *

Peggy woke with a start, knowing so well the sound she could hear, but not understanding why she could hear it now, here. The sound of the BOAC launch, as it left Poole Quay, was so familiar to her and it carried across Fisherman's Dock and in through her bedroom window, into her dreams at first, and then she was fully awake. She looked at the alarm clock on her bedside table: half past one in the morning. There was no good reason for the launch to be out at this time, and yet she knew instinctively who was at the helm and where it was going.

Peggy dressed quickly into her dark-navy slacks and jumper, and, as if it was the most natural thing in the world, grabbed the pistol from under her pillow and stashed it into her canvas satchel, slinging it over her shoulder. She tiptoed down the stairs and crept out the back door to where her dad kept his small dinghy.

If anyone on Ballard Road noticed anything strange on the beach out the back of the houses that night, it wasn't enough to stir them outdoors. Within a few minutes, the dinghy was in the water, the Seagull engine had been fetched from the shed and attached to the boat, and Peggy was disappearing into the moonlight, two crisp, white lines of wake wash separating eternally behind her.

24

POOLE – MAY 1941

Peggy held the tiller of the little outboard engine firmly and willed it to act something more like the motor in the launch than the little dinghy outboard it was. Already, the launch was way out of sight, but she was certain of two things: Charlie was at the helm and he was headed for the River Frome.

She passed the Hamworthy quay, and was soon near to the RAF base, but she was careful to stay out far enough from shore that her face wouldn't be seen. The night was dark now, the moon having been covered over with clouds that had been rolling in from the west, and the harbour looked as black as an oil slick. The town was blacked out too and Peggy could see virtually nothing, but knew instinctively where she was, how to avoid the many sandbars, and which way lay the mouth of the river.

Soon the sound of the engine grew louder because she'd reached the more enclosed mouth of the river. Peggy immediately slowed down to well under the regulation four knots speed limit, and watched the left and right banks in turn. She knew that Charlie was bound to hear the engine from her boat, but he wouldn't know it was her. She was prepared to cut the engine at any moment.

Peggy scoured the bank as she crept along, trying to look and sound as if she wasn't in any particular hurry. There were a couple of houseboats, all shut up and dark – no way of knowing if there were people living aboard or not – and some of the usual small sailing boats, and one or two fishing dinghies. She saw the flash of movement on the right bank from the corner of her eye and cut the engine immediately. It was still another fifty yards ahead, but there was the BOAC launch, moored up beside another boat, which had a tarpaulin cover pulled over it like a tent.

Peggy stealthily picked up the oars, one at a time, and slotted them silently into the rowlocks, as the dinghy drifted towards the bank. She held one oar out to fend off from the riverbank but let the dinghy drift into the reeds from where she could see – and hear – what occurred on the boat.

Charlie's voice reached her first, and she could tell he was angry, but she wasn't quite close enough to hear the words.

Peggy rowed carefully out from the reeds and along the river a few more yards and slipped across to the right bank. Then the voices became clearer.

'I *will* speak English, Klaus, because I *am* English now. I don't want any part of what you're doing, and I won't allow you to ruin my life! I have a job, and friends, and a real chance to start again and I'm not going to let you stop me,' spat Charlie through gritted teeth. 'Take my boat, if you want it, but give me the damn papers and get out of here, then leave me alone!'

Klaus responded with something in Dutch, which Peggy couldn't understand, but whatever it was, Charlie lashed out with his fists in response, hitting Klaus so hard that he cried out in pain.

'Klaus, you are on the wrong side! I should never have suggested to you what I did back in Rotterdam. It was wrong of me, and foolish – but it was all I could think of at the time as a way to protect my family. Germany is not the right side – whether they win or lose, you must not give in to that weakness.'

'It's far too late for that, Hans. I've been German all my life, and now that Germany is going to rule Europe, I know which side is the right side. And you forget – you're German too!' he spat, waving papers in his face. Charlie snatched for the papers and nearly fell into the water, as Klaus tucked them away again.

'But why me, Klaus?' Charlie said, sounding exhausted and desperate. 'I hardly knew you! What can I do for you now? You learnt what you wanted about those visiting politicians without even asking me! And God knows how many people lost their lives in the havoc that air raid brought on so many innocents!'

'Hans, you are so stupid. How can you think these pathetic English will ever win? You have the chance to join the side of your father, and help. You are already close to that woman who seems to know a lot about the passengers on the flying boats. And if you don't help me, I will turn you in as a spy – I have the German ID papers here to prove it, then this lovely little provincial life you yearn for will be over for good,' yelled Klaus.

Hans lashed out again and the two men fell to the bottom of the boat, where they fought so fiercely, Peggy was sure at least one of them would take a fatal blow soon.

As the two tussled and grunted in the bottom of the boat, Peggy moved her dinghy closer and tied it up to the side of the launch, thinking fast. She knew now that though Charlie was not who she'd thought he was, he was certainly not the trouble Fletcher had imagined. It was this Klaus who really needed to be caught.

Peggy was frustrated at not being able to face Klaus directly, but she had to act fast. She tied the dinghy as securely as she could to the BOAC launch then climbed aboard, quiet as a cat. Charlie – the man she knew as Charlie, she thought wryly – had left the key in the padlock on the cabin latch, at least. She crept around the edges, staying low so as not to be seen, checking for ropes. It was only tied, quite loosely, to the Dutch boat by one rope. She re-tied it in a way that she could lift it from the cleat in a hurry and crouched at the wheel to listen again.

'No! Give them back! What are you doing?' yelled Klaus and Peggy heard the ripping of papers.

'These are my papers and I'm doing what I should have done in Rotterdam – destroying them! I want nothing to do with Germany, Klaus!'

There was a thud and a sound that Peggy was convinced must be vulgar swearing in Dutch. Knowing that one of them had taken a hit that had slowed them both down, Peggy took her chance and jumped up onto the Dutch boat, aiming her pistol at the mangle of men in the bottom of the boat.

'Hold still, both of you; this is loaded and I'm not afraid to use it.'

Both Klaus and Charlie turned towards her, stunned, holding their hands raised. And now, for the first time on this strange night, she was properly afraid. She breathed deeply and took stock. She held a gun, and neither of them did. She had the key to the BOAC launch, and they were both below her. Charlie looked to be bleeding from the side of his head. She held the power here and she was going to keep it.

'Now, you're both going to calm down, and tell me what the hell is going on here, because you, Charlie, have got everyone at BOAC convinced that you're English, and now, after believing you when you said you were Dutch, I hear you are actually German! What is your real name?' Peggy demanded.

'Peggy, my *Nederlander* name was Hans. Hans Meyers – but I left him behind in Rotterdam, and I am not German. My father was German, but I was raised as a *Nederlander* by my mother. Klaus here is half Dutch too, just like me, but he's decided to become German, for some reason of utter madness, and help the enemy.' Charlie sighed deeply and sat down before continuing. 'He took my German identity papers, which I should have destroyed months ago, and he was going to hold them against me. As I told you, he is demanding that I share information about passengers on the flying boats, or he will turn me in.'

'And I suppose I hold you, Klaus, responsible for the air raid that was designed to kill our leaders recently?' Peggy asked, daring to find out the truth.

Peggy watched as Charlie looked naturally surprised at all she knew, but Klaus simply scoffed. She turned the pistol fully onto Klaus and held it with both hands.

'So why am I the only enemy now?' he demanded. 'Hans here is more of a liar than me. I'm just doing my part for the Third Reich who will be here in England in no time at all and then women like you had better—'

Charlie gave him no opportunity to finish his disgusting speech and knocked him to the floor.

For Peggy, time stood still as they fought. Charlie had thumped Klaus to the floor and was reeling back from the effort when, in a blink, Klaus was up on his feet and holding Charlie by the throat. Peggy froze as she saw the panic in Charlie's face, while Klaus held both hands around his neck, squeezing tighter and tighter, and then she heard the gunshot, and it was as if the world had tipped on its axis. She saw the smoke spill from the end of her pistol and heard nothing more as the blast rang in her ear. She held her eyes shut tight and then, as her hearing returned, she heard something heavy fall into the water, and then again. Both men must now be in the river, and she had shot at least one of them. The floor of the Dutch boat was slick with blood.

'Charlie! Charlie, where are you?' she cried, peering over the edge of the boat into the water and reeds below, where small splashing sounds still mingled with grunts.

'Charlie? Is that you?' She moved to the other end of the boat, trying to see the men in the water, and as she moved, she kicked something hard and solid on the floor. She bent down to feel for it. The pistol. She must have dropped it after she pulled the trigger. She knew it had held six bullets to begin with, and so she held it carefully, sticky with blood as it was, in her shaking hand, and called for Charlie again.

'Charlie? Where are you?' she called desperately and leant over the side of the boat. A hand reached up and she caught it, pulling with all her strength, hoping against hope this was Charlie's arm and she could pull him out of the water. But the arm was stronger than her, or the pull was heavier than she'd expected, and she slipped and fell.

As Peggy fell into the water, being pulled by her left arm, the gun in her right hand went off, and then she was under the water, tumbling into the inky black night of the river.

25

***

Peggy relaxed in the stillness between sleeping and waking, not willing for the night to end and for the day, with all its yet to be revealed troubles ahead, to start. She relished the comfort of her bed and shut her ears to the sounds of planes overhead that were beginning to encroach upon her dreams until, eventually, reason kicked in and she understood that if she could hear planes, she had no business resting in her bed and should get to the shelter, and fast.

She rolled onto her side and gasped with shock, allowing river water into her mouth, understanding nothing. She choked and coughed and scrambled for a firm hold of something – anything – but felt only reeds that cut her fingers as she grabbed for them.

She was not in bed, but floating in the river still, and she could not tell how long she'd been that way. The night was still black as coal and, thankfully, there was no wind at all, but each part of her body that was raised above the level of the water now felt the sting of chill, wet against the cool night air.

Slowly, memories began to return. The launch, the chase, the argument on what she now knew as Charlie's Dutch boat, the gunshot, the sound of two men falling into the water, one after the other. The hand that had reached up and grasped her arm, and how she'd hoped it was Charlie and wanted to pull him out but had fallen into the river herself instead.

She lay on the riverbank, having pulled herself out by finding a foothold in the muddy clay and pulling on the reeds. She held her hands as close to her face as she could, and tried to decide if the darkness that spread over her palms was mud or blood. Her head ached and she touched a hand to her temple and found a sizeable bump there. *Enough trying for now*, her mind told her. *Rest a while*, and she dozed.

When she woke, which might have been a few minutes or an hour later, the night was still dark and the planes she'd heard earlier were gone. She sat up, waiting for her eyes to adjust, and then looked about. All three boats were still tied up together and there was no sign of anyone else. Her clothes had dried out considerably, and she was missing one shoe. She stood and lumbered around the riverbank calling for Charlie. A few minutes later, she tried a tentative call for Klaus. Nothing. No one. Where the hell could they be? There had only been the one gunshot – except for the second shot that she now remembered firing by accident.

Peggy made her way to the launch, checking inside, in case one of the men had made it on board. Then another thought occurred, and she bent over the side of the Dutch boat moored beside her launch. Curled on the floor was the shape of a body. Her heart quickened and she looked around for the gun, which lay on the cockpit floor where she must have dropped it before she fell in. The memories were vague and seemed to come to mind in the wrong order.

She took ten deep breaths, while remaining perfectly still,

watching the body. It could be Charlie, though in this darkness, it could also be Klaus. She crept silently over the sides of the two boats and into the cockpit of the Dutch boat – Charlie's boat as she now knew it to be. The body did not stir. She crouched down and picked up the gun, and, remembering her accident, checked the safety switch was set correctly. Then she reached out and shoved him on the shoulder. He did not stir. She leant closer to the face and pushed harder to turn him over, which he did with a lifeless thump on the floor of the boat. She jumped back in horror, and heard herself whimper. Klaus was dead.

So where in this hellish night was Charlie? she asked herself as she scanned the water, which was easier to see now that her eyes had grown more accustomed to the darkness.

'Charlie!' she called again and listened. Something moved on the bank but it was small. Probably only a vole, or a water rat. She thought through the possibilities about the situation she was dealing with now. The true spy was dead, at her feet, and quite possibly by her hand, if he'd been shot. The innocent, half-German, half-Dutch Hans/Charlie for whom she had come to know great affection might well be dead, but was, at the very least, missing. And Darrell, the honest, fun, lovely, trustworthy, helpful Australian airman without whose love she could not imagine going on, had absolutely no idea she was out here alone, and probably thought she'd been cheating on him with Charlie. This thought was enough to switch up the gears in her brain and begin a rescue plan.

Within a few moments, she had untied the launch from the Dutch boat and started the engine, backing it slowly – ever so slowly, because Charlie was still unaccounted for in this river water – out from the riverbank. Her dad's fishing dinghy was still tied firmly to the side of the launch and she adjusted the rope so that it towed a safe distance behind. Then, when she had travelled a few hundred yards downstream, she let the throttle go and, defying the speed limit, drove the launch at full speed back in towards Poole Quay.

At the Custom House steps, she worked quickly to tie the boat up, and pulled the dinghy in close again, locked the launch cabin and took the key with her, throwing her one shoe back into the boat and going barefoot. The quay was deserted. She heard the church clock strike for a quarter past three, and then, the sound of planes overhead again. She could run for her parents but what was she to tell them? She couldn't share any of the details about who or why or what owing to the nature of what she'd been tasked with doing by Fletcher. And, besides that, if she arrived home looking like this in the middle of the night, that would be the end of her trying to do anything to find Charlie.

There was nobody in the Customs House or the harbour master's office at this early hour of the morning, so she knew not to bother there. She ran to the police call box at the bottom of the high street, and picked up the receiver, but put it down again immediately, thinking about her options of who she could talk to about what, considering the secretive nature of her mission with Charlie. As she stood beside the police call box, the air-raid siren went off, and within moments, there was movement in the street, with people running to take cover in the public shelters.

Rose Stevens. She lived just a short run away and Peggy needed to see Rose, or Major Carter. She couldn't divulge much information, but as head of Field Security, he would understand, surely. He lived somewhere in Parkstone – miles away – but Peggy knew that Rose lived with her sister, Daisy, in Market Street, just near the Guildhall, and so she cut through the lanes to Church Street, ran alongside the churchyard and on into Market Street, pausing for breath outside the almshouses before pushing on again, the siren wailing the whole time.

'Excuse me, miss, do you want to shelter with us?' called a man from his front door as Peggy ran by. She must have looked as though she was desperately trying to find cover from the air raid.

'I'm going to my friend's house, thanks. I'll be all right!' she called as she ran on.

When she reached Rose and Daisy's door, she loudly rapped the knocker four times, and then waited as the siren wailed and Home Guard men ran past to take their places at the anti-aircraft guns, shouting to one another all the while.

She knocked again, six times, and louder. Still nothing. The shelter, she realised. They would have gone out their back door to their shelter.

'You need to take cover, love!' called an old Home Guard soldier, stopping when he saw her at the front of the house.

'Just going round the back to the shelter now,' she cried in reply as she ran down the lane beside the house where Rose lived. She found the shelter and pulled open the door, much to the shock of the women inside it. Daisy Carter, Rose's sister, was resting along one of the beds on one side, with a pillow behind her and a very pregnant belly before her.

'Peggy! What on earth?' asked Rose, moving to make room for Peggy as she slipped inside the shelter and pulled the door shut behind her. They still had a candle lit, having only been there themselves for a few minutes, getting settled.

Peggy regarded Daisy and looked again to Rose, unsure what she could say in front of Major Carter's assistant's sister, let alone what she should reveal to Rose. She gathered her thoughts and decided on a version of the night's events that shouldn't interfere with the promise she had made to hold these affairs secret.

'I followed someone who had stolen the launch boat, Rose, all the way up the Wareham River. He had another boat kept there, and was with a man who is not from around here,' she said with a pointed look, glancing at Daisy, who had shut her eyes and seemed to be trying to sleep.

'In fact, as it turns out, the man I was following is not from around here either,' she said. 'There was a gunshot, or two, and I was in the water – look at me, my clothes are still damp, and I lost my shoes,' said Peggy, for the first time in the whole affair beginning to feel a bit the worse for wear. Her feet were sore and thrumming with pain now, she realised.

'Where are they now – these others?' asked Rose, glancing at Daisy, who was breathing deeply in sleep by this time.

'That's just the problem, Rose,' hissed Peggy. 'All three of us were in the water at one stage. One man is dead in the cockpit of the boat on the river, but I've no idea where —' She stopped herself just in time. 'Where the man I was following is now. He might be near the river, he could be injured, or worse. I need help to find him, Rose, and I also need to use the telephone at the pottery to make an urgent call,' she said and then, as if the final act of asking for help had switched a valve, the tears began to fall, and Peggy sobbed.

Rose breathed hard and fast while she considered the options, looking about the inside of the Anderson shelter as if the answers were written on the tin walls.

'We need Major Carter's help,' Rose said, getting up to push open the door and peering out of the shelter. 'It doesn't sound as though this is coming to much out here, Peggy. Come on, follow me. Daisy will be all right,' she said, more to comfort herself as she left her heavily pregnant sister in the shelter.

'We'll have to stick to the lanes – the Home Guard boys won't like us being out during a raid,' said Rose as she led Peggy to the lane that ran between the terraced houses in Market Street and those behind.

Peggy was breathless as she ran to keep up with Rose, who

had forgotten Peggy had no shoes, and was calling her plan as she ran.

'We'll go to the pottery and I'll call Major Carter from there. If he doesn't answer, I'll raise the navy at Sandbanks, and the RAF at Hamworthy – or both. But the major will have more sway with them, you see? And you can make your call there too, whatever that's about,' explained Rose as they reached the open quay and she led Peggy around to a back door. Here she felt behind a loose brick where they apparently kept a spare key.

Within minutes, Rose had spoken to the major, who'd instructed them to wait there for his call.

Peggy picked up the receiver and gave the operator the White-hall number that Fletcher had told her. It rang twice and she began to wonder if anyone would be manning the phone at this hour, when a prim voice answered. Peggy gave the coded message that meant she had found a spy and needed backup. The curt response was simply. 'Very well, thank you for your call,' and then the phone went dead, leaving Peggy perplexed.

Peggy went over to the window, looking out across the harbour. The decoy fires on Brownsea Island were lit, but all else was darkness, until she saw a flare go up from the lifeboat house. The night was calm, still no wind, and there couldn't possibly be any ships in danger.

'That's odd, Rose,' she said. 'The lifeboat is going out – look, here they come now,' she said as men ran from the darkness of surrounding streets and into the lifeboat house. Just a few minutes later, the boat was launched and headed out, not to the harbour entrance and out to sea, but to the inner harbour, west-wards towards the Wareham River. The time was now nearing four in the morning and Peggy could see the first light of dawn creeping up over the harbour entrance in the east.

The telephone rang and Rose answered it at once, just as

Peggy saw one of the small Royal Navy seaplanes taking off from Sandbanks and heading west too. Rose indicated the phone call was for her, and when she answered, she heard the familiar voice of Fletcher.

'Well done, Peggy,' he said, after she'd checked Rose was out of earshot and briefly relayed the night's events. 'Major Carter has already had the lifeboat launched, and the navy are sending out a search plane. Patricia from the harbour master's office is being called, and she will meet you at the launch. You're to go back with her up the river to the site of this Dutch boat,' Fletcher explained. 'And have the major's assistant wait for a phone call from me.'

'Yes, sir. We'll catch up to the lifeboat pretty fast – the old *Thomas Kirk Wright* is not known for her speed, but can handle the shallow water better than our launch. They'll be able to explore more of the inlets than we can,' said Peggy, shifting into practical boatwoman mode.

Peggy ran down the front stairs and out the foyer doors, which Rose locked behind her. On the quay, there was still no sign of activity, but as she ran along to the launch, the all-clear sounded. That was something, at least, that they no longer had to worry about.

Patricia met Peggy at the launch, and they were as breathless as each other while Peggy explained where they were going. She untied her dad's dinghy and tied it up to the quay, hoping it would still be there when they got back and knowing her dad would have her guts for garters if she lost it. They set off at high speed in the launch and were soon on the tail of the lifeboat and shouting instructions as to where exactly to find the Dutch boat.

When the lifeboat pulled alongside the Dutch boat, Peggy held the launch back, expecting at any moment to see them lift the dead body of a man aboard the lifeboat. But they did not.

Peggy crept the launch forward and called out to ask what was going on. There was no response except to wait.

The lifeboat crew were searching the boat and some had jumped ashore and were looking around the riverbank.

'What's happening?' called Peggy. 'The body of the dead man is in the cockpit of that boat!' she called.

'No, it's not, love. There's blood on the sole 'ere, but no body. Are you sure he was dead?' asked one of the crew, looking down into the base of the cockpit. Peggy thought back to a short time ago, when she was last here. She had seen a lifeless body. She had turned him over and seen it was Klaus. He had not moved. But had she checked his pulse, or listened for his breath? She couldn't be sure now.

'There was another man here as well – and we were all in the water at some stage,' she said, wanting them to direct their search to Charlie. She knew now that he was innocent, but had some more interrogating of her own to do with him.

The search went on for several hours, with lifeboat men walking up and down the banks, swimming across the river, checking between the reeds. The seaplane swooped overhead again and again, checking the meadows beside the river.

And they found nothing. Not even the body of Klaus. As the sun began to rise on a fresh new day, Peggy's hopes fell further with each passing moment.

26

POOLE – JUNE 1941

Peggy woke with that ever-present heavy feeling in her chest that she'd been carrying since the night of the fiasco on the Wareham River. For the last two days, she'd been aching for news, trying to go about normal business, and unable – prohibited by law – to share the details with her family. She'd been called in the night on official business for BOAC, she had told them, and could not tell them any more than that. The loss of her shoes, and the painful state of her feet, as well as the knock to her head and the fact she'd obviously spent considerable time in damp clothes and risked a chill were all of major concern to her mum, dad, and sister.

'And where's young Darrell when you need him?' demanded her mother. 'If a young man is worth his salt, he will be there for you when times are tough, Peggy.'

'Mum, leave him be. He's in the RAAF, for goodness' sake, and has a lot more to think about than looking out for me or bringing me grapes when I'm at home with a cold,' she'd said, doing her best to put her parents off the scent that something much more serious had been going on, and she'd not seen

Darrell since their strong words on the doorstep a few nights ago.

'A head cold, you call this? If you're not in bed with pneumonia by tomorrow, I'll be surprised,' said Mrs Symonds, patting Peggy's hand tenderly.

'I'll be fine, Mum. And he'll be here soon. You'll see,' Peggy said with such brightness in her voice, nobody would have guessed her pain.

But that afternoon, when Patricia called to visit, she brought with her a gentleman whom Peggy had never imagined would visit her at home. Mr and Mrs Symonds retreated to the kitchen with Molly to allow Peggy a private chat with her visitors in the front room. Molly shut the door as she left and caught Peggy's eye as she did so, her own eyes wide in wonder at what on earth was going on.

'Good to see you're holding up well enough, Peggy,' said Fletcher before lowering his voice. 'You're quite sure we can't be heard in here?' he asked her.

'Quite sure, Mr Fletcher,' answered Peggy. 'I do apologise for being rested up on this settee, sir. Mother is worried, and I must admit I feel a bit too chesty. I've no idea how long I was in that water, but my guess is a couple of hours at least.'

Fletcher and Patricia both nodded, and Peggy glanced at Pat, wondering what she knew.

'Has anything been heard of Charlie, or even this other fellow, "Klaus"? I can't believe he is on the run – I was sure he was dead when I last saw him,' asked Peggy.

'We've come to update you, Peggy, and it might be a little upsetting,' Fletcher said. Peggy's mind immediately turned to Darrell, and she braced herself for the worst possible news, holding back the tears she felt gathering in her throat.

'A body was discovered floating under the lifting bridge in the early hours of dawn today, and we needed to make sure of exactly who it was,' said Fletcher.

Peggy held her breath, her hand resting on her chest, waiting for this era of her life to be ended. She wondered in that moment if there'd be a sound, like a gunshot that would mark the moment, and thought again of the gunshot she'd fired herself, not knowing if it had met any mark at all.

'Is it Klaus?' she asked, hoping that Charlie might still be alive, somehow, somewhere.

'We aren't certain. It could be either Charlie or Klaus, or even someone else. We'd like you to come and help identify the body. For security reasons, it is being held at the RAF base in Hamworthy,' Fletcher said.

Peggy felt her legs shaking and she began to feel quite sick. They had found a body. It was probably Klaus – the bringer of all the trouble, but might also be Charlie. And if it was Charlie, what on earth had happened to Klaus?

Peggy gathered her shoes and outdoor coat, for although the month was now June, the day was cool and damp, and she was already quite unwell. She didn't realise how weak she felt until she walked to the car outside, and was glad to sit down again on the ride to Hamworthy. At the gates, she saw a familiar face, who gave her a meaningful nod. It was one of Darrell's friends she'd met in the pub, and at the dance hall.

Once inside, they were directed to the medical rooms of the base, and asked to wait on hard, wooden chairs in a draughty corridor – a fact Fletcher complained of at once, owing to Peggy's delicate state of health. Once inside the clinical room, the body seemed like a marble statue under its white sheet on the raised table. The RAF doctor peeled back the sheet and Peggy, who only realised now that she was fully intending to see the face of Klaus, was shocked to see Charlie lying there.

She stared for a few seconds, tears running freely down her face, before Fletcher prompted her.

'Can you confirm if you know this man, Peggy?' he asked her.

'Yes. Yes, this is Charlie Edwards – the man we know as Charlie Edwards. But I believe his real name was Hans Meyers,' she added.

'You're quite sure? This is Charlie, and not Klaus?' he asked.

'I'm certain, sir. This is Charlie, who I've been working with these past months, and getting to know extremely well in recent weeks.' Overwhelming emotions overtook her now and whether or not it was grief, exhaustion, regret, or relief that her mission was now over, she could take no more. She slumped into a chair and held her head in her hands as tears streamed down her face and she gasped for air between sobs.

* * *

In the corridor outside, Darrell had positioned himself to watch through a narrow window. He'd heard that Peggy had arrived on site, and that there was a body being held in the medical rooms. He had waited and watched to see Peggy's reaction, and now he knew. This was Charlie, this dead man. And Peggy was completely devastated by the loss. Darrell choked on the thickening in his throat and one lone tear escaped as he watched with a trembling lip the woman of his dreams grieving for the man she loved more than him. He spun on his heels and went straight to his group captain's office, knocking firmly on the door, before entering on command.

'Sir, you mentioned more men were needed in Plymouth?'

'That's right, Flight Lieutenant. There have been some movements and some extra staff are needed on hand there.'

'I'd like to be put in for a transfer, sir, as soon as possible,' said Darrell, speaking quickly before he could change his mind.

'Are you sure? I understood you had a young lady here in Poole that you wished to be close to?'

'I did, sir, but not any more. When can I leave?'

The group captain sat back in his chair and saw the determination in Darrell's face.

'We can have you there tomorrow, if you like. If you're certain?'

'I'm quite certain, sir. Thank you,' Darrell said, saluting and turning to leave the office and walk across the yard, his chest burning with a pain he'd never known before. He daren't look out across the harbour to where he knew he would always imagine Peggy, her blonde curls blowing in the breeze as she flew across the water.

* * *

Back in the medical room, Peggy raised her head as a question occurred to her. Did she really want to know? What if this had been her fault?

'How did he die, sir?' Peggy asked, so quietly, Fletcher asked her to repeat herself.

'Charlie,' she said clearing her throat and speaking up. 'How did he die? Surely not from simply falling into the water during a fight?'

'It would seem he had a gunshot wound to the shoulder, and he'd lost of a lot of blood. There's also a nasty knock on the back of the head, so he was possibly unconscious when he entered the water. Without help, he didn't have much chance of survival, and he drowned, one way or another,' the doctor explained.

And who had been responsible for that gunshot? Peggy's own

untrained and stupid, accidental shot. She'd managed a hit to Klaus, which she had been intending, she was sure, but somehow, she'd accidentally killed innocent Charlie.

* * *

Despite the trauma of the last few days, Peggy slept deeply and peacefully that night, and the threatened pneumonia never came. Two days later, she had recovered from her head cold, and felt well enough to go to work.

'There are things to do, Mum, and planes to meet. The sooner I get back to it, the better,' she'd said as she put on her cap and left for the routine walk up to Poole Quay. Nobody had to know that she was dying on the inside, that she had killed an innocent man, and her heart was shattered. And she needed to find Darrell, and explain as much as she could, but she had to speak with Fletcher first.

At the Custom House steps, she felt for a moment that she'd seen a glimpse of Charlie, crossing the quay quickly and disappearing up one of the lanes, but she knew her mind was playing tricks on her. The Dutch boat had been collected, cleaned, and impounded by the harbour master and it was moored up along the quay just a few yards from the BOAC launch. Peggy went along to look down inside the boat, to the place where she'd seen what she had been convinced was Klaus's dead body. Where could he possibly have gone? Had someone come to help him? She was sure he was dead, and yet it was Charlie lying cold in the mortuary. Charlie who'd seemed so good, and so heartbroken, and yet hopeful for a future in Poole Harbour. With her. It was all wrong.

The day went by in a dull dream, and everything Peggy saw before her was covered with a mist that seemed to come from her own mind. By the afternoon, she was exhausted, and when Patricia called her in to take a phone call from Fletcher, it was the last thing she wanted to do.

'Thank you for all you've done, Peggy. I know you're still struggling, but we have news that might interest you,' he said.

'Peggy, you'll be aware that your mission was to follow Charlie Edwards – as we knew him – to try and ascertain if he might be a spy,' Fletcher began, not expecting any answer. 'And you did an excellent job of uncovering not only his true identity, but also leading us to another person of interest whom we had not imagined was at all connected. Klaus Schmidt was indeed a German spy and we have discovered that it was he who was responsible for leaking the information about our VIP guests, which led to the air raid, aimed to kill them all. Thankfully, this endeavour failed, and our leaders survived, although Poole took a terrible hit that night.'

'But he is still missing, isn't he?' asked Peggy.

'Not any more. The marines conducted a deep search of the marshes, and found our Klaus injured, but alive, and had him taken in for questioning. We have now been able to ascertain that Mr Klaus Schmidt had been harassing our friend Charlie who, although Dutch and of German descent, was not an enemy at all, but a man determined to fight against Germany,' Fletcher continued. 'And so this little venture is at an end. However, Miss Symonds, we have been singularly impressed by your bravery and professionalism, and would ask you to consider coming on board for more formal training for future work of a similar nature,' he said.

Peggy held the receiver with both hands and stared out the window across the harbour and towards Brownsea Island. She thought of all the trauma of the last few days, but of how in the end her involvement had led to the capture a German spy – and the death of an innocent man. Did she want more of this? Or did she long to settle down with Darrell for a life of homely comfort? She sighed deeply before responding.

'Mr Fletcher, do I have a choice? Because I do have a gentleman friend that I intend to marry, and settle down with. If the country can do without me, I think I would rather decline.'

'That is a great disappointment to us, of course, but yes, it is your choice. However, should you ever change your mind, just call that number in Whitehall and use the same code to get back in touch,' he said, and ended the call.

* * *

That evening, Peggy sat at the corner table in the Antelope, in exactly the place she'd been sitting when she first met Darrell. She was sure the airmen would be along soon, and within minutes, she heard their familiar accents fill the bar. She dared not look up, though she knew Darrell would be among them. But as the minutes wore on, and he didn't come to her side, she dared to look around. She could not see him, though many of his friends were there. At last, she saw one of his closest friends and made eye contact, and he came over to sit with her.

'Looking for Darrell, are you, love?' he asked kindly, and when Peggy nodded, he frowned and continued. 'He's left Hamworthy – got a transfer elsewhere. Went yesterday.' There was no easy way to say it, and the Australian way was straight up – right between the eyes.

'What? Where? Why?' demanded Peggy. 'He must be coming back, though? How do I reach him? He didn't even say goodbye,' she said, tears pricking her throat.

The Australian coughed and put his pint down.

'From what I heard, he knew you were seeing that other

bloke, Charlie, and that turned the milk for him, so to speak. Never mind though, love, plenty more fish in the sea, hey?' He laughed, nodding in the direction of his fellow airmen who were playing a rowdy game of darts in the back of the pub.

Peggy tried to smile, but instead picked up her things and left the pub in a hurry, the tears flowing freely now. She ran to the quay, and on beyond the activity of all the pubs, down to the dark lifeboat house. She sat on the wall there, legs dangling over the edge of the quay, looking across the black harbour to Brownsea.

This life of hers, the harbour, the boats, even the excitement of the flying boats, would be meaningless to her now if she couldn't share it with Darrell, she realised. She had her mum and dad, and Molly, and the baby would be here soon, but how could she go on as before after all this? After she'd known the man whom she'd wanted to share her life with, and lost him?

She sat there, in the dark, until the tears ran dry, then thought again of all the action of these last few weeks. She felt in her bag where the pistol would have been, if she was still in service under the secret ministry work. And she made her choice.

The next morning, Peggy went straight to Patricia's office and asked to use the telephone. She asked the operator for the number in Whitehall, and gave the code words.

'Mr Fletcher,' she said when she was finally through. 'I've changed my mind. Where do I go for training?'

27

BRISBANE – DECEMBER 1998

Rebekah and Paul sat in the car outside Darrell Taylor's small home. Rebekah held the file and the letter on her lap. She took a deep breath and looked at Paul.

'He's expecting us now. We'd best go in,' she said, opening the car door and hoping they weren't about to cause an aged man undue grief.

When they knocked on the door, they heard a surprisingly sprightly footstep in the hallway, and when the door was opened, they saw before them a man who was still tall, slim, and with the unmistakably suave bearing of a man of the air force. Rebekah realised she had been expecting someone very elderly, which she now knew to be stupid: Peggy had been seventy-eight when she had died, but that was from cancer. She was still fit enough to help with gardening before the illness had weakened her. Darrell was probably no more than eighty himself and seemed to be fit as a fiddle and looking sharp too.

He welcomed them in, through the small home and out to the little patio at the back where he had laid out plates, cups and saucers for morning tea.

'I've made us some scones – my wife's pumpkin scone recipe, and it never fails,' he said, as he went back to the kitchen.

'Thank you so much for agreeing to see us, Mr Taylor. I'm aware we might be dragging up history that could be difficult for you to revisit,' began Paul, who was more used to this kind of thing than Rebekah.

'Whatever it is you want to share is all from a very long time ago,' Darrell said. 'There's probably not much you can tell me that will be news,' he added, buttering the scones and pouring coffee for them all. 'But I'm all ears, just the same.' He smiled.

'You mentioned your wife,' said Rebekah. 'Is she here today?' she asked, looking around and wondering if the mention of a past lover might cause problems.

'Sadly, no. Beryl passed away a few years ago now. We'd been married since 1948 – almost made it to our golden wedding anniversary, but missed out by a couple of years,' he said, turning to show them a wedding photograph that hung on the wall inside.

Rebekah cleared her throat and decided to plunge right in.

'Mr Taylor, during the war, when you were in England, did you know a Miss Peggy Symonds?' she asked and saw the flash of something like horror in Darrell's eyes as he nearly dropped his cup. He coughed a little and looked over his shoulder as though there was someone behind him.

'I knew Peggy Symonds very well. I was in love with her. I intended to marry her, if the truth be known. But she cast me off for some other bloke she seemed to like better. He died, actually – up to no good and probably a spy, I think, but he died and Peggy loved him more. That's all there was to it. So, I cleared off – got a transfer out of Poole as soon as I could. No good hanging around a woman and playing second fiddle to a dead man, is there?' he said, rather gruffly.

Rebekah and Paul exchanged glances and wondered how to continue, but Darrell helped them out.

'So, what news do you bring me? Something about Peggy, is it?' he asked.

Paul began with what he had uncovered about Peggy's life, and how she had lived from 1941 onwards. He had discovered that she joined an undercover government agency, been trained as an agent, and had worked mostly in Dorset, but occasionally in France, throughout the rest of the war.

'Peggy? But she was a fisherman's daughter – a sharp and beautiful one, mind you, but just a boatwoman. She worked on the launches for the flying boats when I met her,' Darrell said.

'Yes, that's right – and that remained her cover for most of the war, when she wasn't off in action elsewhere. But it seemed that at one stage, she had reason to believe her life might be in danger, and she wrote a letter to be passed to you in case she lost her life. We have that letter here for you, Mr Taylor,' Paul said, handing over the envelope.

Darrell took the letter and opened it, patting his top pocket, looking for reading glasses which he had to go inside to find. Back at the table again with them, he opened the envelope and studied the date first.

'Hmm, that's the time I got to know Peggy,' he said, and settled back to read the letter. As they watched him, Rebekah saw the emotion in his face change from interest to delight to a kind of horror and then disbelief. As he finished the letter, he looked up at them both, and then, open-mouthed, read the letter again.

'She was a spy? She was casing Charlie for the government, not flirting with him? I don't believe it! But when he died, she was devastated – I saw it with my own eyes,' he said, resting his head in his hands. 'Unless... unless she was just overcome with the trial of it all. And I didn't give her chance to explain.' He laughed, mirthlessly. 'We could have had it all – a whole life together, and I gave it up on a stupid assumption,' he said, and sighed.

'But life turns in strange circles, don't you think, Mr Taylor?' asked Rebekah, worried now that he would suffer terrible regret. 'If you hadn't moved away, you might never have met and married Beryl, and you'd have missed all the joy of those years.'

'You're right, but all the same, it is good to know this,' he said, clutching the letter to his chest. 'I held such bitterness for many years over Peggy, you know, and it was all needless.'

Another thought seemed to occur to him now.

'What happened to her after the war? Did she make it to the end?' he asked.

Rebekah swallowed, unsure now of the wisdom in passing on this news.

'She did. She worked for the agency until the end of the war, and then, she moved to Australia. To Brisbane. She was my next-door neighbour in Bracken Ridge when I was growing up.'

'Well, I never. Here in Brisbane, all that time? What a small world,' he said, and Rebekah felt calmer to see that his mind was more happily reflective again.

* * *

For the next gloriously hot and sunny fortnight, Rebekah showed Paul the best of Queensland. She drove him up the mountains into the slightly cooler climes of the rainforest in Lamington National Park, where they enjoyed the welcoming hospitality of O'Reilly's guest house. There Rebekah connected with old friends she had known from her days as a Queensland Parks and Wildlife ranger.

'Tell me, Rebekah,' whispered her friend Lydia while Paul was deep in conversation with the guide who'd led them on their waterfall discovery walk earlier that day, 'are all the men in England this hot, or did you just pick the best of the crop?'

The women laughed out loud, drawing the attention of more than a few dinner guests around them.

'You know me, Lyds, I never really noticed what any of them looked like – even the hot ones. Not until I met Paul. He's just so different, and I don't think he even knows that he's good to look at,' she said.

'Like you, you mean?' said Lydia with a knowing smile.

'I'm nothing special – you know that. I'm just a girl who likes a good walk in the outdoors. I've never been into that "look at me" kind of life. And I never even wanted to attract a man, anyway,' Rebekah said.

'Exactly – and that is why they were always all mad for you!' Lydia replied, a little too loudly for Rebekah's liking.

'Who was always mad for you?' asked Paul, returning to her side and putting on an arch look.

'Nobody! But Lydia here would have you thinking every guy at university was after me!'

'Well, that I can believe,' Paul said. 'But I'm glad you never fell under any of their spells.' He kissed her then, and for Rebekah, the world disappeared for a few moments like it always did when they locked eyes and lips, however briefly.

Lydia left them to enjoy their dessert and coffee, and went to mingle with other guests.

'She's lovely – and she's very fond of you. They all are,' Paul said, signifying the other rangers and guides who helped guests feel at home in this gorgeous rainforest retreat. 'They give me the impression that Queensland was sorry to see you go when you left for England – and they're surprised you've stayed so long. Mitchell there was asking me if you're coming back for good now.'

'Really? I was only working with them for a short while, after university that is. But I did love my time with them. I'd always intended to go to Poole though – they knew that,' she said.

'And how do you feel about staying now? In Poole, I mean?' he asked her as he ran his spoon around his dessert bowl, licking up every last drop of rich chocolate mousse.

'It's so strange, coming back. I do love it here, and the smell of the forest, the birdsong – the family – all of it tells me I'm home. But Brownsea feels like home, too. And you're in England, Paul, and you feel like home most of all,' she said and he kissed her again.

'You feel like my home too,' he said taking her hand and grabbing a quick breath as if he was about to say something else.

'Coming to watch the film tonight, you two?' cried Mitchell from the doorway, not realising what he was disturbing. 'We've got the lyrebird film to show you, in readiness for the dawn walk tomorrow. Starting in five minutes,' he said, and as Mitchell left the main dining room, Paul sighed and looked a little flustered.

'We should watch it, and then you'll know what you're looking for in the morning – or listening for, more like. It really is something special,' Rebekah said as she left to freshen up before going into the small dining room that had been set up as a private movie theatre for house guests.

'Something very special indeed,' muttered Paul to himself, as he watched the most beautiful woman in the room leave his side.

* * *

The dawn walk did not disappoint, and as they crunched stealthily over the humus of the ancient forest floor, the scent of damp eucalyptus, fresh after an overnight rainstorm, filled their senses. At first, it seemed all they could hear was the sound of their own footsteps but the guide brought them to a standstill to listen for a moment. Rebekah whispered to Paul, the nearness of her breathy voice in his ear making him shiver and tingle.

'Can you hear that high-pitched tinkling sound?' She spoke under her breath, not daring to make a sound.

'Like bells?' he asked.

'Exactly like bells – that's the bell miner, or bellbird. And if you listen carefully, you can hear another call that sounds similar, but several tones deeper – that's the eastern yellow robin – we'll see some soon I expect. They're not shy.'

'And the louder sound, like a whip cracking?' Paul asked, listening intently for a moment.

Rebekah nodded. 'A whip bird,' she said.

'Pretty imaginative with your bird names, aren't you?' he joked, and Rebekah struggled not to laugh out loud. She'd already had to deal with him joking about the rainbow lorikeets, so named because they wore so many different colours – a vibrant green back and wings with a cobalt-blue face, orange beak, yellow and orange breast, and a blue belly. When they gathered in a flock to feed from the bright-red bottlebrush flowers in her mother's backyard, they created a storm of colour like fireworks.

'Hey,' she breathed, 'we're Australian – we tell it like it is,' she said and poked him gently in the ribs before they walked on.

The guide indicated they should squat down to wait for a while as he'd heard a lyrebird in this area in the last few days. Rebekah closed her eyes and focused on nothing but the sounds, then she gasped lightly and snapped her eyes open, mirroring the guide's reaction.

The expression on Paul's face showed her that he'd recognised the sounds, but only she and the guide knew that he was mistaken.

'A kookaburra? Whip bird... the king parrot?' he asked

growing confused and knowing Rebekah had taught him all these bird songs in the last few days.

'Well done. You're learning fast, but you're wrong, I'm afraid. All those sounds are being made by the Albert's lyrebird. It's a fantastic mimic and often repeats seven or eight different calls – all ones that you would hear in the area. Listen up,' she whispered, holding up a finger to ask for silence while she concentrated on the forest sounds.

'There, did you hear that? The deep, rich whistling, and then chirping?' she said, again so quietly that nobody but Paul could hear her. The guide had raised his hand and indicated to the other walkers that this was their prize – the Albert's lyrebird. He waited until they all had heard it and then they crept, like soldiers on a secret mission, around the next bend of the forest path until he froze them again.

Rebekah squatted behind Paul and put one hand on his shoulder, her face pinned close to his, cheek to cheek. She pointed into the thick undergrowth towards the flash of some long feathers, determined he would be able to follow her line of sight. Someone behind them stumbled over a rock and the sound was enough to frighten the bird, which froze for a second before running deep into the forest and away from them.

'Did you see it?' she asked him, breathlessly.

'I saw long feathers moving in between the ferns,' he said, more in question than with confidence.

'That was it! Not many people get to experience that, you know? You're a very lucky guy,' she said, as always, not understanding how incredibly blessed Paul felt to have this rare prize in his life.

* * *

After the rainforest retreat, where Rebekah could have stayed for months, and Paul grew fond of hand-feeding the wonderfully tame scarlet and cobalt coloured crimson rosellas, they drove for two days to reach the tropical gateway to the Whitsunday Islands, Airlie Beach. They had booked ahead and arranged a three-day sailing tour around the islands, with snorkelling gear all included.

'Rebekah, this place is absolute heaven,' he said as he relaxed in his swimming trunks on the deck of the yacht, eating sliced mango, dragon fruit, and cherries, while sipping a glass of chilled Champagne. They had spent the morning snorkelling on Hook Island Reef and then enjoyed a delicious lunch of cold meats and salad – the routine they'd grown used to over the last two days while they'd been exploring different turquoise waters alive with fish and coral all around the island group.

'Everywhere is heaven when you're on holiday,' she said thoughtfully, 'though I do admit, even if I was working, this place really is paradise. But so is Brownsea Island. I've been obsessed with Dorset and Poole Harbour all my life, thanks to Peggy, and it still feels like a dream to wake up and see Corfe Castle and Old Harry Rocks from my bedroom window every morning.'

'It must be wonderful for your work to also be your joy,' Paul said, finishing his glass and lying back with his hands behind his head.

'Would your work have been your joy if you'd continued with music, do you think, and gone professional?'

'Probably, yes. Though I do enjoy what I do. And it has all kinds of bonuses. I have a lot of flexibility to follow leads that interest me, and I travel a lot, and meet some great people. Some are particularly wonderful,' he said, shading his eyes from the sun and smiling up at her. 'And I think that joy in work is all about being grateful for the small things – making the most of all the situations life throws at you.'

The details that Darrell had revealed to them about the life Peggy had lived during the war were scant, and he'd left some gaping holes that Rebekah was eager to have filled. But the simple facts had left a lasting impression: Peggy had been a capable boatwoman, a beauty without compare, and a woman who was prepared to take risks for the good of her country. She'd obviously had nerves of steel and skills that had been used by her country in ways that probably nobody would ever really know.

'When we get home, to Brisbane I mean, I think I'd like to offer to take Darrell to the cemetery where Peggy is buried. He may not want to go, of course, but I'll offer all the same,' said Rebekah.

* * *

Rebekah made her phone call to Darrell once they arrived back in Brisbane, and they agreed a good day for the trip to the cemetery would be Christmas Eve. The day began, hot and sunny as ever, and Paul waved Rebekah off as she set out to fetch Darrell. Paul watched the car disappear around the bend and went to finish his coffee on the back deck, where Helen joined him.

'And how are you going to fill your day, love?' she asked him.

'Is there anything you need help with before tomorrow? I'm happy to go and fetch groceries, and can make myself useful in the kitchen?' Paul offered.

'That's very kind of you Paul, but it's all done. We keep our Christmas preparations very simple here. The weather is looking glorious for a day under the mango tree tomorrow – not too humid,' she said.

'If you don't need me, there is something I'm keen to do – but

I'd need to borrow the car and probably have a good lesson in navigation to get there alone. I'm hoping to visit the antique markets at Paddington. Rebekah told me about them, and partly as a historian I'm interested, but I'm hoping to do a little Christmas shopping while I'm there too,' he explained.

'Why don't I come with you, if you don't mind, that is? It's a pig of a place to get to, navigating from here on your own, and it's been a few years since I went for a look around. If you don't mind the company, I can drive you if you like?' Helen said, and a short while later, they were stepping over the threshold to the old cinema that had been converted into an antiques market.

'Wow, there's a lot to discover in here,' Paul said as they walked in.

'You can spend hours here – and I often have done. I'll go this way and leave you to it – come and find me if you need anything,' she said as she went off to rake through the vintage clothing section that she loved.

Paul was amazed to discover antiques from so many different parts of the world, a fact that signified the widely multicultural society that Australia had become since its colonial beginnings – very recent history in the timeline of Australia's ancient civilisation. But he had never expected to find treasures from Poole. One of the first sections he browsed had a glass cabinet full of distinctive Poole Pottery from across the twentieth century. Paul picked out a display plate that was painted with an ancient map of Poole Harbour, with all the islands labelled and decorated with pine trees. He traced with his finger the route he'd taken around Brownsea Island the first night he'd met Rebekah, and smiled, taking it to the front counter to keep safe until he'd finished browsing.

Each individual collector's area had its own style, designed to showcase the different kinds of pieces each focused on: lamps, clothing, military memorabilia, china, and jewellery – the real reason he'd come.

The antique rings were as widely varied as all the other delights in this real treasure trove. There were Australian opals aplenty, as well rings featuring pearls, many of which would have been harvested in Western Australia. But it was the ruby and sapphire gemstone rings that caught his attention, and for a while he couldn't decide between the two colours, until he found the perfect combination.

He paid for his purchases at the front counter and had them both gift-wrapped so they could be placed straight under the tree back at the Martins' home when he arrived.

* * *

When Rebekah came home from the outing with Darrell that afternoon, she was exhausted. The day in itself was not particularly tiring, but the emotional journey had been draining. Both she and Darrell had wept at Peggy's graveside and Darrell had been quiet on the drive home again. But he had thanked her for bringing this news into his life, and told her how it had lightened his heart to know there had never been anything to hold against Peggy after all.

That night, Rebekah dressed carefully for dinner. Paul had booked a table for them at a restaurant that Tim had suggested – with a perfect view of the city at night from the top of the lookout at Mt Coot-Tha.

'I'll drive, Rebekah, but you'll need to navigate to get us there,' he'd joked as they got into the car.

At the restaurant, he had taken Tim's advice and booked the corner-most table for two where they sat with their backs to the other restaurant guests and a picture view of the whole city lit up at night.

After they ordered, and sat sipping their wine, Paul tentatively introduced the subject that had been on his mind for the last few weeks.

'I could happily spend the rest of my life like this, Rebekah.'

'Mmmn, so could I – holidays and travelling and eating out in posh restaurants – it's marvellous. But we'll have to get back to normality in the new year,' she said.

'I wasn't so much thinking of the holiday, and all its delights, though this has been the most amazing experience. I'm more thinking of just this: sitting here beside you, watching you look at the world, eating with you, talking to you, listening to you,' he said and she turned to give him her full attention.

'Paul, you put that so beautifully, and I know exactly what you mean.' She grew quiet and he gave her space for her thoughts.

She had drifted back to the night she'd discovered that Ben was seriously interested in her. She had not chosen the long-term acquaintance who offered the security and predictability of a life she understood, but instead chose Paul – the out-of-town stranger who thrilled her with his spontaneity. Gabriel Oak and Frank Troy came to join her in her thoughts again.

'Have you read *Far from the Madding Crowd*, Paul?' she asked, and from the startled look on his face, it was hard to tell if he was unsure of the book or just thrown off course by her sudden change of subject.

'There are two main characters who vie for the attentions of the heroine, Bathsheba Everdene. One is a playboy who excites her with his wild ways,' she said, raising an eyebrow which made Paul chuckle. 'The other is a farmer, steady and plain, who promises her nothing more than constancy. He says this wonderful line when he describes their future together, "And at home by the fire, whenever you look up, there I shall be – and whenever I look up, there will be you,"' she finished and sighed.

'That's a lovely picture, and one I can certainly relate to,' he said, taking her hand. 'Was that his proposal to Bathsheba?' he asked, daring to utter the word for the first time.

'It was part of it, yes, but she didn't take him – not then at least. She preferred the excitement of Sergeant Troy.'

'The cad you mean? Why?' Paul asked, incredulous.

'Because she thought she wanted more than security.'

'And who am I? The playboy or the reliable one? Do I want to know?' Paul asked, uncertain now where this might be leading.

'That's the interesting thing. To begin with, you were the excitement – the spontaneity – the way you turned up in the night and thrilled me every time your plans changed. But now that I know you, now that we're such good friends,' Paul winced at the way this little speech was going, 'now that we can be together so happily whatever we do, I realise you've become my Farmer Oak.' She smiled gently.

'The dependable one?' he asked.

'That's right. Now you're the only person in the world I want to sit beside on a cold evening, and look up and see you there.'

Paul heaved a big sigh.

'This is very good news. Because all I want to do for the rest of my life is look up and see you there beside me, too.'

Rebekah reached out to stroke his cheek and leant across to kiss him, long and slow, and with a tenderness that had the power to connect their souls, bonding them as if the precious gold from two jewels had been melted together and remade into a newer, stronger treasure.

28

BRISBANE – CHRISTMAS DAY 1998

On Christmas morning, Paul woke with the dawn, still startled by the sounds of the kookaburra chorus and the cicadas that began to sing as soon as the sun spread its light. Rebekah slept soundly beside him so he quietly padded out into the living area and made himself a cup of coffee. He browsed the photographs on the walls, and found himself looking through the bookshelves when an idea occurred. He soon worked out the library system for the Martins' books, and when he found the classics, it wasn't too long before his fingers rested on their copy of *Far from the Madding Crowd*. He pulled it from the shelf and sat out on the old settler chair on the back deck with his feet crossed up on the stool.

An hour later, Paul heard the screen door behind him open and turned to see a sleepy-faced Rebekah smiling down at him.

'Good morning, early bird,' she said.

He put the book down and stood up to wish her a merry Christmas, with a long hug.

'Sit yourself down, and I'll make you a cup of tea, love,' he said, knowing by now that she preferred tea first thing in the morning. While the kettle was boiling, he went to the tree and took out the tiny packet he'd hidden in the branches yesterday, slipping it into the pocket of his gown. He carried the tea tray out and popped it on the table beside Rebekah, and sat down again, waiting for her to enjoy the first few sips of her morning nectar. He needed her to be fully awake before he began.

'Rebekah, that conversation we had last night, at the restaurant? About how much we enjoy being together?'

'Hmmm?' she responded, leaning back in the chair with her eyes closed, as she sipped her tea.

'I've been thinking about it this morning, and there's something I'd like to say to you.' She opened her eyes and looked at him enquiringly as he got up from his chair and knelt on the deck before her. He pulled the little wrapped package from his pocket and put it carefully on the arm of her chair, then took her tea, and rested it on the table. He took her hands into his and watched as her jaw dropped.

'I found your copy of the book,' he said with a nod to the paperback resting beside his chair. 'I've read how Gabriel Oak felt about Bathsheba, and although I'm not very far into the story, I know exactly what he means. Rebekah Martin, just being in the same room with you is a delight to me and I want you to know this,' he said and closed his eyes, frowning briefly to make sure he remembered the words exactly as they needed to sound. 'I want to make you a promise – "I shall do one thing in this life – one thing certain – that is, love you, and long for you, and *keep wanting you* till I die."' He watched as Rebekah's face turned from surprise to joy and into a deep understanding of Gabriel Oak's words from the book.

'And I shall do that one thing whether or not you are beside me, because I will never stop wanting you, Rebekah, to be in my life as my best friend – my guide – my lover. Will you marry me?'

* * *

One week later, on New Year's Day, Rebekah's mum and Tim drove them to the airport. They had all opted for a quick drop-off, so as not to draw out the goodbyes, but still there was time for some heartfelt words.

'Next summer on Brownsea Island then?' said Paul as he shook Tim's hand and gave Helen a warm hug. 'Thank you for everything, and most of all for sharing your precious daughter with me,' he said, and they gave one last wave as they pushed their luggage trolley into the departures lounge, chilled by welcome air-conditioning.

After check-in and passport control, they found a nice coffee shop to sit and wait for their plane's boarding time. Rebekah spread the fingers of her left hand out on the table beside her coffee cup, still grinning not only because she wore Paul's ring, but because it felt so right to be committing to a life spent beside him.

'You still like it?' he asked, breaking into her thoughts. 'You know if you'd prefer something else, you can choose whatever you'd like.'

'It's perfect, Paul. I'd never even considered myself with an engagement ring and wouldn't know where to start with choosing one. This one is wonderful,' she said, flashing it under the bright overhead lights.

The ring was an antique gold setting with a red ruby, a blue sapphire, and a string of small diamonds that wove between the two coloured gems, just like a sparkling mountain creek. Paul had explained to her, after she'd tearfully accepted his wonderful proposal last week on Christmas Day, that the red and the blue had reminded him of the crimson rosellas they had hand-fed while at O'Reilly's guest house in Lamington National Park.

'Their colours were so vivid, and these gems seem to be just the same shade,' he'd told her. And she couldn't think of a better memory with which to seal their engagement, those precious days when she'd shown him who she was before they'd met – when she'd been a Queensland Parks and Wildlife ranger.

'I don't think I'll ever stop looking at it.' She laughed just as they heard their boarding being announced.

29

BROWNSEA ISLAND – JUNE 1999

Rebekah gazed through the open window of her bedroom in Rose Cottage, across the pine tree stands, to the Isle of Purbeck and over Studland beach to Old Harry Rocks. The gentle breeze teased her hair and brought a welcome cool rush. She was standing as still as she could while her mum buttoned the back of her dress – forty pearl buttons, which, Mum had joked, was going to take Paul an age to unbutton later this evening.

Rebekah held up her left hand to the light and twisted the ruby and sapphire ring so that it caught the sunlight and twinkled.

'There you are, all done,' said Helen as she smoothed the full, satin skirts of Rebekah's wedding gown and stood back to admire her beautiful daughter.

'You look absolutely gorgeous, my darling. He's a lucky man,' she said, wiping a stray tear that had escaped.

'Don't start that yet, Mum; we've got to get to the church first, at least.' Rebekah laughed. But yes, she thought as she looked in the floor-length mirror at the bride before her, Paul was a lucky man. He'd had his life plans turned upside down by tragedy

when he'd lost his mother, and his chance meeting with
Rebekah, who hadn't the smallest idea of ever looking for a man
she might like to marry, had been the very thing they'd both
needed.

And she was a blessed woman, too, Rebekah considered,
fortunate to have not only a wonderful mum who had raised her,
but an extra grandparent in Peggy who had inspired her to
become a conservationist, and to travel to Poole – right here to
Brownsea Island – the very place where she'd met Paul. She and
Paul must have a guardian angel watching over them, and for her
part, Rebekah was sure the angel's name was Margaret Symonds
– the young woman who had become a skilled boatwoman for
BOAC and undercover agent working for the British Government
throughout the war.

Peggy had morphed in Rebekah's mind from the kindly,
elderly neighbour she loved as much as her own mother, into a
powerhouse of an undercover agent who'd risked her life while
working to save the lives of others.

Rebekah had learnt from further discussions with Darrell
that this Charlie was really Hans, a Dutchman who was believed
to be a spy. She knew the history of the Dutch refugees who had
been processed here on Brownsea but had never imagined
someone so close to her had been part of any ensuing action. And
now, when she watched the ferry crossing the harbour to Poole
Quay, it was as if she could see the ghosts of the flying boats and
Peggy's launch in the mists of the distance.

'Sit on the bed, love, and I'll help you pop these pretty shoes
on,' said Helen, bringing Rebekah back to the morning of her
wedding day.

Waiting at the garden gate, the old hay wagon from the
museum had been decorated with ivy and roses, and was hitched
to the jeep that was operated by the rangers.

'Oh, how pretty!' she cried when she saw the gorgeous decorations that had been created by her team at the island reception. Her mum stepped up into the wagon first, then helped Rebekah climb up and took care of the train of her dress.

Rebekah was surprised when they took the long way around and realised this was for her benefit – a good, long look at the island she loved and chance for all the day visitors and campers to wave to her as if she were a royal princess passing by in a parade.

At the church, the vicar was waiting at the door and greeted them with a broad grin and a wave, before ducking inside for a moment to tell Paul and the waiting guests that the bride had arrived.

Rebekah climbed down from the wagon and Helen arranged the train before giving her a kiss and going to take her seat in the church where Tim was waiting for her. Rebekah had chosen to walk independently into the church, and climbed the steps up to the church path and into the door from where she could hear one of their faithful volunteers playing the old reed organ for guests while they waited. The instrumental hymn came to an end and the vicar asked the congregation to stand for the bride's arrival.

Paul had organised for some of his London friends to play for the ceremony and Rebekah saw the string quartet raise their bows to play Pachelbel's *Canon*. She held her breath as the music began and Paul turned to watch her walk down the aisle and, from that moment on, all of the organising, the planning, the shopping, and the anticipation came to a sweet end and she felt she was floating on a calm sea, the colour of joy.

Later that afternoon, the bridal party and guests were all ferried via the *Castello* and the *Enterprise* to the Haven jetty, where a bus took them on the short trip down the peninsula to the Harbour Heights Hotel, the only possible venue that either

Rebekah or Paul could imagine now they'd learnt so much about the history they'd discovered together.

Guests gathered around the bride and groom on the terrace for Champagne and photographs with the most stunning backdrop in the world: Brownsea Island and Poole Harbour. The wedding breakfast was served in the main dining room, and late in the evening, Paul and Rebekah held each other close as the music slowed, and the lights dimmed for their first dance together.

* * *

The next morning, Rebekah woke before Paul, and kissed him gently before slipping out of bed and over to the picture window, pulling back the heavy drapes to admire the view. The sun sparkled on the harbour, and she could see a light breeze playing with the tops of the trees on Brownsea. In the distance, there were some rain clouds over the Isle of Purbeck but Corfe Castle shone in a pool of sunlight, as it often did. Looking west towards Wareham and the river, she saw a few light clouds scuttling across the sky. It was going to be another beautiful day in paradise.

As Rebekah leant on the windowsill, she stared at the scene until her eyes grew misty, and she saw as if through to another time, another dimension, a harbour full of moored flying boats. A flotilla of Dutch boats was making its way in through the harbour entrance and around the southern side of Brownsea Island. A Sunderland flying boat in RAF trimmings came in to land near the base at Hamworthy. A smart launch boat raced from the quay to Salterns Marina, and out to one of the waiting flying boats. When the launch pulled away, the flying boat's propellers were already spinning, and it began to move forward, slowly at first, and then so fast that its stern was covered in sea spray until at last, it broke free of the water and rose up into the air with a roar like a million bumblebees and disappeared into the sky to the west.

Helen had unearthed an old card that Rebekah had received from Aunty Peggy on her twelfth birthday, and the message in it now seemed to say so much more than she had ever imagined it could mean. She kept it now in her own journal, and pulled it out to read the words again, though she knew them by heart.

For my darling girl, Rebekah,
May you live for your dreams, fight for those you love, and use your courage to change the world.
With all my love, Pig xxx

EPILOGUE

Peggy snapped her suitcase shut, and checked her handbag one last time. She looked around the bedroom where she'd spent most of her life to date, and through the window, out across the harbour towards Brownsea Island. In the three years since the war had ended, so much had changed.

She still technically worked for BOAC, but most of their operations were being handled out of the Solent again now. The dozens of flying boats that had moored in the harbour during the war had reduced to just one or two. The RAF base was all but closed down and returned to the marines at Hamworthy, and the Royal Navy had handed back the use of the Royal Motor Yacht Squadron at Sandbanks to the yacht club members.

The barbed wire had gone from the beaches, but there were still some enormous concrete blocks that had been put in place to stop the advance of tanks that might have landed during the invasion that was always feared and never came.

Over the last couple of years, Peggy had spent lots of time in London, as there was less work on the launches and no work with the agency, but plenty of diplomatic paperwork to be dealt with by those already sworn to secrecy. But when her family had begun to suggest she should really think about finding a husband and settling down, Peggy realised that she could never be happy with that kind of life.

The excitement she'd known, and the places she had been, left aching holes in her soul that demanded to be filled by more adventure. Nothing, she knew, would ever equal the adrenaline rush of running across a dark field at night in Normandy, racing to meet the incoming Lysander that would take her and her missives back to England from France. Perhaps, if Darrell had stayed... But no. Would the routine of married life with Darrell have satisfied her?

So why, now, she asked herself wryly, was she heading to Brisbane – the very place where Darrell was likely to be if he had even survived the war? Was she leaving herself wide open for the greatest rejection of her life? He might well have moved on, and found someone much better than she, anyway. But Australia was vast, and beautiful, and ripe for discovery, so why not go there, as much as anywhere else?

When her term of service with the agency had come to an end, they had offered her a rehousing arrangement for just about anywhere in the world. They would pay for first-class flights, and help her get set up in a home, all as thanks for the way she had served her country so self-sacrificially throughout the war. Her beginning with the agency in Poole had been just the tip of the iceberg, she thought now as she remembered some of the places she'd been and people she'd met. And all because of Charlie.

Major Carter himself brought a car to the front door, and collected Peggy, after she'd said a tearful goodbye to her mum, dad, Samuel and his new wife – Peggy's work-mate, Nora, Molly and Bill and all their children. He dropped her at Saltern's

Marina where Eileen was waiting with the launch to take her and the other passengers out to the waiting flying boat.

Peggy delighted over the smell of the sea water and the feel of crusty salt on the railings as she stood near Eileen at the helm, feeling the wind rush through her hair as they made their way out of the marina.

'Go on, Peggy, take her from here,' said Eileen with a wink. 'Just one last trip?'

Peggy needed no persuading to take the helm and her mind ran with memories of all she'd been through since starting with BOAC, and thoughts of all the places she might go next.

As they approached the waiting vessel, Eileen took over again, and Peggy was soon stepping aboard, being shown to a window seat by the hostess, ready for the first leg on this two-week trip, bound for Sydney.

As they taxied around and readied for take-off, she could barely hold in her excitement as she had a good view of the quay, with Hamworthy beyond, and as the engines picked up speed, she felt the thrill she had always known she would, as she watched Brownsea Island speed by. Soon, they left the glistening harbour beneath them, and Peggy saw the whole of the beautiful Isle of Purbeck, laid out like a patchwork quilt of fields, with the Purbeck stone of Corfe Castle gleaming in the morning sunshine.

She leant back into the comfort of the seat, closed her eyes, and allowed herself to dream of the adventures she knew would be hers when she made it to Australia. The lucky country.

ACKNOWLEDGEMENTS

Firstly, I must thank the volunteers who have worked to create the *Poole Flying Boats Celebration* website and archives – an incredibly informative and free supply of all the facts one could possibly hope for on this amazing piece of Poole history.

Leslie Dawson is an aviator who has written two wonderful books: *Wings Over Dorset*, and *Fabulous Flying Boats*, both of which have been open on my desk for many months and have provided an incredible wealth of information! Thank you, Les.

Andrew Hawkes, a man famous for his great historical knowledge of Poole, administrates a Facebook group, *Memories of Old Poole & Bournemouth*. Andrew and this group have been an enormous help with extra information, memories, and photos as I've needed them – thank you.

And thank you also to my Poole family who again have read, corrected, advised and encouraged me in my writing, going out to take photos and searching for facts to help me bring this story together.

Finally, thank you to my professional teams at High Spot Literary and Boldwood Books for your support and help with everything along the way. Rachel Faulkner-Willcocks, you are a brilliant editor, and I am so grateful for all your guidance.

AUTHOR'S NOTES ON RESEARCH AND HISTORY

Researching for a novel is a deliciously addictive hobby, and I am happily obsessed! While I was researching for my first novel, *The Last Boat Home*, I was digging deep into information on Poole Pottery when I discovered a tiny snippet of fascinating detail: during the war, when the pottery all but closed down, one of the owners, Mr Carter, became Major Carter and was put in charge of Field Security in Poole Harbour when the British Overseas Airways Corporation moved their flying boat fleet from the Solent into Poole Harbour. The organisation, which would later become Imperial Airways and then British Airways, considered Poole Harbour much safer than the Solent, with its proximity to Southampton, which would be a target for German bombs. The Poole Pottery showroom was used as the Customs Centre, and while the main administrative operations for BOAC were handled at No. 4 High Street (roughly on the site where the current Poole Museum now stands), many passengers went through the Poole Pottery showrooms on their way in or out of the country by flying boat. Guests catching very early flights were also housed at the Harbour Heights Hotel and then ferried via Salterns Marina.

And for a while, during the war, Poole Harbour became the only civilian airport in the whole country and was in fact the first 'air*port*' by nature of the flying boats that landed and took off from the harbour waters.

And, while we are thinking about facts, General de Gaulle did travel via flying boat from Poole, and there was the worst air-raid attack on Poole that night. Spies were suspected to have been involved. Winston Churchill also visited Poole, and particularly Studland, and Robert Menzies visited the UK in 1941, but I fictionalised the idea of these three all being in Poole at once.

When I discovered the amazing archives on the *Poole Flying Boat Celebration* website, it was like stepping into Tutankhamun's tomb – so much rich history is gifted in those pages! There are some wonderful pictures in existence of the seawomen who oper-ated the launches to and from the flying boats and one incredibly striking woman, Mollie Skinner, who always looks more sombre than the others, became the inspiration for my character, Peggy Symonds. These strong and capable women took on roles vacated by the men who'd joined up, and they mostly relin-quished their jobs when the men came home.

It was through the *Poole Flying Boats* website that I also discov-ered another amazing fact: an Australian RAAF squadron was based in Hamworthy, Poole, for just under two years during World War Two. They were there to fly the Short Sandringham flying boats for the RAF. This was such a brilliant opportunity to bring my connection to Australia into the story, that I couldn't resist creating Flight Lieutenant Darrell Taylor, and once I had one Australian, that led me to Rebekah.

While I grew up in Poole, and know all these places in and around the harbour so very well from memory, my parents had travelled to Brisbane as 'Ten Pound Poms' before I was born. I spent the first five years of my life in Brisbane, Australia, before we went home to Poole. I returned to live in Brisbane when I was twenty-five. Rebekah's memories of playing in a muddy creek at the bottom of her garden in Brisbane, and hearing the insects and birds there, are my memories. Rebekah and Paul's holiday in Brisbane is all based on very real places, and a visit to Queensland will prove that it is as spectacular as I've shown on these pages. Come and see!

Brownsea Island is the jewel in the crown of Poole Harbour, a wildlife reserve beloved by thousands of nature lovers, birdwatchers, picnicking families and even Shakespeare playgoers each summer. The history of the island from the time that Mrs Bonham-Christie bought it until she died in 1961, and then it being handed over to the National Trust, who gradually returned it to its natural state, is all retold here as accurately as I could manage.

One extra piece of information about Brownsea that ended up becoming the key starting point for this story was that in May 1940, after the German invasion of Holland, three thousand Dutch and Belgian refugees were guided to Brownsea and billeted there in tents while their identity details could be processed. I don't know if Mrs Bonham-Christie ever got involved with feeding them soup, but I wanted to include her somewhere in my story, along with the Girl Guide leaders and Royal Navy.

The island is now lovingly cared for by the National Trust, and an army of guides, rangers and volunteers work there tirelessly, dedicated to keeping it beautiful and protecting the rare red squirrels that remain.

As in my first novel, *The Last Boat Home*, the streets and buildings of Poole have been written here as accurately as possible, based on old maps and historical notes. Blue Boar Lane no longer exists as it was, but there are many pictures to be found of this very lowly address, complete with the laundry hanging across the lane. My great-great-great-grandfather, John Wills Dominey, died in a house in Blue Boar Lane, in 1860. He was a fisherman and died of tuberculosis, aged thirty.

I do hope you've enjoyed this fictional field trip into a sea of facts and are inspired to enjoy a visit to Poole Harbour, Brownsea Island, and the Isle of Purbeck – some of England's finest treasures.

ABOUT THE AUTHOR

Rachel Sweasey is a debut historical fiction novelist. She lives in Australia, where she was born to English parents, but bases her fiction in Poole where she grew up, which provides inspiration for her WWII stories.

Sign up to Rachel Sweasey's mailing list here for news, competitions and updates on future books.

Visit Rachel's website: www.rachelsweasey.com

Follow Rachel on social media:

 facebook.com/rachelsweaseyauthor

ALSO BY RACHEL SWEASEY

The Last Boat Home

The Island Girls

Letters from
the past

Discover page-turning
historical novels from
your favourite authors
and be transported
back in time

Join our book club
Facebook group

https://bit.ly/SixpenceGroup

Sign up to our
newsletter

https://bit.ly/LettersFrom
PastNews

Boldwood

Boldwood Books is an award-winning fiction publishing company seeking out the best stories from around the world.

Find out more at www.boldwoodbooks.com

Join our reader community for brilliant books, competitions and offers!

Follow us
@BoldwoodBooks
@TheBoldBookClub

Sign up to our weekly deals newsletter

https://bit.ly/BoldwoodBNewsletter

Printed in Dunstable, United Kingdom